TAMSIN

D J COOK

Kerry,

So lovely to meet a 'local'!

Thank you so much for your love + support.

Love
DJ Cook x ♡

All rights reserved. No part of this book may be reproduced without written consent from the author, except that of small quotations used in reviews and promotions via blogs.

Tamsin is a work of fiction. Names, characters, businesses, events and incidents are either the products of the author's imagination or used in a fictitious manner. Any resemblance to actual persons, living or dead, or actual events is purely coincidental.

Cover design by Shower Of Schmidt's Designs
Editing by H.A. Robinson

Copyright © 2020 D J Cook
All rights reserved.
ISBN: 9798683432836

D J COOK ON SOCIAL MEDIA:

Instagram - @author_djcook
Facebook - @AuthorDJCook

DEDICATION

This book is dedicated to Erica.

In a scary world full of change, one of the only things that remains constant is my love for you.
Thank you for being the greatest mum anyone could ask for.

ACKNOWLEDGMENTS

It may be my name that's on the front of this book, but it wouldn't be if it weren't for some crazy talented people, along with my closest friends and family. So here goes:

Heather. If it weren't for you, I wouldn't have started this book, let alone finished it. You waved your magic over this book whilst editing, and prompted me to start writing it in the very first place. You're one of the most selfless people I know. That shows by you allowing me to donate to Macmillan instead of paying you for your editing talent. You are a legend. My legend, forever.

Eleanor. You gave me the book cover I'd dreamed of, and more! Nothing was ever too much for you, and I'm so eternally grateful. I can't wait to get to know you more.

Ruth. Not only are you one of my closest friends, you were a sounding board for the majority of this book. The countless hours we spent together–half of the time using writing as an excuse to get drunk–are times I never want to forget. Thank you just doesn't cut it.

Thank you to all those that constantly asked how I was getting on with writing. It was those little prompts and nudges I needed to get my ass into gear. To name a few: Simon, Jodee, Jamie, Sylwia, Hannah, Potter, Abi, Blaire, Georgie & the list really does go on. I don't have much of a family, but with you guys around, it never feels that way. I'm so lucky to have you all.

And finally, I couldn't forget about my biggest cheerleader of all, Evan. In all of my endeavours, you continue to support me, no matter how big or small. If it weren't for you, I wouldn't have finished this book. You motivated me whilst I was writing, you listened when I needed you to, and you picked me up in the final days of looking over my drafts. You are the best. On a personal note, no matter how many book boyfriends I may write or read about, you're the only one I'll ever truly need. I love you.

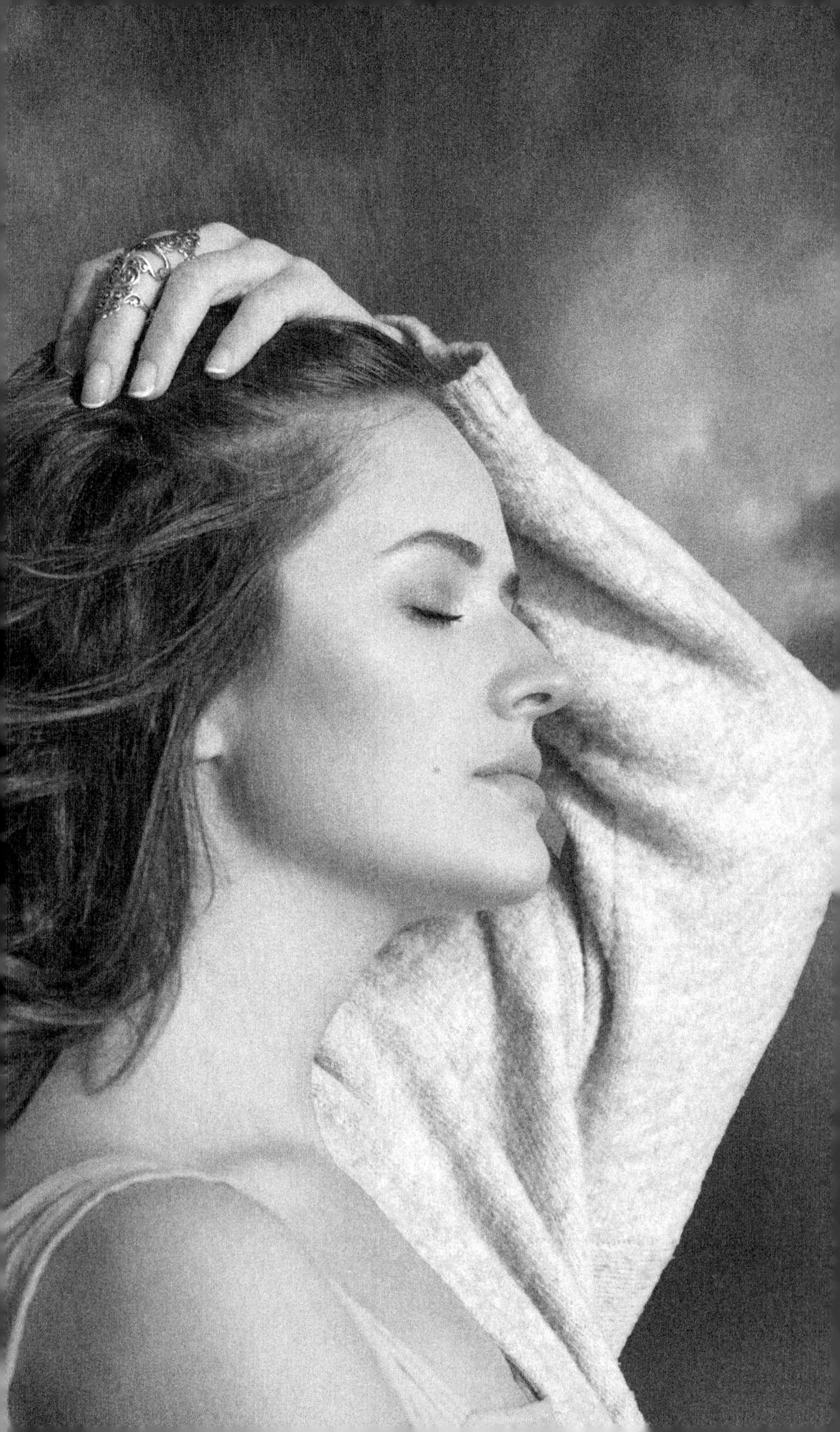

PROLOGUE

"Don't forget the parsley."

The stern words came from my boss, accompanied by an intimidating look. He couldn't have sounded scary if he'd tried. His Irish accent made him too lovable. I couldn't resist it. Aidan was a great manager, and as passionate as they came when it came to his pub, especially the presentation of the food. I didn't dare serve fish and chips without a sprig of parsley; I'd never have heard the end of it. I guess it was good that he never gave me the chance to forget to put a sprig on.

"Oops. Sorry, hun. It's parsley my fault." Liam said laughing at himself.

"He's right. He was talking too much. It's his fault. Punish him!" I yelled dramatically.

"Parsley your fault? That pun doesn't even make sense," Aidan said as I pulled a sprig and placed it on top of the battered fish. I then battled to balance the hot plates on both palms, ready to head out of the kitchen.

"Yes, it does. It's a food pun. The word parsley is used instead of partially. Get it now?" Liam argued back in a joking way. He had been the class clown for as long as I'd known him, always finding new ways to make me laugh. Liam was my closest friend, and very gay. I think that made me love him more, and was the reason we got on so well. We were a perfect match. Typically, males intimidated me and I didn't have many female friends either, aside from the ones we went to high school and college with. They were the only girls I could stand to have a conversation with, although we always knew their loyalties lay with each other and not with us.

"Stop trying to make food puns happen. They are not going to happen," I said, mocking him. He chuckled at my attempt to adapt his favourite film quote.

The Rusty Tap wasn't the classiest pub in Chester; the name said it all. It was a proper local British pub– good grub in the day, televisions tuned into sports all day long and as soon as the clock struck nine pm, the tables would be moved to make way for the dance floor, no matter the day of the week. I loved my job so much that I regularly offered to work longer shifts because I genuinely couldn't get enough of working there. I couldn't get enough of spending time with Liam, so after I'd worked there for three months, I recommended him for a job. The money wasn't too bad either. It paid for the steady flow of alcohol while I was at university at least. The thing I was most thankful for was the working environment which helped me come out of my shell. My confidence was growing and so was my experience of a working business. Part of me wanted to work at the Rusty Tap forever. I think Aidan wanted that, too, but deep down I knew it was a means to an end. Until then, I was thankful for my job, the people around me, and still working on my confidence. I had to; otherwise I wouldn't get a word in edgeways around Liam.

"Tamsin, we've got a delivery. Aidan wants us to sort it." Liam leant over the bar to tap me repeatedly, knowing it would irritate me.

"Be there in a sec'. Just gonna finish cleaning the bar."

"Okay. Owl wait," he said, holding up his hands.

I couldn't help but laugh at his animal pun. I couldn't not love him. It was a good job as we were inseparable. We danced together. Worked together. Lived together. I couldn't count on one hand the times I'd gone home to a toilet roll fort, or the number of times I'd got home to Rihanna's album playing full blast, yet somehow Liam managed to sing louder than the music. We walked down to the cellar together and began lugging huge kegs and cases of beer into place. Aidan was precious about how everything was placed in there.

"What time are you in 'til today?" I asked Liam. Fridays were my long day in work, but it meant I could go home most weekends to see Mum. I hated the thought of her being left alone. Me being at university was the longest we'd ever been apart. She kept herself entertained, mostly with shopping online and going for short walks, but I knew she got lonely. She didn't have many friends, aside from the people she saw out and about. I was all she had, and Liam too, for that matter. They got on like a house on fire. I often wondered if Liam was the son she wanted but never had.

"Until seven today. So glad because I need to go out! My assignments are killing me at the moment. You coming out?" Liam loved a night out, especially a Tuesday night. We wouldn't dare miss a night out on a Tuesgay. Gay nights were the best, although my Wednesday morning lecturer never thought so. I'd missed most of her lecturers in first year and every few weeks I'd been copied into emails about lack of attendance. I'd still smashed those marketing assignments, though.

"I can't. In until close, although I guess I could come and meet you afterwards?" I wasn't keen on the idea, as I knew working a twelve-hour shift would leave me a zombie the following day. That hadn't stopped me in the past. I would simply cover the Rusty Tap logo on my work shirt and potter up the street into the nearest club after work.

"Do it! Otherwise I'm gonna have to go out with the girls, and they are fine, but we have so much more fun together. Also, you don't mind if I pull at the end of the night, and the girls always judge me. I need sex!"

"You always need sex. Also, I don't moan because I'm jealous. Seriously, since when is it easier for a gay guy to pull? There are fewer of you," I joked, even though I couldn't get my head around it. It had been months since my last encounter. My problem was I always wanted more than just one night. I wore my heart on my sleeve, and somehow guys knew that. Whether they took advantage on purpose, I wasn't sure, but after a couple of drunken nights and heartbroken mornings, I'd convinced myself that they caused more pain than good. So instead, I'd made a plan. I focused on myself, and the ambition inside that I couldn't dampen. I would meet a guy but before then I would have a house and a nice car. I'd have the perfect job before then and be married before thirty. I had it all planned out, yet every day, my plan felt further out of reach.

"I know. It's not my fault. It's an instinct. Probably the only manly thing about me."

"You said it, Gayboy," I jested, using his nickname with love. He may have been bullied about his sexuality at school, but when you got constant criticism for something you couldn't control, you either became weak or gained resilience. Liam didn't care and I admired that about him.

"Who are you calling Gayboy? Have you seen these muscles?" He rolled up his work shirt, showing off his pale scrawny arms, slightly bulging at the bicep.

I knew that as soon as he finished work, he would be turning our communal bathroom orange, plastering fake tan all over his body. He wore it well, something I was never brave enough to try to cover my own pasty skin.

"You're right. I'm sorry. You are so masc! I'm gonna go get you a pint of Stella and some drywall for you to plaster," I mocked him again. It was one of my favourite things to do.

"Once we're done here, I'm having a break. I don't care if we're busy."

"That's fine. I will pick up your slack as usual." Sarcasm rolled off his tongue.

"You're a dick. You know that?" I muttered as I scraped another crate across the floor into position.

"I know. You love dick, so that's a compliment."

It took around forty minutes of heavy lifting and sarcasm for us to finish putting away the delivery, and in line with my word, once we'd finished, I sat on the step next to the lift we never used. It was where everyone dumped their things when they came onto shift and huddled during their breaks, even though Aidan told us not to. I grabbed my phone, about to open the screen when I saw a missed call and voicemail from mum. She never called, especially when she knew I was at work. I pressed play on the voicemail and placed the speaker next to my ear.

"Tamsin, c... Can you call me back?" She was

crying, sniffing, struggling to speak. Something was wrong.

I quickly pressed call on my phone, listening to the continuous ring, until...

"Mum. Are you ok? What's up?" I panicked.

"Tamsin. Can you come home?" She was still sobbing, and sounded completely different from her usual self.

"I'm in work. Why? What's wrong?" I probed again, worry filling my gut in the form of bile.

"I can't tell you over the phone. Just come home," she pleaded.

I couldn't just come home. What was I going to say to Aidan?

I need to go because my mum told me to.

I'd be laughed at.

"Mum. I can't come home. I'm in work until close. Please, just tell me."

The phone went silent, but I knew she was at the other end of the line. I could hear her slow breaths as she held the phone close to her mouth.

"I... I have... cancer." Her slow breaths grew faster as she struggled to catch her breath. Struggled to string together a sentence. Struggled to say that word. Cancer. As if the word alone was what was stealing her breath.

It was that phone call that changed my life. There were so many questions, so much information I needed, but I couldn't ask. Even if I could have, I wouldn't have been able to process it. Emotions flooded my body. At first, anger took over. The rage inside me made me want to throw my phone across the floor because it was the only thing near me that I could throw. It wouldn't have done any good, though. I wanted to tell her she was wrong, but how could I? Who was I to know? Besides, Mum was never wrong. A dull pain ached through my body–a pain that only a hug from my mum, Theresa, would help heal. She was so selfless. I knew that even though she had cancer, she would be thinking about me. Thinking about how I was feeling.

"Tamsin, say something." She sniffed down the phone.

"I'm coming home," I said, not knowing what else to do, other than to try to hold myself together, hiding my emotions. I knew that my cries would make her worse. She wouldn't want to see me hurt, too. I was her daughter, her best friend, and cancer was making her hurt me indirectly. I didn't want to show the pain I was feeling. I couldn't.

"I love you, Tamsin." A lump grew in my throat. I was breaking. I had to end the call.

"Lots and lots…" I replied, waiting for her to finish my sentence.

"Like Jelly Tots."

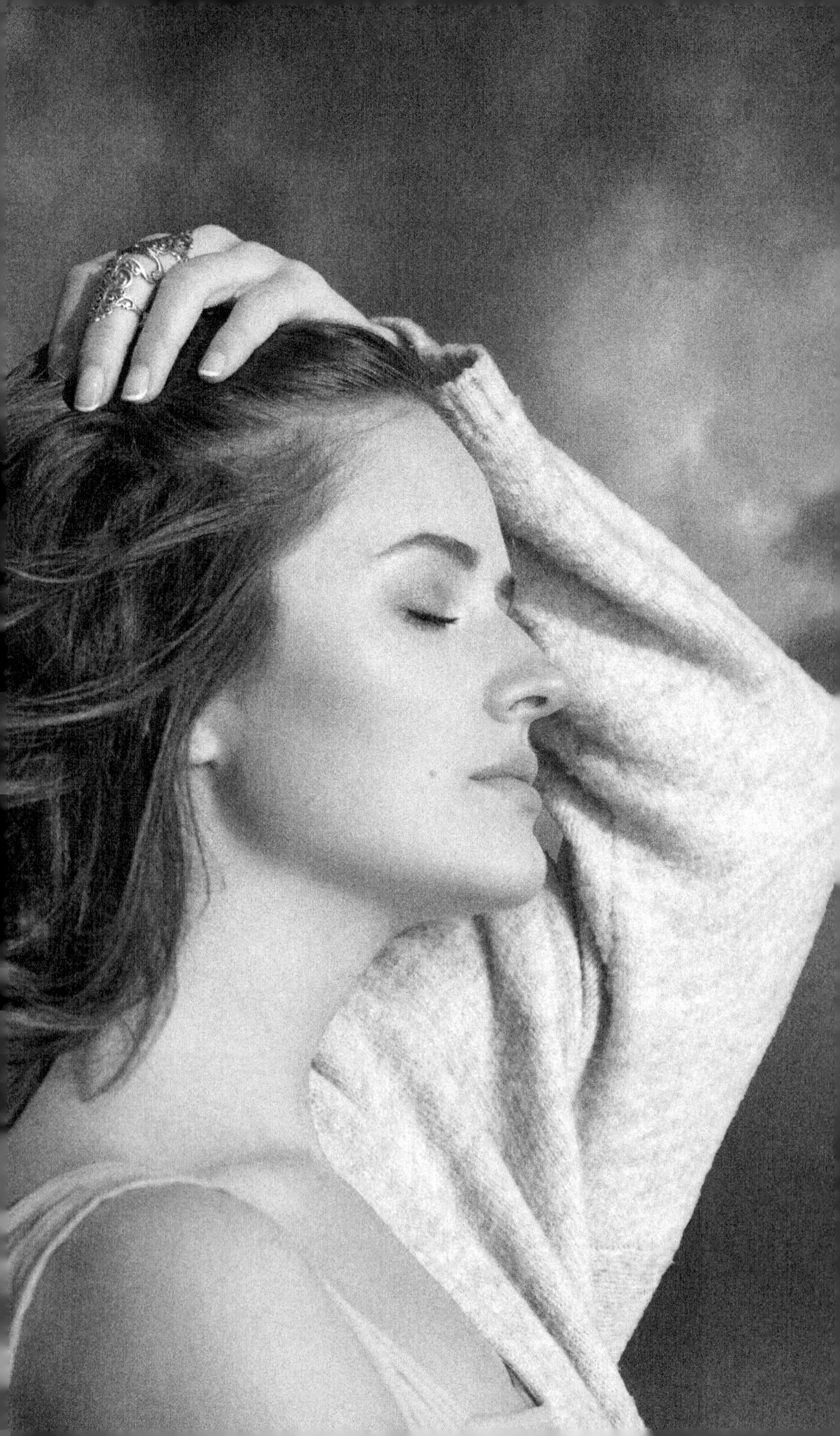

CHAPTER ONE

THREE MONTHS LATER

It was over, and I had no idea how I had managed it. I'd handed my dissertation in, all beautifully bound. Naturally, I'd had a second copy printed and bound just for me. For memories.

'The extent of consumer trust looking at social media sites used to launch a new product, and the factors that influence this level of trust.'

I had worked so damn hard on it. I sacrificed work, nights out, and even a few weekends of seeing mum to complete it. Somehow, I was able to bury the emotions that crept up at the weirdest of times. I'd be sat writing about social media trends and start crying. I tried my best to bury them, anyway. I didn't let my pain, or Mum's pain, get in the way of my future. I just hoped that my degree would be worth something in a world where you needed experience to get you where I wanted to be. I had applied for numerous jobs under the recommendation of my mentor, and with a CV I was trained to write, yet I'd had no luck. Not one single interview. All I could do was wait. Wait for my degree result to be published and wait for a business to contact me back. The thing was, I had very little patience, so I decided to do what any person would do in my position.

"Four double vodkas with Diet Coke and a bottle of prosecco please," I asked politely, still excited to celebrate. Liam couldn't contain his excitement either, even more so as his assessment was due a couple of days before mine. We had been waiting for today, and it felt long overdue.

"How many glasses?"

"Two please." The bar tender didn't flinch. It was nearly eleven am after all. The Student Union bar, or the SU as we called it, was the one place you could go for a drink in the morning without being judged, because students worked there. Liam and I rarely found ourselves in the SU together; he'd be with his course friends and I'd be with mine. We knew we had to make the most of the opportunity and celebrate finishing our degrees in style. The air was stuffy outside, but we couldn't resist sitting in the heat wave that was suffocating the UK. It wasn't often we had weather like this, never mind in April. We perched on a patch of grass outside the bar, with our plastic cups filled to the brim with alcohol and a bottle of prosecco. They wouldn't be filled to the brim for long, though. I basked in the sun that radiated against my skin. A slight breeze carried

Liam's aftershave to my nose, and I tipped my head back. Finishing university allowed a huge weight to be lifted from my shoulders, and I could almost relax. Almost. I grabbed my phone and focused on the screen after looking up at the sky for too long and sent a text.

Mum - ICE 1
25th April 2018

[12:38]

Handed in my dissertation! Can't believe it to be honest. Having a few celebratory drinks with Liam before we start packing tomorrow. I've told Aidan I can only work once or twice a week from now on so I can be at home more. Excited to move back in with you. Love you lots and lots like Jelly Tots xxx

[12:49]

Congrats, Tamsin. I'm so proud of you and Liam, too. Make sure you celebrate. There is no rush to come home. Stay in Chester as long as you want to. I do miss you, though xxx

I was excited to move back home–to see her every day. Worry constantly filled my gut being so far away from her. At least being with her I knew I could help as much as possible. I was going to miss living in Chester, and with Liam, but I knew it was right for me to be back with Mum. It wasn't part of my plan; I'd never pictured going back to Crewe. I'd always imagined I'd work at The Tap with Liam until we both found the job of our dreams. Maybe it had been a little naive of me to assume that would happen, but he'd always followed me everywhere.

"So what's your plan now that you've finished your degree? Are you going to get a job in fashion?" I asked, almost worried that we'd eventually be apart. I didn't like this part of growing up.

"That's the dream. I've applied for a job at the fabric shop in town. Not exactly what I want to be doing, but imagine the discount I'd get on materials." He lay there, rolling a blade a grass between his fingertips.

"So why not a fashion job now instead of the fabric shop? If it's your dream?"

"Most fashion jobs are in London, or abroad if I hit it big time. I'm not ready to leave everyone behind. Couldn't imagine seeing Jade less than I already do. Also, do you really think I could go more than a day without seeing you?"

I laughed and a small sigh escaped my mouth. I couldn't imagine it either.

"Maybe I'll start my own business one day. My bespoke designs could be on catwalks all over the world." He sniggered. He didn't believe in himself even though I knew he had the potential. I never understood his fashion until he sat me down to watch clips of the London Fashion Show. Fashion would strut down the clean white runway, all held up by size zero models. Truthfully, Liam's work should have been up there. He would reel off which designers' work he was inspired by. Most of the time it went straight over my head, but I was starting to appreciate his work for what it was. It was a type of art.

"One day you will have your own label, and it will be worth the hard work. I believe in you." I emptied the last drop of prosecco into my mouth.

———

"Ugh. Why do I have so much crap?" I groaned while pulling a deflated sheep from my canvas wardrobe.

"Suzie!" Liam shouted, snatching the inflatable toy we'd acquired on a night out from my hands. "Remember the guy who gave us this? He was hot. His mouth would have been on this," he stated, then started to blow seductively on the nozzle, pumping Suzie the sheep back up to her former self.

"Liam Wright, will you please help me?" I begged. "The moving van is going to be here tomorrow and my bedroom is a tip."

"I'm well aware the van is coming tomorrow. Half of the van is mine. It's not my fault you are so disorganised," He quipped, laughing at my misfortune and only wanting to play with Suzie. I had asked him to come up and help, but he was more of a distraction. I didn't want to say goodbye to my loft room. The wall above the chimneybreast was covered in six-by-four prints of nights out, patterned in a brick-like formation. I pulled an old box out from the bottom of the wardrobe, while Liam threw the sheep in the air.

"You're not helping," I huffed at him, lifting the lid off the box, which released a cloud of dust into the air. My face puffed and both my hands automatically started to rub my eyes to calm the sneeze about to erupt from my nose.

"What the hell are you doing?" He cried with laughter and started to mimic me.

"It's my dust allergy. I'm trying to stop myself from sneezing." I said bluntly, still trying to tame the inevitable sneezing fit that I was about to have.

"Brilliant. Dust allergy. How did I not know this?"

"Honestly… You keep the house freakishly clean, but you don't clean my bedroom, so I tend to just sneeze a lot up here."

"Should clean more often then, shouldn't you?" he said sharply. He'd always had a remark for any comment I'd made. We kept each other on our toes.

"I always thought you had hay fever when we were younger. Anyway, I'll sort that box, and you start packing up those books, okay?"

"Thank you." I sniffled, my nose streaming. Packing was the worst but I carried on. I had to if I ever wanted to be at home with Mum again. I didn't want to pay for another term of rent either. I pulled the books one by one off the shelf that was secured onto the chimney-breast. I scanned the pictures in front of me, my mind wandering through the different memories they each held. One picture had been taken three years earlier during freshers' week. Both Liam and I were stood soaking wet in the middle of a nightclub during a foam party. Liam was stick thin, enough to make the average person look huge. I cringed at the matted mess of my brown wavy hair and the clothes I had, for some reason, thought would look hot. I was wearing a sky blue shirt and white denim shorts, and was covered in neon necklaces. It was all good fun, but how wrong was I? Looking back, it came as no surprise that I hadn't taken a guy home that night.

I was pulled back to reality as my phone vibrated in my pocket.

"Hello?" I answered. I didn't recognise the number.

"Hello, is this Tamsin?" a female asked.

"Yes, it is. Who's this please?" People always told me I had a phone voice. I could talk for Britain, but I hated introductions.

"Hi, this is Roberta from Farden Hotel. We received your application for the position of Customer Relationship Manager, and we have put you on the shortlist. I know this may be short notice, but would you be free to come for an interview next Friday?"

I couldn't believe what I was hearing. A small part of me had been losing faith in all of the applications I'd sent. I thought there had been something wrong with them. Something wrong with me.

"Oh wow, of course I can. That would be great.

What time?" I asked eagerly, unable to contain my excitement.

"Is ten-thirty okay? You'll just need to sign in with security and then I'll collect you." she asked politely.

"Perfect. I'll see you then. Thank you!"

Adrenaline rushed through me from head to toe. This was the beginning of something big for me; I could feel it. I had to get my arse into gear and pack like I'd never packed before. My future depended on it.

―――

Dawn Street was laced with terraced housing and pathetically sized gardens, but it was home. I'd lived on this street all my life. I remembered playing tag with Liam on the roads around ours; we would weave our way through the parked cars, often setting off the alarms. We didn't care, though. Our parents had given us only three rules to follow or we would be grounded:

1. Once you are out, no traipsing in and out of the house, unless it's for food or the toilet.
2. In for the night when the street lights came on.
3. Stay within the boundaries our parents had set.

We weren't allowed to play past the last streetlight on one side of Dawn Street, and the post office on Liam's street, which was just around the corner. As I pulled up alongside my house in the moving van, the street looked deserted, as did the wooden play area. Children would have flocked to it all those years back, but instead the park sat rotting, only occupied by gangs of teenagers smoking and God knew what else. Times had changed, and how I knew it. Life had been so much simpler back then. I didn't have to worry about mum; she worried about me.

"Thank you so much for helping." The driver placed my last box just outside the house. My things filled our small paved garden.

"You're very welcome. Are you sure you don't want help taking them inside?" he asked. I hadn't been home for a few weeks, and although my mum was quite capable of making her meals and taking her medication, I knew that she'd had chemotherapy a few days before and that made her struggle. I didn't want her to feel like she had to make an effort. She needed to rest and not worry about a stranger coming into her home.

"I'm fine, thank you. My friend should be back soon to help," I lied. There was no way I would drag Liam back here after seeing Jade's little face light up when she saw him. His sister adored him. Who didn't?

I stepped through the doorway and kicked off my shoes, flinging them across the hall amongst the boxes I had placed there. My body slumped down next to Mum on the couch. I held her hand and slowly grazed her skin with my fingers.

"I've missed you so much. So happy to be back for good with you," I said as she smiled weakly. Her skin looked dry and her eyes duller than they had ever been. Cancer was draining the life out of her, and the chemo even more so. But it was helping. The tumour in her oesophagus was shrinking. It was still terminal; the cancer had spread too much by the time they caught it.

"I've missed you, too," she croaked, like she hadn't said a word in weeks. Her sparkle and humour were fading, I just wished I could grab on to them to stop them from disappearing altogether.

This is just temporary.

I shook it off. I did miss her humour, though. Mum said the reason she'd got Cancer was because she would never stop talking. She joked it was someone trying to shut her up. Laughter was the best medicine and we'd always laughed pain away before, but this time was different. I was the clone of her. We laughed the same, loved all the same things, even shared makeup. By share, I mean I took hers and didn't buy my own. Because we were so similar I always knew when she wasn't herself, but it also meant she could read me like a book. I missed the old her, and all her crazy stories, like when she and her old best friend had flashed the postman because he always stared at their chests. If only I had the confidence they had to pull that off, or their cup size. Mine were barely a handful.

"Mum, I got an interview at the hotel I told you about," I said in an attempt to cheer her up.

"You did? I knew you could do it, Tams." Her voice was hoarse, but her smile grew wider than the last one she'd tried. I couldn't wing the interview like I had my Wednesday lecture assignments. I had to prepare, but I had time. I just had to organise myself and take a leaf out of the very organised pages of Liam's book. I would allocate a couple of hours over the next week, in between becoming Mum's full-time carer, and the very few shifts I had at The Tap.

"You'll be wanting my makeup then, won't you?"

"Absolutely! And I will be wearing this." I pulled out a knee length black dress with a white collar to show her. I had packed it separate from my clothes once I got the phone call from Roberta because I knew I'd be too lazy to unpack straight away. I had to look the part, first impressions were everything, so I had every intention of using her makeup.

"You will look beautiful. Go and grab my makeup box," she said with the very little energy she had. I passed it to her and she began to root through it, looking for something in particular. She pulled out a red lipstick–*the* red lipstick–the one I was never allowed to use because it cost her a fortune, and looking at it, she hadn't dared to use it either.

"Take this, and when you go to the interview, make sure you knock them dead."

For her, anything.

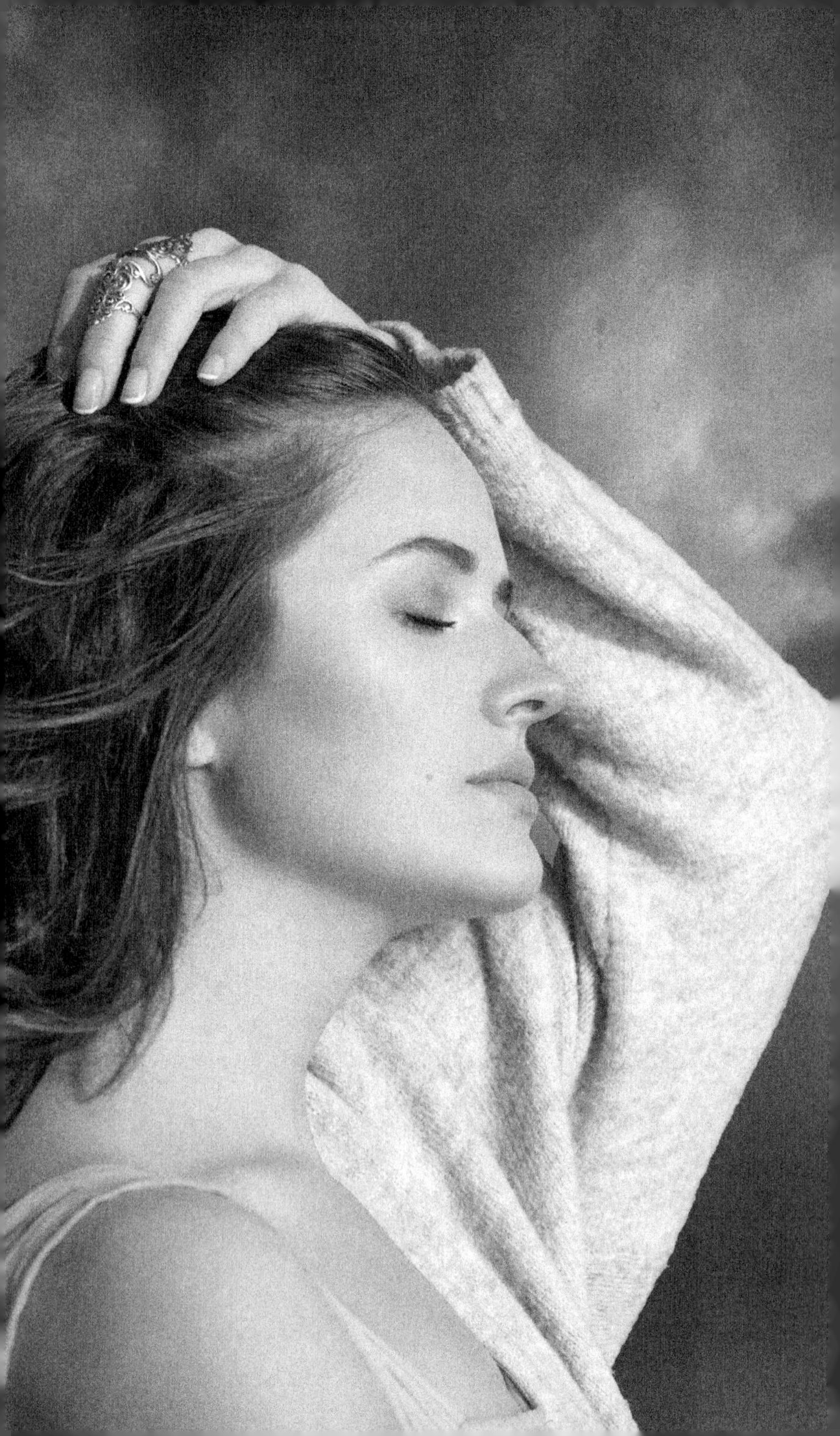

CHAPTER TWO

The white painted room surrounded us, yet despite the crisp clean walls it still looked gloomy. The infamous hospital smell was almost as recognisable as Mum's Sunday lunch. Nurses passed the room now and again, occasionally looking in. Mum's breaths went from deep inhales to shallow gasps for air as I sat next to her, clutching her hand tightly. The beeping of the heart monitor was slowly driving me crazy. What felt like days had only been hours, but each one that passed made it more apparent that this was the end of her journey.

Mum had always said if she were to go into the hospital, she would never leave. She was right. Annoyingly, she was always right, but I had hoped and prayed that this one time she would be wrong. She had to be wrong.

I started to count the seconds in between her breaths, which wasn't the cleverest of ideas. I would panic after *every few seconds, waiting for the next crackle of her breathing. Her chest rose ever so slightly with each inhale, moving the tubes attached to her pale skin.*

"I love you so much. Like Jelly Tots," I said, barely able to get out the words as I tried to hold back my tears. The doctors had told me she would still be able to hear me. I wanted to believe them. My only wish was to hear her say 'I love you lots and lots, like Jelly Tots' one last time. The heart monitor emitted a drawn-out high-pitched noise. My body froze. For a minute, I stopped breathing, too. As much as I'd known this day was on the horizon, nothing could have prepared me for it.

"No... No, this can't be happening," I stuttered as the doctors came in and covered her with a white cloth so I couldn't see her.

"Why are you doing that?" I screamed as my whole body shook.

"Take that off her!"

Everything was blurred.

I panted as sweat dripped from my body onto the sofa. My phone sounded, accompanied by a repetitive buzz that woke me at seven am. Half of the duvet was draped on the floor like I had wrestled with it all night. Mum was lying next to me, sleeping soundly, inhaling slow breaths and making little snores. It was a dream. A nightmare.

A nightmare that will be reality one day.

I had no idea what I was going to do, and the more I thought about losing Mum, the more I felt like I was losing my mind. It was a bright morning. I could feel the warmth already as the sun shone through the gaps in the blinds, creating a dust-like mist around us. I grabbed onto the arm of the sofa, and slowly pushed myself off as my body ached with exhaustion. It wasn't easy looking after Mum, I had no idea how she'd coped all the time I'd been in Chester.

"Coffee," I said to myself as I stumbled towards the pink retro kettle in the kitchen and flicked it on. I couldn't function without a strong coffee in the morning; that and tea were staples of my diet. I put a heaped teaspoon of granules into a mug that read 'Don't be a shoe. Be a hat or a purse'. We'd always watched *Friends* together, so it was a very fitting gift. Liam bought it me after I finished my exams in the first year. Surprisingly, it was still in one piece as I was notoriously clumsy. I put an extra teaspoon of coffee and a sweetener in the mug for good luck. I daydreamed about having a fancy coffee machine with pods, or better yet an assistant to run along and get me an Americano from Starbucks at the click of my fingers like in the movies. But that's all it was–a dream. I didn't *need* them. They were a luxury I could live without. Besides, I needed my own house, there was no way I could have fit one in Mum's kitchen amongst all the clutter.

. . .

Mum was still sleeping peacefully once I had finished tiptoeing around the kitchen, so I crept upstairs to my room to start getting ready for my interview. My bedroom was finally looking like it used to after I had spent the past few days unpacking. I plugged my phone into the Hi-Fi system I'd received for Christmas years before and started to play the *'Getting Ready'* playlist I had saved, turning the volume down low to make sure it didn't startle me. I applied a minimal amount of makeup on top of the layer I should have removed the night before, trying to make myself look more human and less Casper the Friendly Ghost. I was surprised I hadn't broken out in spots with the amount of nights I had slept in makeup recently. I was exhausted, but I couldn't let it stop me. I curled my brown hair loosely to create a wavy effect and then slipped into my black dress. Something was missing.

Red lipstick.

I could see the exhaustion in my face as I looked in the mirror. The cheap makeup had barely provided any cover for my growing panda eyes. The early morning didn't help but it was necessary to tame my usually untidy hair. No matter how much effort I made, I couldn't seem to shake a feeling of envy. My confidence plummeted every time I looked at myself. It was the media's fault. Women were air brushed to perfection or plastered in makeup with teams of stylists to make them look television ready. It did nothing for my self-confidence. Confidence had always been an issue for me, likely another reason why I was still single. As I walked down the stairs, they creaked beneath me.

Mum was stood at the bottom of the stairs, looking up at me in awe.

"You look so beautiful," she said, seeming to have more energy than a few days earlier.

"Thanks, Mum. I honestly don't know what I would do without you." My hell-ish dream flashed to the forefront of my mind. I nearly teared up at the thought of living a day without her.

Could it be days, weeks or months?

I didn't know. No one knew. I knew I had to cherish the rest of our days together, to limit the hurt I knew was coming.

"I'm so proud of you. I love you lots and lots like Jelly Tots." The words I longed to hear in my dream came from her mouth. Tears rolled down my cheeks, thankfully not smudging my make up too much. Overwhelmed, I kissed her goodbye and stepped out through the front door onto the cracked slabs in our tiny front garden. Our next-door neighbour, an elderly lady, was in her garden. She was moving her black bin after the collection that morning. We exchanged a smile and nothing more then I carried myself to the train station.

I quickly arrived at Crewe Train Station. The automatic doors were jammed open with the masses of people who poured in and out. The loud engines roared over the hustle and bustle of the commuters; I could barely hear myself think. Platform five was just as busy, all of us waiting for the next train to Birmingham New Street. I could barely balance in the heels I'd worn in an attempt to appear taller, and not one guy offered me their seat. Chivalry was dead. I stood with one of my hips dropped, trying to balance as best I could in my heels. My eyes scanned the platform and everyone on it. I found myself locked onto a suited man. His lips were small, and his tanned skin was clear of imperfections. One manly hand was wrapped around the phone he was staring at, and the other tapped at his hip in some sort of rhythm. At first, I couldn't tear myself away from his beauty, until his deep blue eyes met mine. He was stunning.

"Hot," I muttered, elongating the word as my gaze shyly dropped from his face, down his blue suit to the floor. That was about as close as I was getting to flirting, if that's even what you could call it. He was meters away, but that didn't stop my imagination bringing him closer. Confidence poured from his posture, as he stood with a worn satchel bag that hung off his shoulder. I looked up again, hoping my eyes would meet his once more, but I had no such luck. Commuters rushed past me to board the train that had pulled in beside me, blocking a view I wished I had taken a mental picture of. Once my line of sight had cleared, he had disappeared. I wanted him. I wanted to bite his bottom lip, feel his manly hands all over me and quiver against his touch. I stood day-dreaming for a while, longing to see him again, and then with disappointment I shuffled my way through the crowd and managed to sit on a seat next to a window. The seat faced backwards, which made me dizzy. I suffered from travel sickness, especially when I travelled by coach, but my mum would always give me ginger biscuits to eat before and on the journey. I missed those school trip days. Everyone would fight for the back seat, and I would be at the front of the bus smugly eating my biscuits.

I sat on the train feeling guilty. Mum was at home, struggling with the disease that was wreaking havoc throughout her body. I was on a train to Farden to try to win over their hearts and give me the job of my dreams. I hadn't even thought of the consequences of getting a full time job right now. It hadn't crossed my mind until then.

Mum would want me to do this. She said she was proud of me.

I tried to reassure myself as fields of green passed by. Sunlight peered between the clouds that had covered the sky since my journey to the train station. Rain droplets started to run diagonally across the window of the train while it moved at speed. To pass the time, I silently bet on which rain droplet would win and watched them race across the glass pane, an oddly satisfying game to play. I blinked and my eyes re-focused, not on the raindrops, but my reflection. My once coiffed hair was flat, but that didn't stop me trying to bring it back to life by vigorously scrunching the curls in my hand as I looked at my reflection. I paused. It was him.

Suit guy.

I looked at his reflection in the window a couple of seats down. Facing backwards had never been my favourite, but with this view how could I complain? He looked up from his phone and faced the window. My heart stopped as our eyes met once more. His lips widened as he smiled at me. I smiled back, and the train slowed and came to a halt. I grabbed my things together and completed my mental checklist.

Phone. Purse. Keys. Bag.

With my things in hand, I quickly walked past a few seats, all empty of busy and rushing commuters, to where he'd been sat. Suit guy had already left, and a newspaper that read *Crewe and Nantwich Guardian* lay in his place.

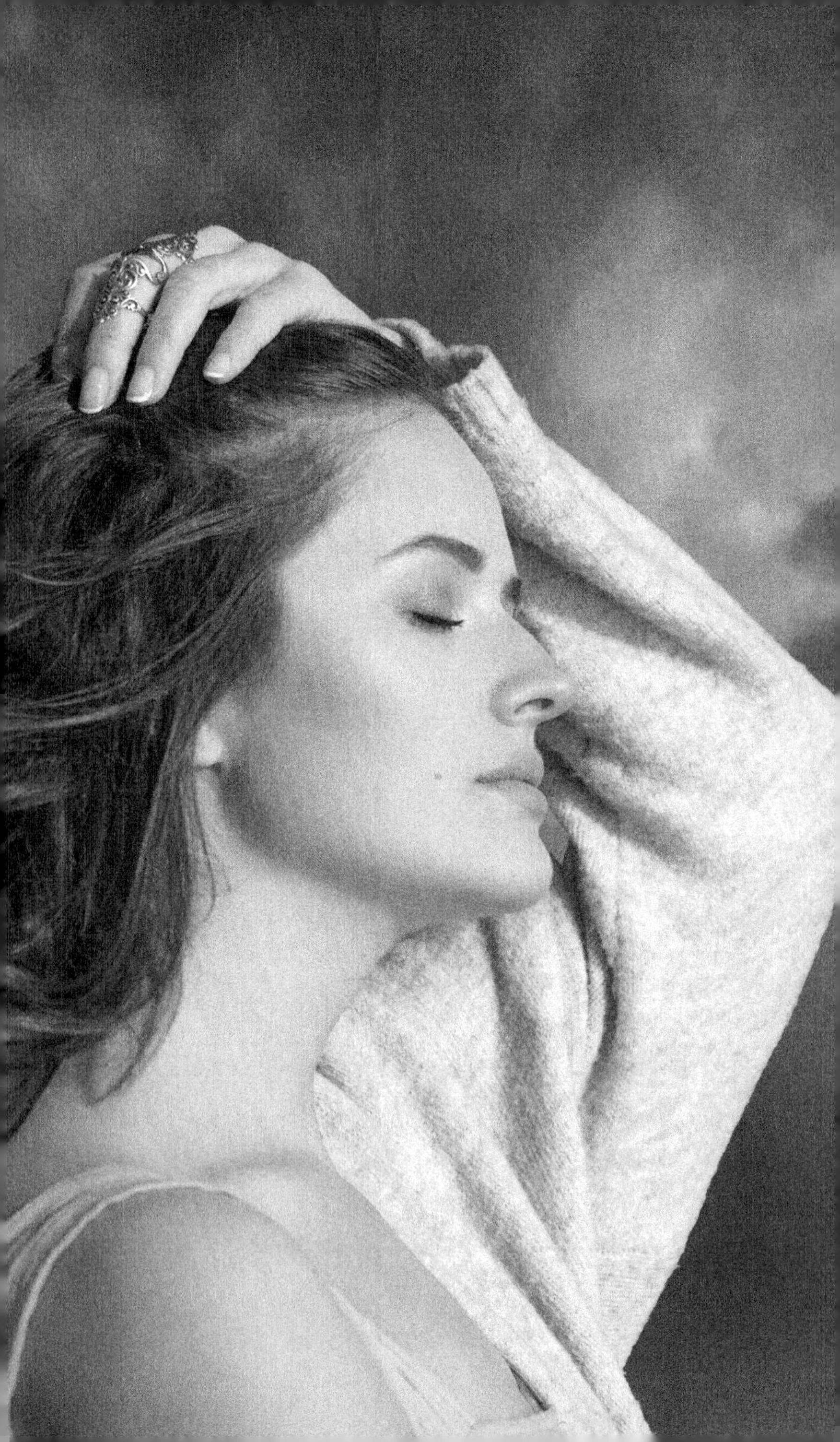

CHAPTER THREE

After scrambling from the train station, through the crowds of people in Birmingham city centre, I arrived at Farden Hotel. I found myself stood alongside a tall, sleek building covered entirely in glass. It was like an Apple Store on ecstasy. I questioned if I would fit in at Farden, as the revolving door swept me into the reception area. I knew I wanted to. I'd researched countless websites in preparation for the interview. This hotel wasn't part of a chain. It was independent and had been run by the Farden family ever since it opened its doors as a small hotel in the late 1960s. Five years earlier, it had relocated, and now towered over Birmingham in all its modern skyscraper glory. It was a shame about the reviews, though. Some of them made me cringe. After a few minutes of waiting and drumming my fingers against a Perspex chair, Roberta finally greeted me.

"You must be Tamsin Cross. Lovely to meet you." She held out her hand professionally.

"Lovely to meet you, too. Thanks for inviting me for an interview." I tried to exude confidence to hide my nerves. It worked. She led me into a lift and escorted me through the twenty-third floor, to an office encased in glass. A male sat in a black leather swivel chair. He was dressed in a grey suit, without a tie, and sporting an open collar. Roberta wore a blouse and a black tubular skirt, meeting just below her knees, and sat in the empty chair next to him.

"Please, take a seat."

As instructed, I sat with my head propped up high, trying to display the same confidence everyone around me seemed to have in abundance. I shook while trying to hide my nerves.

"Good afternoon, everyone." I looked at the clock. First mistake. It was still morning, even if it had felt like I'd been up for ages and it was too late to correct myself.

"Good morning, Miss Cross. My name is Ian, and you've met Roberta." Ian spoke for the first time. Shaken with nerves, I thought back to the last time I'd sat in front of someone like being on 'The Apprentice'. I'd only ever had two other jobs, one of which I'd got from messaging someone on social media, which had scored me a job at a local football ground. The other had been at The Rusty Tap, and Aidan had just questioned me about my favourite alcoholic concoctions, of which the list went on!

I worked myself up, preparing mentally for the interrogation that was about to come my way. In my head, I felt like Ian was about to shine a light in my eyes, to try to get me to confess that my entire three years at university had revolved around drinking and nothing more. I did go to a couple of lectures, I guess.

"So, Miss Cross, what made you want to apply for the position of Customer Relationship Manager?" Ian questioned while Roberta had a pen poised, ready to scribe my answer.

I'm sick of being covered in beer and want to do something with my life.

I held back.

"I've always been passionate about customer service. Whether it's shopping, buying a drink in a bar, or staying at a hotel, I believe that customers deserve to walk away with a smile. I want to be the one to make that happen."

Roberta gave Ian a look. Her eyes told me everything I needed to know. I felt reassured. As the interview continued, I asked them questions about the position in detail. They advised me the role would be the direct line of support for two people–Rach and James–who both worked predominantly in customer service. They also discussed the salary, which was more than I could ever have imagined after just graduating. It was THE dream. I needed to work there. After shaking both of their hands, I turned and walked into the glass wall.

FUCK! There goes that dream.

"If I had a pound for every person that has done that." Both Ian and Roberta laughed in sync. Ian was no longer that professional stiff, but a human.

"You really shouldn't clean these windows!" I mocked myself, trying to hide the embarrassment already plastered across my face. As I stood awkwardly, a lady called Sharon was summoned into the room as she walked past the glass encased office.

"Would you mind escorting Tamsin back to reception?" Roberta asked her in a friendly manner. You could instantly tell they were friends. As we walked through, I scanned my surroundings to avoid clashing with any more glass panels. The building was open plan with rooms on each side. I caught myself peering in each and every room we passed. The majority of people either had their heads down working or were laughing with their colleagues. I knew I would fit in here, but I had done all I could. Fate had to decide. Well, Ian and Roberta did. Just as I was about to sign out, I received a call.

"Hello?" I said.

"Tamsin, sorry to call you so soon. We just wanted to let you know that you have the job. You were the last interviewee, and you outshone all of the other candidates. Congratulations."

"That's incredible. Thank you so much," I said professionally, trying to conceal my excitement with all the power I had.

"When can you start?"

"Next week?" I said, a little uncertain if that was possible. It had to be. Aidan would understand.

"Brilliant, we look forward to it. Do you have to rush off? Roberta and I would love to introduce you to your new colleagues. We have a catch up lunch meeting booked in at the hotel restaurant in about half an hour, and we'd love you to join us. It'll be paid, of course."

"That would be fantastic. I don't have anywhere to be."

Could this day get any better?

I wanted to scream. The day could have gone a little better, I noted as I rubbed my still aching nose. I sat next to the bar, staring at the wide entrance into the restaurant, with my hands wrapped around a tall glass of Diet Coke. I wanted to crack open a bottle of wine to celebrate, or at the very least a glass, but I sensibly resisted the temptation to make a good first impression.

Ian walked in, accompanied by around half a dozen people dressed immaculately. I felt like a trusty Ford compared with them. Each one of them oozed a sense of authority and luxury just like a high-end Rolls Royce. Ian spotted me at the bar and summoned me over to a table with his fingers. I exchanged pleasantries with everyone sat around the table. One woman seemed a little hostile, but I shook it off. After all, I was the newbie. They didn't know or trust me yet. Other than that, I felt comfortable, especially having Roberta sat next to me. She was the friendly face I needed to cope with the most daunting lunch I'd ever had. A waitress brought over a bottle of wine and began pouring it into the glasses already placed neatly on the table.

"Don't expect alcohol at all of our upcoming meetings," Ian announced to the table and nudged Sharon who was sat next to him. You could tell she was a keen drinker. Her glass already held the remains of a good wine after she'd necked it.

"We're just waiting for Darren and Callum to join us, so keep chatting amongst yourselves and we will commence shortly."

I watched Roberta swirling her red wine in a circular motion before she took a small sip and kept it in her mouth for a while. I almost felt sorry that my glass was already half empty.

Almost.

Roberta and Sharon had taken advantage of Ian disappearing to the toilet and started to gossip about their work hours and how they never managed to get out of the office and back home on time. At the time, I selfishly didn't think about the problems that would cause with me caring for Mum. I was just ecstatic I had a job. A proper job. Sharon's hair was a yellow blonde colour, just shorter than shoulder length. She was older than me, around mid-forties, whereas Roberta seemed to look around early thirties. Sharon looked at me inquisitively.

"Tamsin, right?" I nodded while taking another gulp of wine. "Where do you live, bab?" she asked.

"I live in Crewe. It's about an hour's train ride from

here." I was still nervous I forgot to ask her the same thing, although I could tell Sharon was local. She had a strong Brummie accent.

"Oh, you poor girl!"

"Crewe isn't that bad. I–"

Sharon interrupted with laughter. "I didn't mean that. I meant that it's a long distance to be travelling each day."

"Ohhhhh." I giggled. "You're right, it is, but I don't mind travelling, especially for this job." I was so cheesy; for some reason, around my new colleagues I couldn't get out of *'interview mode'*.

"Well, I admire you. I know I couldn't do it. It's an effort for me just walking fifteen minutes down the road to go home." We laughed. I could relate.

"Come to mention it, doesn't Callum live in Crewe?" Sharon looked at Roberta, who nodded with a glowing smile.

"Near Crewe, I think. You could travel together."

Roberta started to play with her black woolly hair. She was a natural beauty, but her personality was enough to fall in love with. I could tell everyone around the table was under her spell. She bit her lip and nudged Sharon while nodding towards the entrance of the restaurant. Her almost flirtatious look grew as two suited guys walked in.

My heart fluttered, trying to keep itself afloat. I was powerless. My heart sank, unsure what to do next.

It was him.

Suit guy!

All of our gazes followed them across the restaurant to the table, my eyes glued to the mystery man.

"Callum's the one in the blue," Roberta whispered to me, almost bursting with excitement to spill the gossip.

Callum is suit guy.

The God-like guy I'd seen at the train station and on the train. I hoped he didn't think I was stalking him. I wondered if he would actually remember me, and recognise me from the reflection on the train.

Callum sat in the empty chair next to me, and the other I presumed to be Darren sat beside him.

Perfect.

My head dropped towards my neck as I tried to shyly hide away from him.

"Callum, this is Tamsin. She got the job they were advertising and is starting next week," Roberta blurted, and Callum's eyes locked on mine. My eyes fell shyly and I found myself looking at his wide smile. I exhaled in lust. He remembered me. Darren peered around to introduce himself, and I shook his hand. He was broad, and older than Callum. Callum extended his arm out towards me, and I felt his grip tighten as it closed around mine. His long gaze left me vulnerable to him, yet I didn't want it to end. I was being stupid. Pure lust was taking over my body. I was not about to lose my integrity and act like a school-girl around him, no matter how strong the power he held over me. I was unaware of how long we'd held on to each other; I was completely and utterly lost in the moment until Ian commenced the meeting. He introduced me formally and explained the role I would be taking on within the business, and then he got everyone to announce themselves in a circle.

"I'm Sharon, Events Manager, and I started last year."

"I'm Roberta, HR manager here at Farden."

"My name's Callum. My role is Marketing Manager and I've been here for a few years now."

"Darren. IT and social media operations." A man of very few words. The others continued to introduce themselves in turn.

"And, of course, you all know who I am. I'm the General Manager of Farden Hotel and Spa," Ian said, tittering to himself. I could tell he liked to have a little banter with the others, but he knew there were boundaries as manager. I couldn't be sure if he was genuinely funny or if I was laughing to impress him.

"I am pleased to introduce Tamsin Cross, a new addition to the Farden Family. As Customer Relationship Manager, she'll be tackling the complaints and reviews the hotel has started to see. Tamsin, would you like to add anything?"

Shit.

I stuttered and stumbled.

"Umm, just that I am happy to be here and help,

and that, umm, if anyone has any advice or can help when I start my role I would greatly appreciate it."

Phew!

I'd had enough stress dealing with an interview already today; I was not prepared to speak in front of everyone. In front of Callum.

Callum turned to me and whispered under his breath, "Far too pretty to be working in an office all day."

I turned beetroot red.

"I'm sorry, what did you say?" I heard him. I could have said the same about him. Too pretty for most things. Working in an office, and definitely too hot for clothes. Despite that, I was still a massive fan of his suit.

"So, T, what did you do before getting this job?"

He had given me a pet name, already. I couldn't cope!

"I work at a bar in Chester, worked there for about two years while I was at uni. You?"

"I went to Chester Uni, had a gap year in America after graduating and then did some volunteering. Been working here for about two years now," he said while everyone else went back to talking amongst themselves.

"Wow!" I gasped, trying to work out his age.

That must make him at-least twenty-four.

"What degree did you do?"

"Business studies, you?"

"Me too!" I said, almost too loud.

"Do you live in Crewe?" he asked bluntly. "Did I see you at the train station today?"

"I do, yeah. Oh, you may have done?" I tried to play it cool.

Callum smirked. My gaze caught his lips as they twitched slightly. I felt like I was about to melt in the warmth that surrounded him. Both of us. His crisp white collar grazed his tanned skin and stubble as he looked down at his phone under the table.

"The first item on the agenda are the planned refurbishments to the hotel to commence next week," Ian interrupted. "The spa will be closed during the refurbishment, set to last twelve weeks. The existing sauna, steam room and Jacuzzi will be ripped out and replaced. It's very exciting." He adored this hotel. He had worked there since before the relocation, so they were practically married and celebrating their twentieth wedding anniversary.

"Looks like you are going to have your work cut out." Callum laughed once Ian had finished enthusiastically telling us about the plans.

"What do you mean?" I asked.

"The spa is going to be closed completely. You're going to be drowning in complaints." He paused.

"That's true, but you haven't seen me in action, yet," I said confidently, the wine providing a small amount of Dutch courage.

"Well, Tamsin, I'll be marketing the new spa, so I guess that means we are going to be spending a lot more time together." He passed his phone to me under the table and grazed my right leg slightly. My whole body tingled as I looked down at it. My name appeared on the screen, with the cursor flashing in the contact number section.

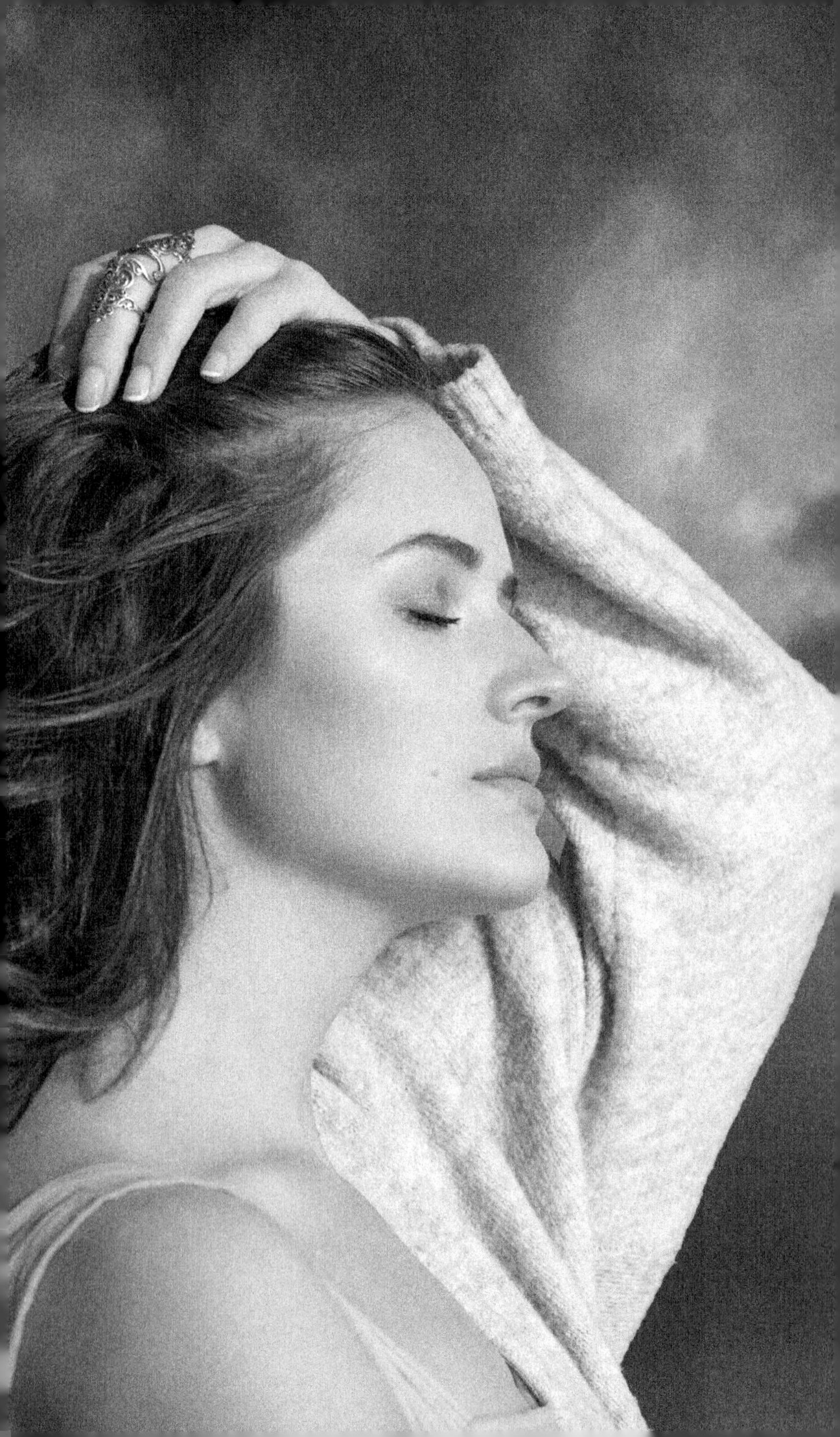

CHAPTER FOUR

I arrived back home, exhausted and overwhelmed from how the past few hours had panned out. An interview and a job offer all in one day. Then there was Callum. I couldn't help but check my phone every few minutes, feeling phantom vibrations in my pocket even though there was nothing. No text or call.

What did I expect? I was reading far too much into the situation. He wanted my number to talk business.

That's what I told myself to cover the disappointment I felt. I was always like this–clingy, needy even. Something had to change. I had a new career to focus on and a place to re-invent myself. This was a big deal, and I wasn't going to let some Adonis ruin it for me. This time, I was in control.

Mum was slumped in her chair with the television flickering in front of her when I got home.

"So..." she said in a worn out voice, turning to me as my heels drummed the floor.

"I GOT THE JOB!" I screamed and ran over to hold her tight. A smile lit up her face and a stray tear rolled down her cheek. It was the first time she had smiled for a while. The chemotherapy was draining the life out of her. The woman who had brought me up, who I adored more than life itself, was fading and it was tough to see. If anything, getting a job was worth it just to see her smile like that. It made my pain go away, and it seemed hers disappeared for a little while, too. She'd always told me I could be whatever I wanted while I was growing up, so I knew how proud she was.

Aim for the sky, Tamsin, but don't stop there.

She always used to say that. It had been my mantra for as long as I could remember. Every day I believed in myself a little more, all because of her faith in me.

"You should celebrate. I will text Liam to get his arse here."

I was shattered. I hadn't even thought about celebrating.

I should celebrate.

This was a big deal. They had put their trust in me. I hadn't even graduated. Hell, I hadn't even got my grade yet. I was going to celebrate, and I knew Liam wouldn't let me down.

. . .

"Heyyyyy!" Liam shouted from the hallway and peered around the doorframe. I didn't need to see to ascertain it was him; his distinct voice gave it away. He had a habit of walking in and making himself comfortable, but he could do literally anything after all he had done for Mum. He had sometimes visited her on his days off from uni, and he went to chemotherapy with her once. He even called her on the phone more than he did me. Liam and I had been best friends since primary school, so mum had known him as long as I had. She would always be on the phone with Diane, his mum, organising birthdays and play dates. His mum had been around every weekend when we were younger, but as time had passed and we'd started to organise our own plans, they'd seen each other less and less.

"Tell me then?" He knew full well I had got the job. Mum and Liam had clearly been conspiring behind my back, which I secretly loved. With Liam around, Mum was never going to be lonely.

"I got the job!"

"Yes, you did!" he said, walking back through to the hallway, and this time peering through with a gorgeous bouquet of flowers, purple calla lilies surrounded by greenery, and a bottle of champagne. My favourites.

"You deserve this, hun." He smiled, walked over to my mum and kissed her softly on the cheek.

"Shut up! They are gorgeous, thank you." He must have spent a fortune on the flowers, and champagne was never cheap. He knew me far too well. I loved to drink a glass of fizz and pretend to be rich.

"Staying for a coffee?" I asked Liam, as I snapped a photo of the gifts to put on my social media.

"Coffee? Are you kidding? Babe, we are going out. Go put on a revealing dress and let's go slut drop on the dance floor." Mum laughed at his humour. "And between you and me, it's been about a week and a half..."

"You horny bugger." My mum laughed with as much energy as she could conjure up. "Try three years, and then I will let you complain!"

"MUM! Too much information." In disgust, I stomped upstairs theatrically with Liam cackling behind me.

Cheesy pop songs filled my bedroom as we made ourselves look pretty, ready for my celebratory night out. A few of the girls from high school were joining us. I hadn't seen them since Liam had told them about Mum. They were worried, and I would get the occasional message from them, but tonight was my chance to show them I was fine, or at least to pretend I had my shit together. I slipped into a black sequin dress with straps that clung to the sides of my shoulders, and then make up was next. I found myself watching video tutorials in an attempt to have my make up better than Liam's. He was always getting complimented on his perfectly shaped eyebrows. It took him forever to get them so perfect, though. I guess I wasn't as committed.

"Liam, can I use your concealer?" A question I asked all too often.

He chucked it to me from across the room while fighting with his black skin-tight jeans.

My phone buzzed and flashed with a text.

Unknown
4th May 2018

[20:14]

Hey beautiful, congrats on today. It was great meeting you. We should do something together. Speak soon, C.

A text. From Callum. I blushed and smiled as I read his text. I'd never been called beautiful before, not by a guy anyway. Liam turned to me and grabbed my phone from my hands.

"HEY! Give it back." Liam ran to the other side of the room reading the text.

"Who's C? And why is he calling you beautiful?" Liam said while holding the phone high above his head, knowing he was too tall for me to reach it.

"It's Callum. He's one of my new colleagues and a little bit of a dream. But to answer your second question, I have no idea why he's calling me beautiful. He asked for my number, though. That's never happened before. You should see him. He looks like he could be a model in an aftershave advert." If I hadn't told him about Callum, he wouldn't have dropped it all night.

"Drop the I'm not pretty act. You know you're fit, babe," He said hugging me tightly. His arms wrapped around my body and held me tightly in place so I couldn't move. I then heard clicking. He was texting. On my phone. *Woooosh*. He'd sent a text.

[20:17]

Hey Callum, thanks so much! Meeting you was a pleasure. Off out to Cassie's in Chester tonight to celebrate. If you find yourself over that way, feel free to join. T.

My heart sank into my stomach. I wanted the ground to swallow me up. I started to chase Liam around my room, playfully hitting him. I wanted to punch him harder, especially for signing the text with a pet name I had somehow acquired over the past few hours.

"Tams, he might actually come. It might be you getting lucky instead of me."

Oh god, what if he does come?

My once slight panic over a text turned into one massive stress at the reality that he could come. I looked in the mirror at myself and for the first time, I worried about what another man would think when he looked at me. For once, the way I looked mattered because of a guy. I gathered my products to add loose curls to my hair, making it look like an organised mess. I bugged

Liam, constantly asking about my outfit, but he just reassured me. He said it was the best I'd looked since my first year of uni. He wasn't wrong, as that was probably the last time I'd really tried.

"I can't believe I'm on a train for the third time today. We could have just gone out in town to avoid this," I said, fed up of sitting on public transport.

"You're joking, right? To celebrate your big shot job? Ridiculous suggestion."

"Alright... I guess you're right. You could have driven us," I joked with him, knowing full well he wouldn't give up a night of alcohol.

"Pft. Right. The girls are getting the next train in. They've just messaged saying they're ready."

I looked around the train station, gazing quickly at everyone around us. I didn't feel overdressed anymore, especially as two girls from Liverpool walked past with their brows penciled on, sporting skimpy crop tops showing too much skin. I was getting old.

Shortly after, we found ourselves in a small bar. Bird-cages hung from the ceilings and walls with candles placed inside. It was only a short walk from The Rusty Tap, too. As much as I wanted a free drink from Aidan, we had to avoid it. I hadn't told him about Farden yet. We ordered a bottle of prosecco with two glasses, and sat waiting for the girls to arrive. The prosecco came in a rose gold wine cooler, which Liam liked a little too much and attempted to fit in my handbag. Music played quietly in the background, people's voices mumbling over it. Everyone huddled together in small groups, like penguins trying to keep warm, while we sat cosy near the bar. We loved to people watch. Our friendship was strong and comfortable. We could sit in silence and it not be the slightest bit awkward. Most of the time, the silences were broken by Liam pointing at cute guys, at which point all kinds of crude comments would spill from his mouth.

"Liam! Tamsin." The girls shouted in harmony across the bar to catch our attention. I had known them since the beginning of high school, but Liam and I had latched onto them during drama class. I'd gone along mostly because Liam had dragged me, but I would be lying if I said I hadn't enjoyed it. They'd all had big personalities, just like Liam, which had helped keep me on my toes. After getting another round of drinks, we all made our way to the dance floor, weaving through the small crowds dotted across the venue. The sound had been cranked up and dance music made sure no once was left in their seats. Liam pointed to another guy in the crowd behind me and I turned to humour him.

"Fuck, he's fit," Liam said with his jaw practically scraping on the alcohol-sodden floor.

It was Callum. He walked towards me, dressed in a tight pair of ripped skinny jeans and a long plain white shirt. His wrists were wrapped in accessories, a gold watch on one and a black weaved leather bracelet with a gold band on the other.

"Hey, T." His head bowed and lightly pecked my cheek–a bold move for someone I had only spent about an hour with.

"Well, aren't you going to introduce me?" Callum said with a grin as wide as a wolf about to eat supper.

"Liam…" Liam eagerly reached out to shake Callum's hand. I went on to introduce the girls to him, too. Courage, in the form of alcohol, filled me, which was a miracle; if I'd been sober I would have been hiding behind something or someone.

"Thanks for inviting me, T," he said while grabbing my hand, swarmed by the crowds of people dancing around us.

Thank Liam.

Drinks continued to flow, and not once did I have to open my purse. Callum clung to my hand as the night continued, kind of like a child who didn't want to lose his mum in the supermarket. I had not felt this good about myself for a long time, or felt as though someone sincerely wanted to spend time with me–to get to know me, for me and not for what was covered by my delicates. I suddenly found myself alone with Callum, as Liam and the girls went to smoke. Liam was a social smoker, but he had clearly asked the girls to go outside to give Callum and me space. I knew the game he was playing. *Operation Get Tamsin Laid.* I played along; I wasn't against it.

"As if you had lectures with Paul, too? An absolute legend." Callum laughed as we both reminisced. Turned out we'd studied similar modules, too. The more we spoke, the more we found we had in common.

"I know. One of the lectures I actually refused to miss." I had to shout my response over the music, which left a ringing noise in my ear.

"Absolutely. Shall we take these drinks some place else?" he shouted back. He didn't have to ask, and I didn't have to think about it. I let go of his hand and texted Liam quickly.

[00:39]

Me and Callum are heading off. Text me in the morning. Get lucky xoxo

"Let's go then," I said confidently, grabbing his hand so he could lead me through the crowds. It felt strange being in a taxi with a guy I hardly knew. We had a lot in common, but our conversations often trailed off into silence, leaving me feeling awkward. His hand rested on mine, his thumb grazing my soft skin. He couldn't have been any closer to the heart I wore on my sleeve. I knew I had to protect myself, and make this time different from how it usually ended up. I had to call the shots, just like all the other guys had with me. So I decided it would be just one night. No more than that. The taxi pulled up outside a detached new build, just on the outskirts of Nantwich. He had a drive, a garage, and a garden that put mine to shame. I tripped over a decorative rock but managed to steady myself as Callum went to unlock the door. He pushed it open to reveal an open wooden staircase and a chandelier that hung from the ceiling and glistened once he flicked on the light.

"Well, what do you think?" Callum asked, as sober as anything.

"It's stunning." I tried not to slur my words, but I was both drunk and in awe of his place. Some girls growing up dreamt of their perfect weddings, others of having children, but I'd pictured a house like this as my own for a long time. It had started when I was younger, circling things in the Argos catalogue and making my dream home on *The Sims*.

"I'll be right back. Wait here." With a kiss to my forehead, Callum wandered into the kitchen and returned with a glass of wine. As I took the drink, his other hand met my waist. His eyes sparkled just like the chandelier above.

How was this happening?

I couldn't believe it. I looked down at the white wine and took a sip.

"You're a slurper." He smirked, still with his hand resting there, his thumb slowly grazing my hip.

"It's one of my many annoying qualities." I giggled and put the drink on a wooden side cabinet next to me.

"I could get used to it. Wait, scratch that. What are your other annoying qualities?" He oozed swag. Of course he would say that. He wanted sex and so did I.

"Haha," I said sarcastically.

His smile widened as his other hand pushed my brown curled hair away from my neck. His touch was sensual, and I felt his warmth throughout my body. His fingers lightly played with the back of my neck and an accidental sigh of pleasure slipped from my mouth. He pulled me closer against his body and kissed my neck, gently pressing his lips from my throat to my collarbone. My body tingled all over. He stopped and looked at me.

"Don't stop." I sighed.

"Sure you want to do this? We're going to be working together. Is this going to complicate things?" His hand never left my waist.

God, yes!

I couldn't think about work, not with his presence taking over my body. I wanted to jump on him and not let go. I couldn't let an opportunity like this go to waste. I wanted him. I needed him.

"Then let's agree. Just one night. That's it." I stretched onto my tiptoes and allowed our lips to meet. His grip tightened around my waist, and he pushed me against the closed front door.

"Okay. If that's what you want. One night it is."

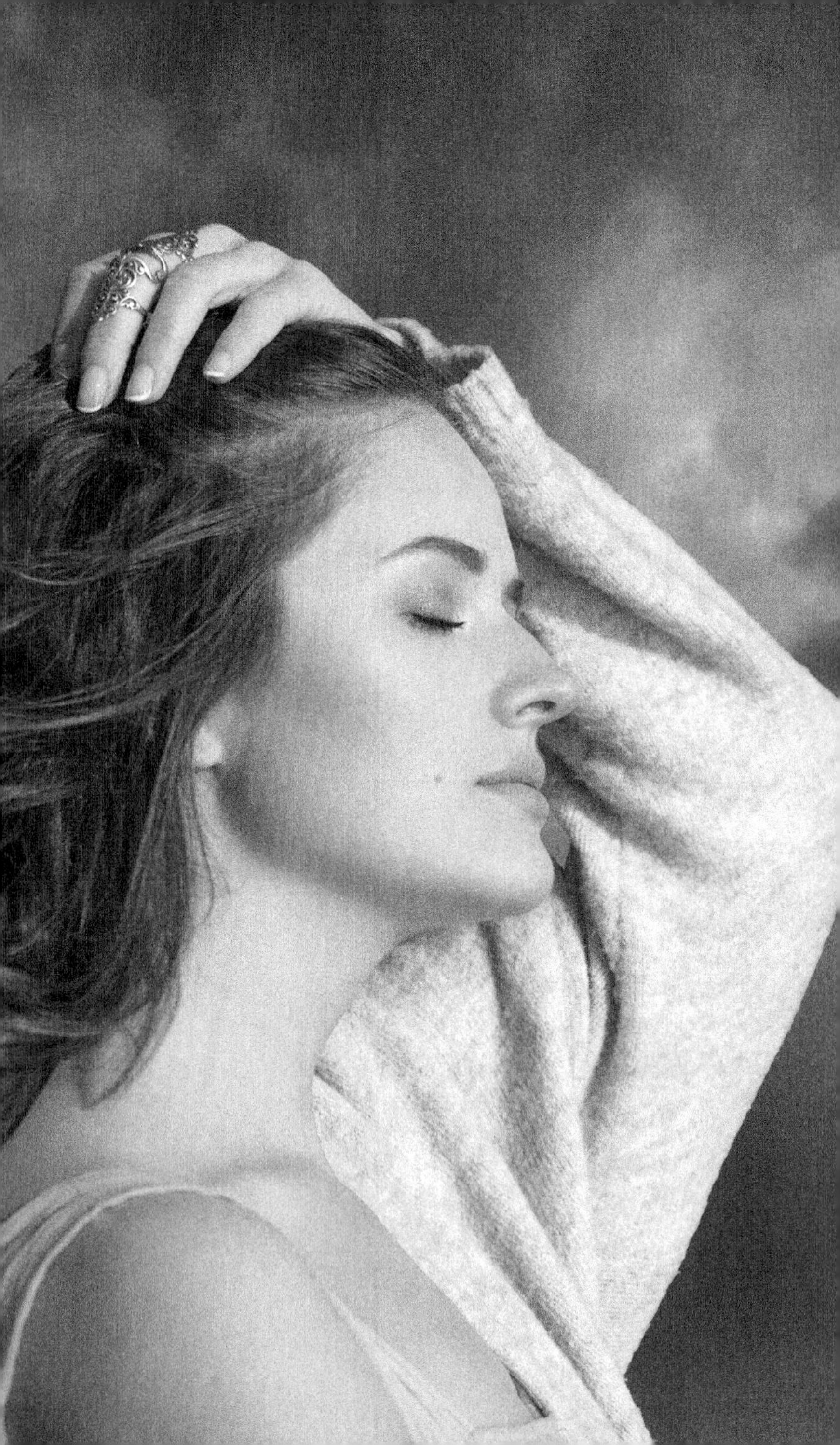

CHAPTER FIVE

Callum had taken me to another world and back—an imaginary world of pleasure where only he and I had existed or mattered. We'd barely slept and now I was paying for it. I couldn't help yawning, my mouth begging for another taste of him. I turned over and lay next to him with one hand resting on the centre of his abs. He slept silently but stirred at my every movement. His bronzed skin looked darker with the plain white duvet just above his waist. In the space of a few hours, he had become my drug. A guilty pleasure I wanted more of, but I knew I couldn't have. I could feel myself being drawn into him more and more the longer I lay next to him. Things like last night didn't happen to me, especially with guys like him. Who could blame me? I started to feel overwhelmed, and question every decision I'd made. My mind and body clashed in a war of emotion versus logic, and I didn't know which I wanted to win. My body wanted to climb onto his lap, straddle him again, and feel a pleasure I had longed for. My mind, however, told me to run. All the Dutch courage from the night before had drained from my body, leaving me with pain, panic and complete lust for the man sleeping next to me.

He's too good for me anyway. I don't deserve him.

I convinced myself he was only going to bring trouble. I had to control the damage or I would be left standing in ruins. My mind won. The next thing I knew, I was leaving his house with my bag clutched in one hand and my phone in the other. I quietly closed the door behind me, tiptoeing in the impractical heels I'd worn the night before. I stood waiting for Liam after texting him frantically to come to my rescue. My hair took a serious beating from the rain, turning my bedhead into a wet, knotted mess. I looked down the street, a sub-urban paradise shrouded by heavy grey clouds. The road looked as if it was a flowing river; cars waded slowly through the water as I dodged the spray from their wheels. Thankfully, Liam arrived at the bottom of Callum's drive in his red Mini Cooper. It was sparkling, even in the rain. I climbed into the front seat, trying not to tear my black sequin dress, and looked back to Callum's house as I put my seatbelt on. He stood at his bedroom window, still topless. I locked onto his eyes, which were filled with sadness. His expression shook me to my core, as I'd only ever seen a look like that once before. I wanted to get out and say sorry, but as the thought crossed my mind, Liam accelerated leaving the house to fade into the distance.

"Are you ignoring me this morning?" Liam said.

"What?" I asked, still picturing Callum's face.

"I've been talking to you ever since you got in the car. I asked if you had a good night?"

"Oh, sorry. I'm still half asleep," I said, trying to excuse myself. "It was out of this world."

"Really? I can imagine to be fair. He's gorgeous." He paused briefly. "So I don't have to imagine anymore... how big?" Liam took his hands off the steering wheel and used them to get an indication of how lucky I had been.

"That's for me to know, and you to never find out." I laughed.

"Well, that's rude," he said in a joking voice. "Right, let's get you home. I think I'm still drunk from last night."

What had I done? I'd walked out on the guy of my dreams, and he'd watched me leave. Without saying goodbye. I couldn't help but allow my mind to wander back, playing scattered images through my mind like a record on repeat. My whole life, I'd made sensible, justified decisions. I was that kid who never got into trouble. Not once. Then I go and do something stupid, now of all times. It was like I'd been waiting to mess up my life. This was something, quite frankly, Liam would do. Countless times he'd fled scenes of pleasure without even catching the other guys' names.

It had been a week since leaving Callum, and I hadn't heard from him. I stepped up to the front of Farden for my first day, dressed to impress with the help of Mum and Liam. My mind was so deep in thought about Callum, I'd gone into autopilot without realising it.

"Tamsin, great to see you again," Ian said holding his hand out to reach for mine as I approached him in the hotel reception. "I know you've seen a lot of the hotel already, but I'll start off by giving you another tour and showing you the rooms and facilities. Roberta will be going through some training and the hotel policies and procedures over the next few days, but the priority is getting you settled. Once we've finished the tour I'll show you where you'll be setting up camp." He laughed to himself and I joined in awkwardly.

"It all sounds great, thanks, Ian." I said, buzzing with excitement. I'd worked long and hard for this–a job I was told I would be statistically unlikely to get because people from council houses had poorer grades. I showed them. Nothing was going to ruin the first day of the rest of my career, and ahead of schedule for that matter. My perfect job had come sooner than expected. I only hoped my perfect man was around the corner, too.

Ian led me around the hotel, visiting the basic rooms up to the deluxe suites and penthouse. The suites were stunning, each with their own unique decor and style. They even had coffee machines. The penthouse had a stunning four-poster bed positioned at the centre of the back wall. Off the corridor, there was a bathroom with a contemporary freestanding bath and two sinks. Opposite, featured a walk in wardrobe, bigger than my front yard. It was luxurious. The spa facilities were nowhere near as bad as the staff made out. It was a huge space with a good-sized pool. There were a few cracked tiles and worn facilities, but I'd seen worse. The hotel just looked well used.

"New tiles here, two new Jacuzzis and a urban themed sauna and steam room over there," he lectured as we walked around the spa nestled in the basement.

"It all sounds great. I'm going to be in here all the time, you know? Well, not when I'm working."

"You do get complimentary use of the spa and wellness centre. You even get discounts on rooms," he said, sounding as excited as I felt after hearing that. Access to the spa and gym, for free! I loved a bargain; Liam knew that. I'd come back with bags of free stuff from the Freshers Fair. Pens, pencils, magnets, vouchers, drinks, even condoms. I'd picked up loads because they were free. I'd never made use of them though. We took the lift back up to the office floor. Glass encased the whole open-plan area. As Ian led me to my desk, each time we passed a room I gazed through the glass pane. I couldn't help myself. Each door had a name and job title just at eye level, etched in white. My eyes caught Callum's name on a door. I looked in to see him sat at his desk, wearing a navy blue suit, with his white cuffs showing slightly at the sleeve. Just as I was about to pass his office, our eyes met briefly, and he immediately looked down. He looked disappointed. Angry even.

"And here we are," Ian said, stopping at the office next door to Callum's.

Oh god. This can't be happening.

"A whole room to myself? I honestly don't mind having one of the desks in the centre, over there?" I tried to avoid being in the room, without sounding ungrateful.

"Don't be silly, Tamsin. It's all yours. It even has a coffee machine." Ian laughed, looking quite pleased with himself.

"Well, I wouldn't expect anything less from this place, Ian. If my office didn't have a coffee machine, I would have taken one from one of the hotel rooms," I joked as I entered my office, nearly blinded by the light pouring in from the windows spanning the room. Ian loved to laugh.

"All that's left is to put your name on the door." I couldn't believe it. My dreams were coming true. I sat in my office chair and spun myself around. There was nothing that could ruin this, not even the awkward fact that Callum was on the other side of the plaster board dividing our offices.

Later that morning, once I had settled into my office and fire safety had been dealt with, Roberta came in to show me how to use the hotel's systems. She was considered an expert at Farden. She'd only been there for a short time, so it was clear she learnt quick. Ian would be the first to admit the hotel would fall apart without her. I knew I was going to get on with her. She had the bubbly sort of personality I was used to surrounding myself with, just like Liam.

"You are so lucky, you know." Roberta nudged me, signalling the fact that we were next door to Callum. I blushed. Sleeping with him had complicated things. I just wished I could have watched from afar, admired his tight pants that hugged his junk without all of this mess.

"You had sex with him, didn't you?" she said confidently.

"How do you...?" I gasped.

I should have denied it.

"Please, Tamsin. It's written all over your face. I was speaking to Callum this morning and when I mentioned you he went all awkward and tried to change the subject. He is always so confident, but this morning, not so much. You've ruined him." Roberta laughed but I had a feeling she was being serious.

There was a knock on the door.

"Oh, I'm sorry. I'll come back," Callum said after noticing Roberta in the room. I looked and smiled to try to make the awkward feeling go away.

"It's alright, I'm just heading back to my office. See you later, guys." Roberta said as she walked out of my room. I hadn't even had the chance to log on to the system.

Great.

I had to do something. We looked at each other, both speechless for a while. Callum played with his fingers nervously. Had I really ruined him? A man with such a confident and hard exterior. I couldn't help but stare at his hands, my mind tracing back to when they were all over my naked body. Even the slightest of his touches made me tremble.

"Callum." I plucked up the courage to speak. Saying his name was kind of pathetic, but it was more than he did.

"T," Callum said in return.

Throw me a bone here.

I tried to force some more words from my mouth to string together a sentence, but it was too awkward. I felt sick to my stomach with regret.

"I can't stop thinking about the other night..." He finally spoke.

Thinking about me?

I remained silent. I just wanted to run into his arms and hold him. I didn't care about what he was about to say or my stupid decision to leave.

"I hope you don't mind me coming in. My mind was going crazy being next door. Why did you leave?"

Damage control.

Thoughts ran through my head. If I had been watching myself in a film, I would have yelled at the screen. Any girl in their right mind would have stayed wrapped in his arms; even I knew that.

"I got scared. We're colleagues. I'm sorry." I had to force the words from my dry mouth.

"Seeing you at the end of my drive..." Callum sighed. "I had such a great night, and it hurt."

I had no idea what to do or say. I contemplated cracking open a window and jumping from the twenty-third floor to escape. I'd never had a guy make me feel the way he did. He was hurting because of me.

"I just need to know, was it just one night? Or do I have another chance to take you out properly?" Callum filled the silence I had left him with.

"It's not often I find myself with a guy asking for more than one night. How could I say no? Just give me the time and place, and I'll be there."

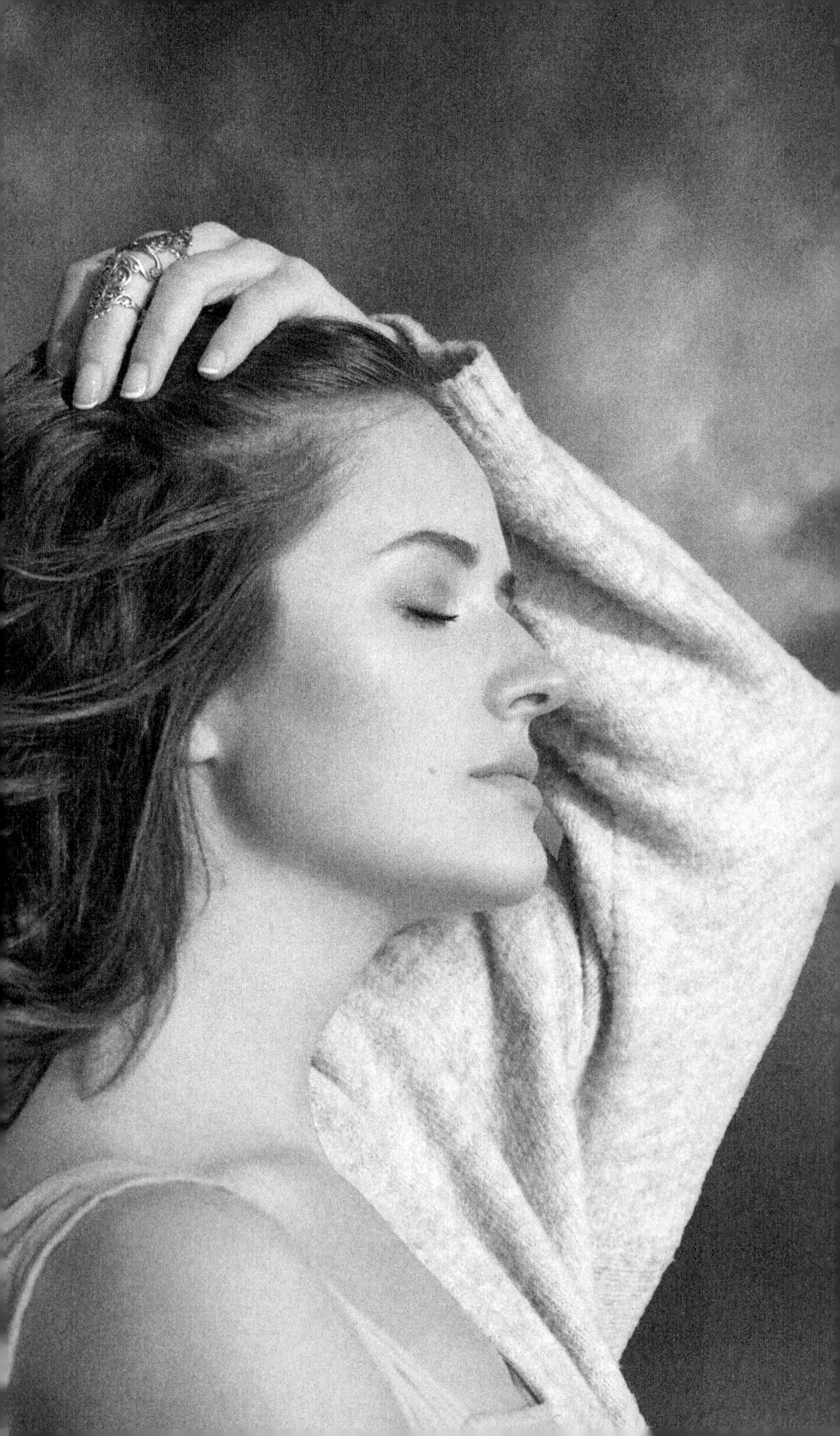

CHAPTER SIX

A whole working week had passed. Things were smoother now that Callum and I had patched things up. The dead air between us had turned back into lust, especially on my part. We constantly found reasons to see each other at work, usually meeting about the upcoming spa renovation or *computer issues*. We had been texting, too, a lot. Mum had even noticed me smiling more frequently, most of the time looking at my phone.

I could talk to Mum about anything, yet some people found that weird. We were best friends after all. As much as she could sometimes share too much information for my *delicate* ears to cope with, I wouldn't have changed it for the world. She listened to every worry, no matter how big or small, whether it was when I had my first kiss, broke up with my first boyfriend at school, or even getting my period. Her face lit up when I told her about Callum. She'd always wanted a happily ever after for me. She said that Callum would be my *Prince Charming*. Heck, even I was hopeful.

My phone buzzed in my pocket.

Callum
19th May 2018

[10:12]

Hey T. Strange not seeing you today after seeing you every day in work this week. These weekends are going to kill me. I have an idea, though. Save me by meeting me at The Country Club tonight at 8.30pm. The table's booked under T x

Hoping helped! I couldn't help but grin like the Cheshire Cat. A proper date. At a bloody snazzy restaurant.

"Is that Callum?" Mum knew me so well; she didn't have to ask.

"Yep, he's asked me to meet him tonight." I pulled my mum from the couch where the cushions were moulded into her shape, trying not to hurt her. She had barely left the house at all because I'd been so busy at work, so we headed to the back garden to allow her some of the fresh air she had been missing. She valued her privacy and didn't want anyone to know she had cancer, so she hid it whenever she could. She'd bought a gazebo and placed it next to the back door, so our neighbours couldn't look over the garden. She didn't want sympathy, not even from the old lady next door. She was a proud woman. She had little, but what she had was enough. I hated seeing her like this. Cancer was killing her, chemotherapy was draining the personality out of her, and having no hair was upsetting her more than the cancer itself. She could cope with the pains in her chest and the aches that led her body to collapse. Nothing could fix the emotion she felt when she looked in the mirror. As the weeks passed, the less she wore the wig around the house. She barely had the energy to brush her teeth, never mind put a wig on. I read the text from Callum to her in full, excited to share it with her.

"He sounds so sexy. If you don't go and meet him, I will."

"Believe me, Mum, I'm going to meet him. I will wrestle you to the ground if you try to take my man," I said with sass as she put her fists up to try to fight me, using all her energy to hold her hands up limply. The smile on my face faded suddenly as I realised I hadn't spoken about Mum to Callum. Not one word. When we were at work, we spoke about work, or flirted. Selfishly, I had divided my life. Work was my only norm, because as soon as I arrived back home I had to care for Mum. The only other time I had a short break was when Mum's cancer nurse came to do a home visit. Her name was Rebecca, and she swept in twice a week like a superhero. She wasn't just there for mum either; she was there for me, too. I tried to turn down as much support as I could. It was my responsibility to look after her, and there were others with cancer who had nobody. Besides, I could manage. I was managing. I worried that telling Callum would drive him away. It was a lot.

He needs to know.

I'd tell him at the restaurant. I had to. Before that, though, it was all about spending some quality time with Mum. I wanted to make the most of our weekend together, as every evening after work I was exhausted and had to do chores. We watched our favourite comedy TV shows and I painted her nails a light shade of purple. That was her favourite colour. I painted my nails, too, choosing a deep red colour to compliment the dress I was going to wear, while she drank her meal replacement.

My taxi pulled into The Country Club car park. It was a small restaurant, just off a busy road near Crewe and it sat in the countryside, secluded and affluent. The sky was a gorgeous orange as the sun set over a field. The restaurant was already lit up with twinkling fairy lights and flickering candles that made the whole building glow as bright as the sunset. It wasn't raining, so customers huddled outside around tables. I knew Callum had already arrived as I recognised his personalised number plate. As I passed the groups of people to the front doors, a small group of men wolf whistled in my direction. Immediately, my head shot down towards the concrete steps. I overheard one guy commenting on how *'fit'* I was, which made me cringe.

Must be the alcohol talking.

I took it as a compliment, although I rarely took compliments well. I'd usually react by arguing and telling the other person they were wrong, or I would blush and get all shy. This time I remained flustered. I looked up to see Callum wearing a navy suit jacket accompanied with a plain white shirt. He sat in a quiet corner of the restaurant with a bottle of champagne already placed on the table. It was like he'd read my mind and knew I loved fizz.

"You look gorgeous." He looked me up and down as I stood glancing in the mirror with panic. I was beetroot red from being whistled at.

"Blushing already? I didn't know I had that effect on you." He laughed and I chuckled along nervously.

"Oh, believe me, you do." I sat down, trying to hide my embarrassment from the guys just outside the patio door.

The men continued to comment outside, looking at me occasionally. Callum turned to them, communicating with his eyes only. "This is beautiful. I wasn't expecting any of this, Cal."

"They won't bother you anymore," he said confidently.

"Don't worry about them. They've probably done it

to every girl who walked past," I said as he poured me a glass of champagne.

"They don't bother me. They were bothering you, though, I could see. Also, don't put yourself down like that, T. You are beautiful. From the moment I laid eyes on you, I knew I wanted more." He grabbed my hand. I didn't understand how he could be so upset about me leaving, yet seemed unfazed by the rowdy guys outside. Who was I to try to understand the complex state of a man's brain? I just hoped he meant every word he said because I was falling for him, hard. Even more than I knew.

Our starters arrived quickly after we ordered them. Salt and pepper calamari for me and baked Camembert for Callum.

"This is delicious. Want some?" he said, already handing over some bread covered in the gooey cheese. I moaned with pleasure as I took a bite.

"That's so hot," he mumbled as I continued to dig into my food.

As we waited for our mains, I tried to find the best time to tell him about Mum. It was difficult as we barely stopped talking.

"To us!" He raised his glass to mine.

"I need to tell you something, Callum," I blurted, interrupting his toast.

"What is it?" He looked concerned and set down his glass in its original place.

With hesitation, I told him about Mum. About how close we were. I must have rambled and told him our life story to try to avoid telling him about Mum's cancer. I didn't want to burden him.

"And, she has cancer. It's shit." The truth finally left my mouth in a casual way, as if it didn't bother me. But it did. It wasn't often I spoke to anyone about her cancer, like I denied the reality of what the disease was doing to her. As we spoke in more detail, I felt tears filling my eyes.

Callum grabbed my hand again to comfort me, although this time I felt sadness grow over me, instead of butterflies.

"I can't imagine what you're going through, T. I'm here for you, okay?"

A huge weight lifted from my shoulders, so heavy it had been pressing on my chest. I'd carried it around for no reason. It didn't matter after all. I leant back in my chair as I relaxed into the evening.

"So, tell me about your parents? Your childhood?" I asked. After talking so much, I needed a break, otherwise I would have driven myself insane.

"My childhood was fine. I had everything I could have ever wanted–a warm home, good friends at school, and crazy parents. One day, you could meet them?" He smiled back and continued to hold my hand, the tip of his thumb grazing against my skin.

"That would be nice."

Our main meals arrived and we tried to eat in between the flowing conversation. Talking to him had become so natural that I could have sat there all night. Once we'd finished, the waiter passed us a list of desserts and cleared the plates. My fingers brushed along the spine of the menu as I gazed down at all of the choices.

"Don't do that to me. You've been teasing me all evening. You can't lick your lips like that."

"What are you on about?" I looked at him seductively.

"Are you asking for trouble? Right, we're going back to mine. We can have dessert there."

He quickly paid the bill, and before I knew it, he'd escorted me out of the restaurant, holding onto my hand. The men who had whistled earlier were still sat in the same place outside, more and more intoxicated, but this time remained silent as Callum wrapped his arm around the small of my back.

"Get in."

The more forceful he became, the more I wanted to disobey him. My body ached with desire, with a need to be close to him. I'd never met a guy who had the ability to make me feel as comfortable and confident as I did in front of them before–well, apart from Liam. In no time at all, we were buckled in and driving towards Callum's house.

"I need to apologise in advance because when I get you home, I won't be able to control myself." Until those words left Callum's mouth, I thought the sexual tension between us had peaked. I was wrong. My thoughts flicked back to the last night we'd spent together, as anticipation and confidence oozed from my body. It was like I was a different person, possessed even.

"Who's to say we need control?"

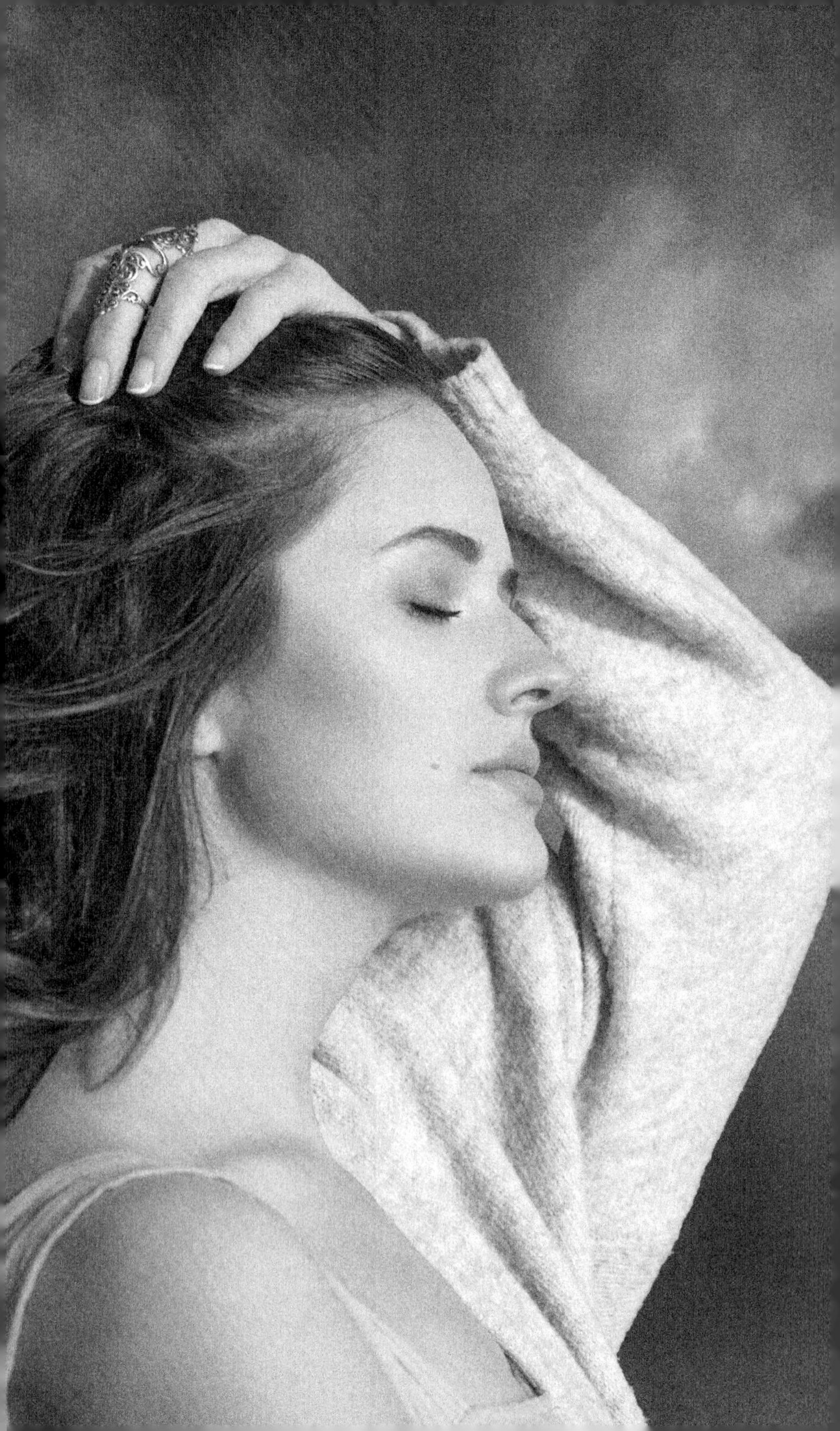

CHAPTER SEVEN

Light poured in through a gap in the curtains, my eyes burning from the bright light. The pure white bedding was hung over my body, and my hair met the pillowcase in a mess of knots. It wasn't just the bedding that looked familiar; the whole room left me with regret from the last time I'd been there. Not because of Callum—I couldn't regret that—but because I'd left. I lay in Callum's bed once more, only this time he wasn't next to me. I picked up my phone to check the time and responded to the countless texts I had received from Liam with a picture of Callum's room. I then messaged Mum.

Mum - ICE1
20TH May 2018

[09:39]

Hey mum. I'm safe. I'm with Callum. Will be home soon xxx

I knew she'd worry about me. I then mindlessly scrolled through social media until the door opened. The smell of a cooked English breakfast filled the room before I caught sight of Callum. He was wearing a tight white t-shirt and black boxers that wrapped nicely around his trunk like thighs. He carried in a tray of food and placed it in front of me.

"But, why?" I asked him, in awe of what he'd done. I could have wept.

"I woke up early so you couldn't leave without me knowing again. I made you breakfast because I know you're a foodie and I want to keep you here for a while longer." He smirked more than usual while opening the curtains wide, allowing light to stream in.

"You shouldn't have."

"I know, T. In all seriousness, you deserve it. You've been caring for your mum, but who's looking after you? Let me help." Callum sat on the duvet covers beside me and looked deep into my eyes. Now he had me smiling more than ever. I was living a dream and I didn't want to wake up.

"So, you told me about your mum last night, but what else do you have to tell? What about your dad? Boyfriends? Committed any crimes?" His grin grew as mine faded.

My hunger had gone. Not because of the boyfriends

he wanted to know about, or lack of for that matter. Or even because I had streaked across the university campus with a sex toy in my hands, and ended up breaking my toe to escape a police car that came around the corner. I wasn't hungry because I hadn't spoken about my dad in years. I didn't have to.

"I don't know who my dad is. I don't want to either. For a long time I thought Mum went to a sperm donor to have me. That's what she'd call him anyway." A small smile grew on my face. "But as I grew up, I started to ask her more and more questions and I found out that she was protecting me." I paused and Callum looked at me, confused.

"Protecting you from what?" he asked, and moved closer to me on the bed as the food became colder.

"He left Mum because of me. When he found out she was pregnant, he got drunk, they argued and he packed his things." I looked at him nervously.

"That's so shit, T."

Bile churned in my stomach the more I spoke about him. Callum didn't say anything. Instead, he continued to listen and grabbed my hand.

"So that's why Mum called him the sperm donor. She said it was the one good thing he did for her. I'm lucky to have her, you know? Now I'm lucky to have you, too." I smiled warmly at him.

"You're wrong. I'm the lucky one, T." He leant in and kissed me softly. "I'm always here if you need anything, okay?"

I looked at him in awe. Normally, I'd have looked away and blushed, but this time I couldn't look away; I didn't want to. He lay next to me, his eyes lustfully scanning my whole body. I still hadn't moved from the imprint I'd left on the mattress underneath me, which was perfectly moulded to the shape of my body.

"So, what about you? Tell me more about this perfect childhood of yours."

"Umm, well, it was pretty perfect. My mum and dad were great. Mum comes from quite an upper-class family, and quite religious at that, although she's probably the most spontaneous person you'll ever meet. She'd book a holiday the night before and pack their bags to go in the morning. She's a loon, although I'd never say that to her face. And, well Dad goes along with everything Mum says. He's just a really decent guy. He thinks the world of her. They even helped me get to North America for my gap year..." He stopped speaking after a while, looking awkward. I could tell he felt guilty talking about how great his life was, even though he had no reason to. Of course, I was a little jealous. Who wouldn't be? As much as I didn't have a conventional family, it didn't mean I wasn't happy. My childhood had made me the person I was.

"I guess that's where it all went wrong."

"What do you mean?" I leant in and rested my hand on his arm.

"Well, I met this girl in a bar in New York at the beginning of my gap year, and cutting a long story short, she ended up travelling with me to each of the places I'd booked to go to across America. Towards the end, we were in a pretty serious relationship. I loved Louise. So about a month before I was due to go home, we arrived back in New York. That's where I proposed to her. We were standing next to the Ghostbusters fire station, her favourite film, and she said yes."

"That sounds amazing. This isn't where you tell me you're married, is it?"

"Ha, no." His laugh was blunt, and his face looked as serious as it had when he'd seen me at the bottom of his drive. "The opposite actually. Two weeks after I proposed, she disappeared and I've not seen her since. I woke up to a note saying that there was stuff she had to deal with. There was no trace of her. Her phone number had changed. No sign of her on social media. She'd vanished."

"Shit, Callum, I don't know what to say." I didn't. I could hear the pain in his voice as if the memories were replaying on repeat as he told his story. I wanted to grab hold of him and never let go, but instead I listened. I let him pour his heart out to me. He needed it.

"It was shit. For a long time, Louise was all I could think about... but yeah, that's me. Not many people know about her." Callum changed his tone and snapped out of the pain he was feeling. I could tell he didn't want to speak about her anymore. He had a taboo subject just like me. Hearing all of this made me realise why me leaving that night had affected him so much. It was because of her, because he'd been walked out on before. That wasn't going to happen again. I was going to prove that not all girls ran away, restore his faith, and never leave his side. I just wanted to know if he missed her. I needed to know if he still loved her, and if he did still love her, would that remove me from the picture?

"Come on then, let's get you home," Callum said, getting off the bed to get ready, leaving the food untouched behind us.

I stepped out into the rain and embraced the mild breeze and the shower that fell lightly onto my bare shoulders. Callum followed behind after locking the front door, looking pristine as ever dressed in a long khaki top that hung below his waist. He was wearing black ripped skinny jeans to compliment, which sat very well on his tush. I had already thought about buying him a pair of grey sweatpants. They left very little to the imagination. Callum wasn't overly chirpy, but I wasn't surprised after he'd gushed emotions about his runaway *nearly*-bride, but that didn't stop him from reaching over and softly pressing his lips to mine while he wrapped the seatbelt around me. The short drive home led us down weaving country roads, past a quaint ice cream shop, which prized a large straw sculpture in the shape of Peter Rabbit.

This was the part of Cheshire I loved.

Callum whistled along to the radio and it wasn't long before he pulled up curbside opposite my house.

"Before you go, what are you doing over the next couple of days?" My hand was over his, resting on the gear stick.

"Today, I'm going to spend some time with Mum. I feel like I've hardly seen her. Then I'm working at Farden in the week, nothing in the evenings."

"Tomorrow it is then. I've got to stay late at work, so I'll pick you up at eight, if that's okay?"

"Great. I'll see you then and in the morning for work." I leant over and kissed him. I knew I'd miss him as soon as I got out of his car, so I made the most of it. His tongue wrapped around mine as we became lost in each other. Louise didn't matter, and it seemed Callum didn't care either.

"I'm home!" I swung the door wide open with an enthusiastic shove. Usually I'd have been interrogated by my mum as soon as I walked through the door, but instead the house remained silent.

"Mum?" I continued to shout through the house, but there was no reply. I panicked and once again kicked my heels across the room and threw my bag on the floor. My breaths became short as I rushed to each room, tripping over furniture as I went. I couldn't help but think this was it. The end. It wasn't supposed to end like this. It wasn't supposed to end at all. In a moment of panic, I heard the downstairs toilet door creak, and behind it she was sat on the floor sobbing.

"Where were you? I've been sat here for hours." She sobbed further, as tears began to puddle on my cheeks.

"What happened?" I grabbed her hands and slowly helped her to get up.

"I didn't have the energy to get up. I fell last night and couldn't move. I couldn't reach the door handle." Tears streamed down her face, trying to rid her of the embarrassment she must have felt.

She lay silently on the couch with a cover draped over her, barely glancing away from the television. That evening, she was different, the worst I'd seen her. She wasn't in pain physically, but she was ruined emotionally. It was like someone had started to drain the life out of her, like the symptoms in the early days of chemotherapy weren't wearing off anymore and the effects had taken up permanent residence. It killed me to see her in that way. Her usual caring, loving, optimistic self had become dull, emotionless and cold. I grabbed boxes of tablets and organised them in the order she had to take them. It was a chore, but I knew it was keeping Mum alive. Seeing her helpless had left me exhausted, my emotions still running high after talking about my dad. I collapsed into bed that night and lay in the darkness, waiting to fall asleep. Waiting for the day to be over and for the thoughts that had run wild in my mind to stop. My phone lit up and buzzed simultaneously.

Callum
20th May 2018

[21:47]

Hey beautiful. Can't wait for tomorrow evening. I've spoken to Ian, and I've moved stuff around in my work calendar. Fancy travelling home together after work? xxx

[21:53]

Hey! I'm so sorry. Mum isn't great at the moment. I need to be at home with her. Can we reschedule? xxx

I lay awake for what seemed like hours, waiting for a reply after I had let him down. I didn't want to, but I'd have been selfish to just leave Mum after seeing the state she was in. I knew he'd understand, but I still struggled to switch off. My phone vibrated occasionally, alerting me to new emails. If I hadn't had some control that night, I would have continued to text his phone for a reply. I hated letting people down. I always said yes, but I had to prioritise the person who meant the most to me, and make up for abandoning her the night before. My life could wait; it didn't matter as much as Mum's.

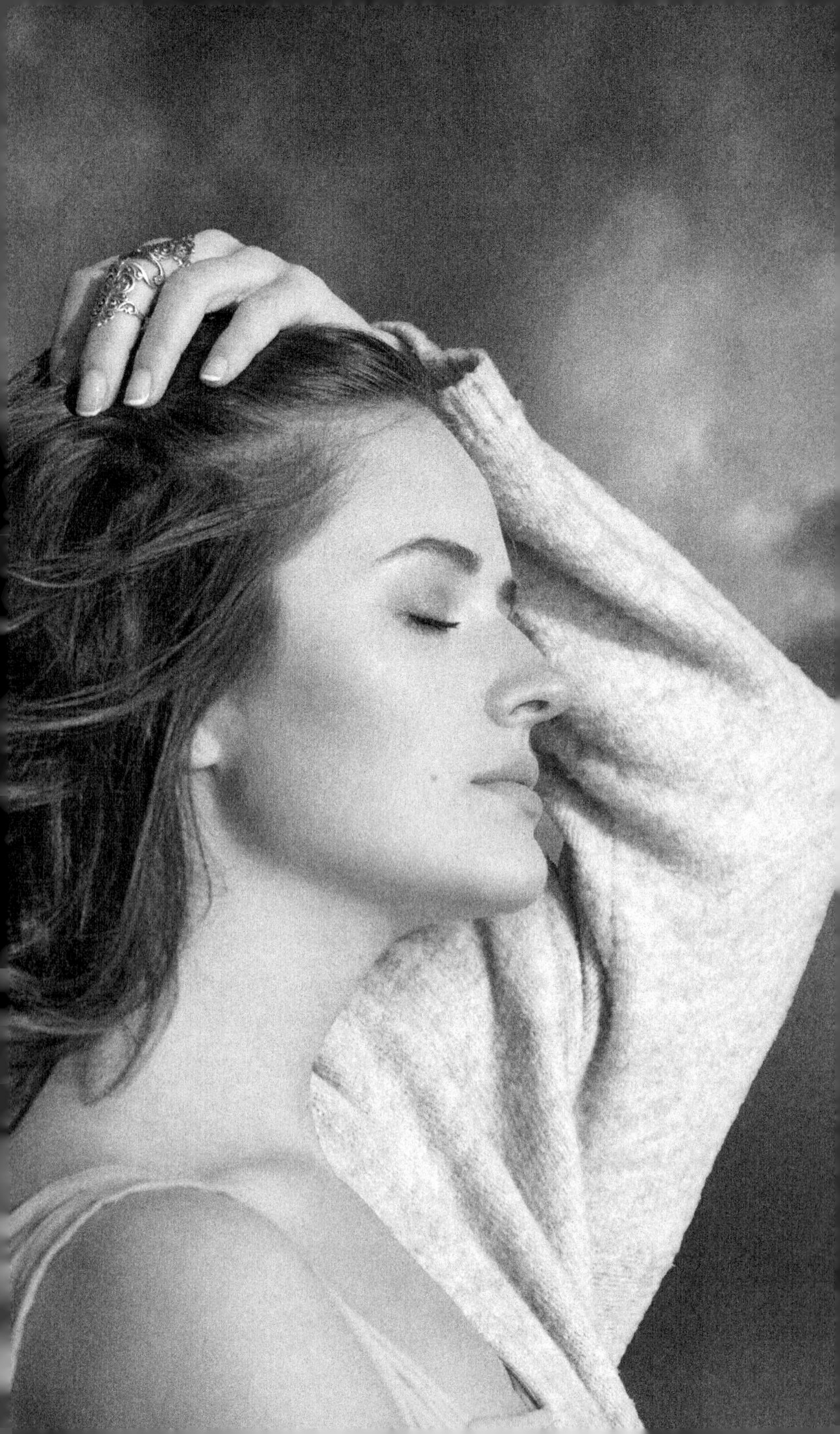

CHAPTER EIGHT

Woken by my alarm the next morning, I looked straight at my phone to check if Callum had replied. My eyes struggled to adjust to the light at first. I was not a morning person.

CALLUM
21ST MAY 2018

[05:42]

HEY BEAUTIFUL. SORRY I FELL ASLEEP LAST NIGHT, I COMPLETELY UNDERSTAND. HOW IS SHE DOING NOW? DO YOU NEED ME TO COME HELP OUT? I'LL SEE YOU AT WORK SOON, T XXX

I sighed with relief. He'd just fallen asleep and I'd been panicking for no reason. I was my own worst enemy sometimes. I jumped out of bed quickly to avoid the temptation of snoozing my alarm and sleeping some more. The willpower I had! Mum's medication slipped across the kitchen counter as I placed them in the tablet organiser, still squinting in the light. Sorting medication was hard, but applying makeup while tired was almost impossible. I looked at my reflection–my tired eyes drooped more than ever, and no matter how hard I tried, there was no covering them.

"I'm sorry about yesterday, Tamsin," Mum said, peering into my room, seeming more rested and less distressed.

"You have no reason to be sorry at all. I'm the one who should be sorry. I shouldn't have left you for so long. I'll finish early again tonight so we can spend some time together, put on a good film and cocoon in our duvets."

I kissed her goodbye and was out of the door by quarter past six. I collapsed against a seat on the train, already exhausted. The past few days had drained me.

It's only Monday.

I cursed as I struggled to keep my eyes open. If I'd been a character in a cartoon, I would have had matchsticks propping them open. I arrived at work just over an hour later, gasping for a strong cup of coffee from the hotel's cafe. Coffee was the only fuel my body would accept in the mornings; not even the fresh scent of a warm croissant could tempt me to take a bite.

"Morning, sleepy." Roberta crept up behind me, enough to make me jump out of my skin. Luckily, I hadn't grabbed my coffee. Otherwise, it would have been all over both of us.

"Hey, you," I croaked. "Want a coffee? I've just ordered one but I could bring you one up."

"Sure. I'll meet you up there then," Roberta said. She swung her bag over her shoulders and headed towards the lift. Roberta and I spent most of our workdays together as she'd been showing me the ropes. We'd become good friends, although she still hadn't grasped that I wasn't a morning person.

"Ah, the late morning joys of customer complaints," I said sarcastically, sifting through piles of printed complaint emails ready to delegate to Rach and James. Sleep deprivation was making me hate Farden, which no amount of coffee could solve. I zoned out briefly as I thought about my very own dog hotel in the middle of the countryside, far from anyone complaining about a closed spa. Changing Farden's reputation seemed like an impossible task, but I couldn't give up.

Rome wasn't built in a day.

"It can't be that bad, Tamsin." Roberta tried to make me feel better with little success.

"It doesn't end here, though, on paper. No, that would be too easy. There's more emails and don't get me started on these review sites."

"I'm sensing a lot of sass today. Emotions running high?" Roberta said as she slid her chair out from under the desk.

"You have no idea. Just two more hours to go. I'm going to have to go to my meeting. I've already told Rach and James to come up, but when they get here can you give them these to sort? I need to go and get a head start on the pitch." I continued to gather my things in a hurry, as time ran away quicker than I could catch up with it.

"Sure thing, sugar." She smiled and waved me off.

I waited in Conference Room Two patiently until one o'clock. Callum waved eagerly through the glass panels surrounding the room. Our cancelled date night had almost slipped my mind with the mad rush preparing for the meeting. He came in and sat at the front, just close enough to graze my inner thigh as I sat waiting for everyone to arrive.

"Feel good? Don't worry, I'll stop when everyone's here. I'd hate to put you off during your first ever pitch." He winked and kept his hand on my thigh.

"Hey, who knows? I'd sound really excited if you do it during the pitch. I just hope Ian likes it."

My pitch was controversial. I wanted to run a campaign across the social media platforms to encourage good reviews. In return, Farden would give out free day passes to the brand new spa, along with having a VIP list for the first week.

"That's if I can actually get this thing to work. Don't you just hate it when the icons at the bottom start randomly jumping?" I asked rhetorically, shouting at the laptop. "I didn't click on you."

Callum got out of the seat and jokingly backed out of the room, looking at me like I was a crazy person. He was fast becoming my ray of light. He always knew how to cheer me up, and when I needed it.

"Finally!" I yelled as the presentation started to work, as Ian walked into the room. I looked at him with embarrassment. Ian looked startled, as it seemed I had yelled at him for being late.

"Not you, sir, the computer. It's been one of those days." I tried to recover.

"Tell me about it, Tamsin," Ian said looking deflated and tired. It wasn't like him at all. He'd usually had a smile plastered on his face.

Shit. He's in a bad mood. He's going to hate my pitch.

"Oh no. Is there anything I can do or get you? Shall we reschedule the meeting?" I had all of my limbs crossed wanting him to reschedule. I was hoping my personality could sweet-talk him into submission. He couldn't hate my pitch!

"No, I'm fine. Let's just get Darren and Sharon in here and get started." Callum trotted off at Ian's order to gather the troops.

I'm screwed.

I had worked so damn hard on a presentation that was going to be a flop just because my boss was having a tantrum. Callum walked back through into the office.

"Ian, Darren and Sharon are both at home. Darren is working from home and Sharon has a sickness bug.

I've just checked with Roberta. They're on the ends of their emails, though."

"Well, just send the pitch via email. Tell everyone I want their thoughts by the end of tomorrow," Ian said as he got up in a fluster and walked away. Callum had saved me from today without even realising. He was a hero. My Hero.

"Thank you so much, Callum. I was literally shitting bricks."

"I wasn't the one who gave Sharon a stomach bug. But now you best crack on with that email and convince the others that this plan of yours is going to work."

"I'm on it."

I sent the email. The decision was out of my hands. I just hoped I'd done enough to convince everyone. Most of my life, I had dreamed of becoming a hot shot in the business world. Why was it that when I'd imagined my dream job, I'd never thought of the stress it was going to bring? I loved working at the hotel, but today I was buckling–buckling under the pressure of my job, my emotions and my life. I couldn't wait for my shift to be over so I could get back home to Mum.

After falling asleep on the train home and nearly missing my stop, I'd arrived at home and snuggled on the sofa. I was nodding off, resting my head on my mum's shoulder as a knock at the door made us both jump. We turned to each other confused as no one ever knocked, especially at this time of night. Liam would just walk in, so it wasn't him.

"Ugh, my back. I'm getting so old and achy."

"Old? I must be ancient." Mum looked at me disapprovingly as I went to open the door, unable to look through the peephole as I had covered it with the famous *Friends* picture frame. Callum stood on the doorstep looking fantastic as usual. A man bag hung from his shoulder and he held a large picnic basket and a bouquet of purple calla lilies.

"I know I should have called first to make sure this was okay, but I wanted to surprise you. I've brought our date to you. Also, I want to meet Theresa." He smiled and looked to the ground shyly. "I want you to know I'm here for you, no matter what. Whether you need help with your mum, whether we are a thousand miles apart or even if we argue and fall out, I will always be there to try to make everything right again."

I looked at him, startled by the bouquet that lay on his bicep and in awe that he wanted to meet Mum. Aside from Mum and Liam, I hadn't had someone want to be there for me this much. He was fast becoming my rock. I did wish I'd known he was coming; I was wearing a grey sweatshirt and joggers that I'd thrown on once I got home from work.

"My favourite colour, they are gorgeous. Thank you." I pressed a kiss to his lips after looking lustfully at him for an uncomfortable amount of time, and invited him in, taking the flowers out of his muscled embrace.

He placed his bag in the hall after asking for permission, even though he had no reason to.

"Who is it?" Mum croaked from the living room.

"Just me, Miss Cross." Callum stepped in ahead of me and leant over and kissed her on the cheek. At the time, I didn't know how Mum would feel. She hadn't seen anyone in months.

"You must be Callum. Please, call me Tessa. Tamsin hasn't stopped talking about you. She goes on and on..." She laughed. Her wit was still intact, at least.

"MUM!" I said dramatically, and picked up Callum's things from the hall to take to my room. It was like she enjoyed embarrassing me, like most mums. I took his leather bag and black suit jacket upstairs, and quickly dashed around my room to tidy it before he came up.

Gayboy x
21ST May 2018

[19:56]

Callum kissed Mum on the cheek when he met her!!! Isn't he a babe?

Liam responded quickly, telling me that Callum better not steal *his* Tess from him. I continued to pick up after myself, laying his bag on my bed, and hung his suit jacket on the wardrobe as I admired the soft material. A small leather book had slipped from the bag and onto the bed. A ribbon marked the latest page of what seemed to be a journal.

> IT'S BEEN A WHILE SINCE I HAVE WRITTEN IN HERE. THERE WAS A TIME I NEVER THOUGHT ABOUT ANOTHER PERSON. DAYS I LONGED FOR YOUR TOUCH. MONTHS I WANTED YOU TO GET IN TOUCH. ALMOST A YEAR I SEARCHED FOR YOU. MAYBE I STILL WANT YOU. I DON'T KNOW. I DO KNOW THAT I'M FALLING HARD FOR SOMEONE ELSE, THOUGH.

I dropped the book in shock as Callum yelled my name from downstairs.

"Coming," I shouted back, my voice a little high pitched after reading his journal.

Did he still want her?

I shouldn't have read it; I had invaded his privacy. I walked downstairs to find Callum sat snugly next to mum on the sofa. I wanted to ask him about the journal, but I couldn't. It was personal. I could barely look him in the eye.

"Just prepping Mum's food. Be right back," I said awkwardly, desperate to excuse myself.

"Do you want help?" Callum said, about to get up from his seat.

"No, no. You stay there. Relax. I'll be back in a bit."

I swiftly made my way into the kitchen feeling more flustered than ever, leaving the door ajar. I couldn't help but eavesdrop. I could hear them talking about his parents. Callum told her about how his parents had both grown up in Crewe, and they were a similar age. His mum had gone to the same all-girls school as mine before she moved down south; they were just a couple of years apart. Mum loved to reminisce, so I knew she was happy. I could hear it in the tone of her voice. He was making her smile and laugh, something I'd struggled to do myself.

I guess it's okay to ask for help.

"You should meet my parents. They would love to meet you. Well, they need to meet Tamsin, too."

"That would be lovely, and you are too kind, but I don't think I'll have the energy to meet them, not yet. I'm embarrassed you've had to see me like this to be honest. If only you could have seen me, as me, and not consumed by this monster."

"It's only me." Liam could always be heard before he was seen. I opened the kitchen door to see Mum's smile grow wider. He greeted mum in the usual way, with a high-five and a kiss on each cheek. I just hoped he wouldn't do that to Callum, and knowing Liam, he would have. I glared at him from the kitchen as a warning, and he smirked at me. Callum rose from the sofa and wrapped his arms around Liam like they'd known each other for years.

"Missed you, babe," Callum said in a clear flirtatious way. He'd already figured Liam out. The way to my heart was food. The way to Liam's was hot guy flirting.

"Sickening." I laughed and looked at them both.

"You're just jealous. If you aren't careful, I'm stealing your man." Liam touched Callum seductively on the arm. Naturally, Callum didn't flinch, like he was used to all of the attention.

"Not before I do." Mum laughed.

"Hey, there is plenty of me to go round. I won't leave anyone out. Especially you, Tessa." Callum held onto Mum's hand. He was serious about her, and serious about us. I beamed knowing that Mum approved of him. I had my three favourite people all in the same room. I couldn't have been any happier.

"Did you open the card?" Callum asked with a cheeky smile as I shook my head. Callum led me to the kitchen where I lay the flowers ready to place in a vase. A white envelope was hidden snugly between the stems of the lilies, which I quickly opened.

T. It's time you took some time out and looked after yourself. That's why I've booked us a weekend at a spa retreat. It's not until October, but I want you to know I'm serious about us. Callum xxx

I was wrong. Three of my favourite people in the same room, and then a weekend away with one of them. My happiness grew uncontrollably. Was it the words written on the card that made me smile, or the thought of spending time away with Callum alone? It felt almost too good to be true.

Mum...

Dread filled me as I realised I'd be away from Mum again, for a whole weekend this time. I couldn't go; there was no way.

"Don't worry. Liam is going to be here with Tessa. You have nothing to worry about. It's handled." Callum could read me like a book. He must have seen the rush of anxiety on my face.

Callum called Liam into the kitchen, and in he came, enthusiastically skipping and jumping. He took the card from my hands and placed it to one side.

"Callum and I have been talking behind your back to organise this, and you had no idea. Step one of operation *steal Tamsin's man* is complete!"

"Why are we even friends?" I said, the sarcasm rolling off my tongue.

"Because you love me. And I love you. There is no getting rid of me, hun. Besides, Tess and me are going to have so much fun she'll not want you to come back."

"Haha. Dick." I couldn't help myself.

All I had to do now was wait. Patience had never been my strongest skill. October couldn't come soon enough.

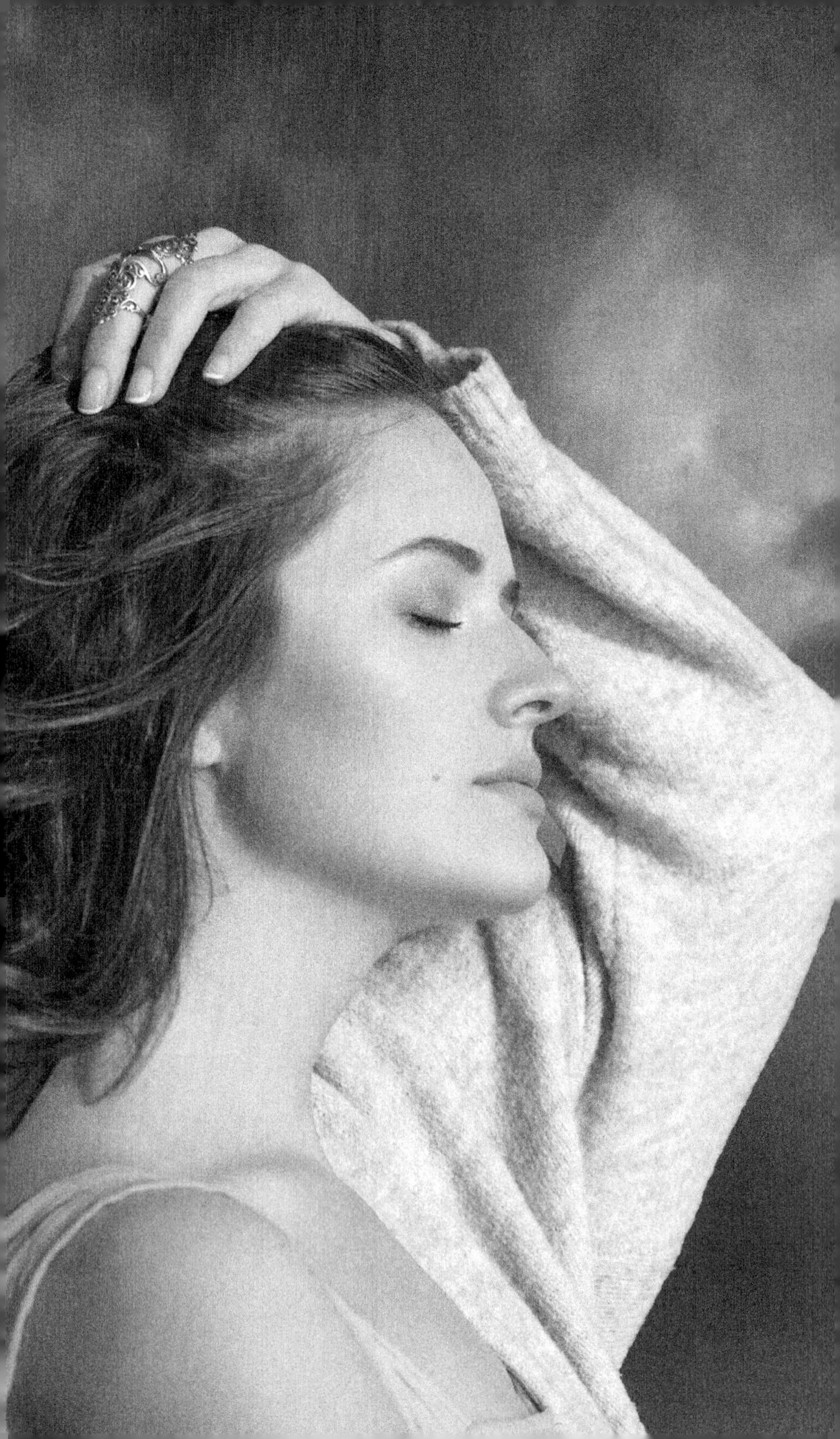

CHAPTER NINE

OCTOBER 2018

You've got to be kidding.

Not even a pinch could wake me from the dream-like surrounding I gaped at in awe. The pool glistened under the sun as the cool autumn breeze left ripples in the water. Buildings surrounded the pool, made up of columns two storeys high and wrapped in vines. A couple emerged fresh from the pool. Liam would have thought the guy was fit and probably would have pounced like a dog in heat.

"Oh god." I let out a small squeal as Callum placed his hands on my waist from behind. I hadn't noticed him coming out of the changing rooms. I didn't understand how I'd got ready quicker than him.

Probably too busy doing his hair.

The clean white cotton gown hugged his skin perfectly, like it had been tailored to him. His slight tan seemed darker, and his skin looked clearer than ever.

His black swimming shorts clung to his thighs. As much as I loved his tight white boxers, I also liked that now there was nothing concealing his modesty but a thin piece of polyester.

"It's just something else, isn't it, T?" I nodded in agreement.

"You're telling me. What are we waiting for? Let's go enjoy it before we go back to our room."

"We've got all day. It's only eleven am." Callum laughed as I pulled him excitedly to the closest of the spa experience rooms. I shut the door, trying not to let steam out, and then sat watching it fill the room around us. I could barely make out the shape of Callum sat next to me. He moved closer and placed his hand on my thigh, kissing my cheek, which was covered in water droplets. In my opinion, the first room was the best and not just because of the kiss, but because the steam smelled like *Vapour Rub* and it unblocked my allergy prone nose. I could breathe.

We continued visiting each experience room, walking clockwise around the pool, only a couple of minutes before the anticipation of the next room took over.

"Shall we go in the pool now?" I asked quietly, surrounded by people relaxing in the sauna, overlooking the pool.

"Not yet, T. I have another surprise. Come with me." I put my gown on over my bathing suit, and followed him into an open, modern restaurant connected to the spa itself. We weaved our way around the tables in the restaurant to have someone greet us near the exit.

"Reservation for Dunn." It wasn't often he used his last name. Damn, it was sexy.

Callum Dunn. Tamsin Dunn.

"This way, please." A small suited man escorted us to a secluded purpose-built cabin nestled between the burnt orange trees. Falling leaves made the area look like something out of a fairytale. We perched on the cushioned chairs and curled up next to each other underneath a fur blanket to hide from the bitter October weather. Heaters buzzed with a glowing heat so we didn't feel the cold at all.

"Surprise!" Callum kissed me again as I watched the man pour fizz into the champagne flutes on the table, then disappeared to get us some menus.

"Do you want to know the best bit? We're booked onto a Rasul Mud Treatment later. We can lie there and relax and spread mud on each other. Together. Naked." He looked at me seductively. I wanted to jump on him, and feel the fur on our bare skin, but I couldn't. Not with the waiter already on his way back to the table. That would have been awkward.

"We have the food that you pre-ordered. Can I assume there are no amendments?" the waiter asked. Callum nodded kindly, still oozing a sense of authority. A platter of food arrived not long after, and the champagne continued to flow, poured by a waitress who continued to check up on us. Callum's eyes followed her as she left the cabin for the second time. She was hot; there was no denying it. Her short blonde hair sat just above her shoulders, and her figure was the perfect hourglass shape.

"You aren't very subtle, you know?"

Callum looked at me and I grinned at him.

"What do you mean?" He squirmed.

"I saw you checking out that blonde. It's okay, though. She's gorgeous." He looked at me, puzzled. I assumed he was wondering why I wasn't having a go at him, or trying not to look turned on that I had called another girl hot.

"I don't know what to say. You aren't jealous?"

"Why would I be jealous? I'm sat here with you, aren't I? Besides, jealousy does not look good."

"Noted. I'll bear that in mind if I see you checking out another guy." He laughed, wiping a nervous bead of sweat from his forehead. Once we'd finished our platter of food, and the waitress resisted coming in and filling our glasses, I led him to the pool. I decided to save my three-some remark for another time. I didn't want him to spontaneously combust with excitement. It would have shown way too easily in those skimpy black shorts of his.

"Shut up! As if they have water beds," I exclaimed, bouncing on the balls of my feet as I prepared to jump on one of the beds. Callum climbed onto the one next to me, and once he had covered up, his hand reached out to grab mine.

"You are gorgeous. You know that, right?" Callum smiled at me, and I knew if I could have seen myself, I would have looked bright pink. A section of hair fell in front of my face, sodden by the steam from the last room we'd surrendered ourselves to. I moved my hair to the place it seemed to belong, and his eyes followed my every movement. I couldn't help but want him to climb onto me. The water beneath me moved my body in a certain rhythm and it tempted me to run my finger down the hem of his gown, grazing his abs until I met the top of his swimming shorts.

"Now, that's teasing," he said as his shorts began to bulge. His face filled with disappointment as I took my hand away. I wanted to carry on, I did, but I knew the women only a few beds away would undoubtedly wake at an inappropriate time. I couldn't resist temptation for long, though. My hand returned to his shorts and I continued to trace my finger across them. I could feel his excitement rising at the lightest of touches. I couldn't help but continue to play in that one area, making sure his gown covered his modesty. The more I held back, the more I wanted him, and seeing the pleasure on his face encouraged me further.

"Our room. Now," I commanded. I didn't need to beg. I had him in the palm of my hands.

. . .

We lay in our circular bed, which stretched further than I could reach, yet we couldn't have been any closer if we'd tried. The room was quirky, with pictures of animals dressed in suits hung precisely on the walls. My head rested on Callum's chest along with my hand, which was stroking his bare abdomen.

"I'm having the best time here with you. Thank you." I exhaled, lifting my head to kiss him for the thousandth time. I was smothering him with affection, but I didn't care and he didn't either. He was the first guy, in my experience, to want to show me how much he loved me. We pulled the cold duvet over us to cover our bare skin to help cool us down. Nothing could have made us separate, not even the sweat between us that I would usually have avoided by tucking the covers between our bodies.

"Tell me about it." He paused. "You're my weakness, my kryptonite. Do you know that?"

"Isn't a weakness something you want to get rid of?" I looked at him in horror.

"Most of the time, yes. Everyone wants to become stronger and not have any weaknesses, but you aren't a weakness in the conventional sense. You affect me like kryptonite, but in a good way. You make me open up. I've told you things I've not told my closest friends. You affect me in a way I never thought was possible. I don't ever want you to stop." In my mind, I begged for him to never stop talking.

"I love it when you speak romantic nerd to me." I

held him tighter than I had before. I couldn't help but laugh and mock him a little.

"Speaking of nerds... I brought my laptop with me." Callum eagerly pulled out his laptop.

Who brings work with them to a spa retreat?

I rolled my eyes. He proceeded to plug an HDMI cable into the back of the hotel room TV and opened a collection of films. He really was a nerd.

"I think the most important question I'm yet to ask you is *Marvel* or *DC*? Which do you prefer?" I hesitated, knowing it was a test. I'd always thought DC had the edge years before, but you couldn't beat Marvel. Their films were something else. And then there was my love for Chris Evans as Captain America, though. I didn't think I should tell him about that.

"Old DC, new Marvel," I said in an uncertain voice. Callum smiled at me.

Did I pass?

I must have been right, especially as he then went and put on *Thor: Ragnarok*. Chris Hemsworth was another hunk I wouldn't have kicked out of bed, and I had to sit there trying not to imagine him all over me. Me, Thor and Callum all in the same room. I must have been dreaming.

A dull hum from the room opposite woke me, with what must have been a vacuum cleaner banging on the skirting boards. I glanced at the alarm clock on the bedside table, which read '12.30'. Light crept in between the gaps in the blinds. I hadn't slept until the afternoon since the last time Liam and I had been to Tuesgay. Guilt choked me; we should have been making the most of the spa.

"Clearly that '*shhhh, we're sleeping*' sign we put on the door handle last night was a figment of our imagination." I turned to Callum who was also awake. He smirked at me and kissed my forehead. I went in to kiss his lips, but he pulled away.

What had I done?

I racked my brain for a reason why he didn't want to kiss me. I worried that I'd probably been screaming Chris Hemsworth's name in my sleep.

"Sorry, T. I must have some rank breath at the moment." He jumped up wearing nothing but his skin. I tried to pull him back onto the bed playfully, but I lacked energy and effort. He walked around the bed, teasing me unintentionally. I wanted him, bad breath and all. I reached to the floor for my phone to try to snap a picture, to find I had three recent missed calls from Liam.

"Oh god, who's he slept with now?" I said to myself while the phone dialled out and rang continuously.

"Liam is not available to take your call at the moment. Please leave a~" I hung up.

I fell back into the pillows, my head sinking deep into them, and then scrolled through my phone when a picture of Liam flashed up as he returned my call. There was a lot of background noise, and Liam's voice was muffled. I could hear voices I didn't recognise in between sirens. I could hear sirens.

"I didn't want to call you, Tams, but you need to come home. I'm with your mum, and we're heading to the hospital."

I dropped the phone instantly, without responding. The smile that had lingered all weekend had disappeared. My world slowly came to a grinding halt, and there was nothing I could do. I was two hours away from home.

"Are you talking to yourself again?" Callum walked in from the bathroom. I just sat there. Motionless. The only movement were the tears streaming down my face.

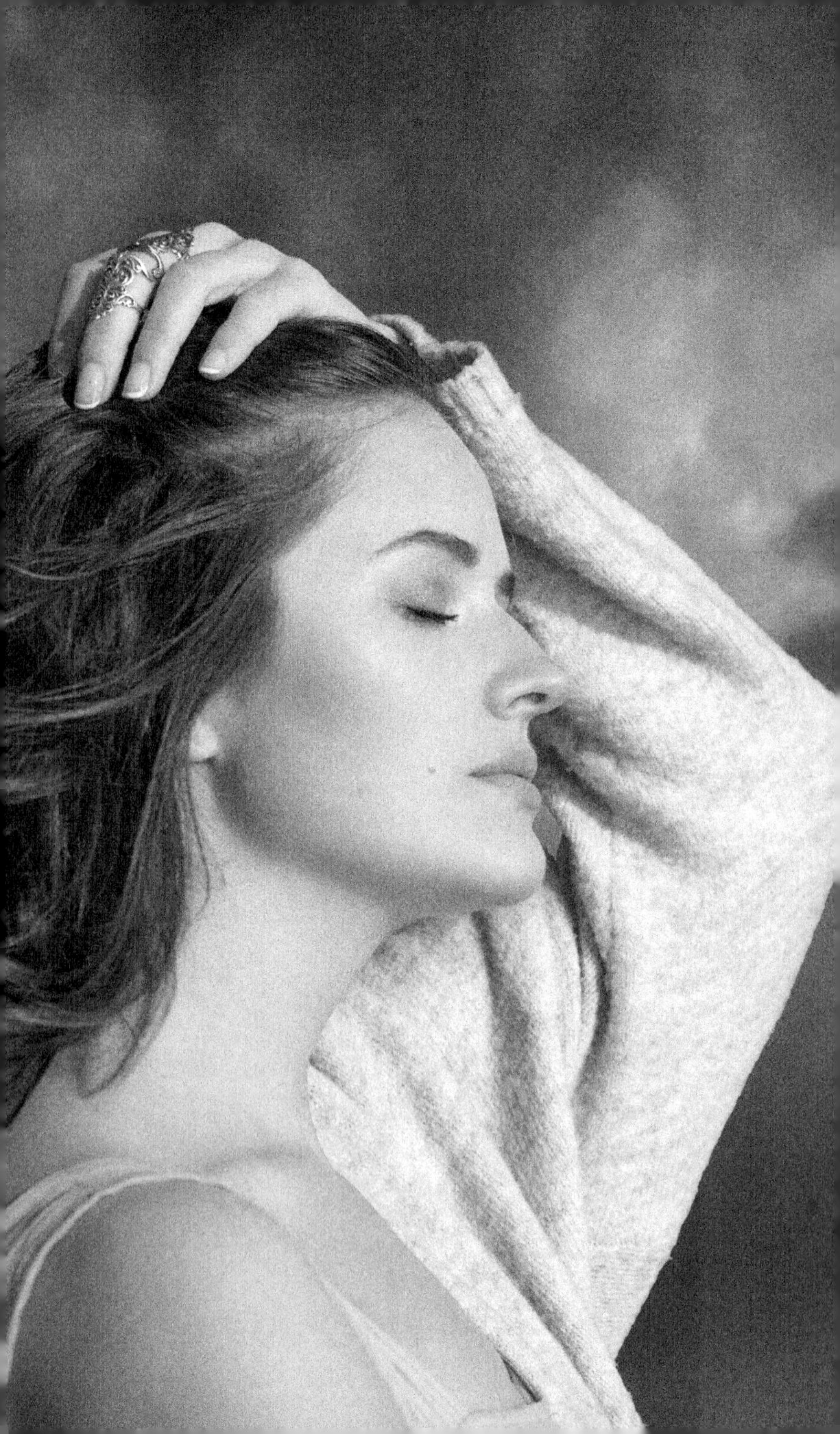

CHAPTER TEN

It's hard to describe heartache. Is it a pain in your chest or is it a numbness or an ache? I know how I felt. I felt like two children were fighting over a piece of Play-Doh, pulling and yanking at it in turn. The thing with Play-Doh is that it doesn't return to its original shape by itself. My heart had been torn once or twice before, but I was completely unaware that it was about to break in two.

I couldn't talk. I was speechless. Lifeless. Lifeless on the outside, but losing my mind on the inside. No matter how hard I tried, there was no switch I could flick to stop the thoughts from spinning around in my head. It felt like the car was in motion for hours. My senses amplified the haze around me as if my body were fighting to keep itself alive. Adrenaline rushed through my body and yet time seemed to stand still. Callum placed his hand on my lap, comforting me while pulling me from my subconscious. I'd not seen him drive that way before. It was dangerous, but I didn't care. I wanted him to drive faster. I needed him to know how much I loved him, but the lump in my throat was growing, stopping my every word. I guess that didn't matter. All that mattered was Mum. I wondered if she'd be pretending to cope with the pain, like she had for so long. As I continued to drown in my own thoughts, trying desperately to catch my breath, time stopped around me once more.

I clambered out of the car before Callum could align it between the tight spaces and frantically weaved my way across the car park. I stood at the entrance, filled with panic. The signs merged into a blurred mess as sweat dripped from my forehead, down my face as if I was crying. I wasn't crying. I was too anxious to cry. Callum caught up and grabbed my hand, leading me down a corridor that stretched on as far as the eye could see. The disinfectant smell was as eerily accurate as the hospital smell in my dream. My stomach churned.

My dream was coming true.

I struggled to catch my breath as fumes from the disinfectant choked my lungs. I was living in a nightmare, yet not even Callum pulling me through the hospital could wake me. People, doors and hospital beds seemed to pass slowly, like a scene from The Matrix, as bullets passed in a blur. They were lucky. They could dodge the bullets that were being fired, but I'd been hit. Being here was like a bullet had struck me in the chest.

Mum. There she was lying on the bed. I was awake yet my nightmare was only just beginning. I couldn't bear to count the tubes and wires attached to her arms and chest. An oxygen mask covered her face as she struggled to inhale. I let go of Callum's hand after my nails had pierced his skin, and ran over to the hospital bed.

"Mum," I croaked. I could barely speak. All I wanted to do was comfort her, to tell her how much I loved her. I could only manage to hold her hand. My head fell to her shoulder gently. She pulled the clear mask off her face.

"I'm okay, Tamsin. Drugs," she said in between breaths, pointing to one of the tubes that fed her medication.

"What happened?" Liam sat twiddling his thumbs as if it was the only helpful thing he could do.

"The morning you left she kept on getting wheezy, so we gave her the inhaler as usual, but nothing was making it go away. I called an ambulance early this morning because she was really struggling. They said it was best to take her in." Liam spoke slowly, trying to stay calm. He was shaking, still playing with his thumbs nervously. I could tell he didn't want to be in the hospital as much as Mum.

"So, it's a chest infection then?" I tried to diagnose her to make myself feel better. It didn't work. I knew any type of infection couldn't be good, especially for someone with cancer.

"I'm not sure. I guess we've just got to wait," Liam said uncertainly as I looked back at Mum. She smiled weakly at me, and likely wanted me to stop talking about her and talk about the spa. I smiled back and sat at her side. I knew what I had to do. I buried my emotions as deep as I could and spoke. I rambled about everything, something I was very good at. I knew she was happy. Mum's face brightened as I told her about the spa. I didn't need her to say anything.

"I love you lots and lots, like *Jelly Tots*," I said, holding onto her hand like it was going to be the last time.

"Don't speak... It's okay." I held back my tears for her. It was the least I could do. My gaze turned to the corner of the room where Callum was holding onto Liam. He was feeling as much pain as I was. They were both talking quietly, under the beeping of the machinery, but I could only see Callum's lips moving as his head rested on Liam's shoulder.

"I'm gonna go. Callum's here for you and I'm at the other end of the phone if you need anything. Just remember that she's in the best place right now." Liam wrapped his arms around me. His tight grasp lingered. He didn't want to leave me. I nodded back, emotion backed up in my throat in the form of tears, and Liam left. I hadn't seen a serious side to Liam in a long time, not since the beginning of university anyway.

Callum stood calmly at the other side of Mum's bed, his hands tucked together, which made up for the angst

I had every time someone walked past the room. I craved answers.

A nurse in a blue gown approached us with a grin, took Mum's chart from the bottom of the bed and checked the tubes and screens surrounding her. She didn't say much at first, not until she had scribed her notes in the file. I wanted to snatch it off her to find out what was really happening.

"Tamsin, is it? My name's Rose." I anxiously stood up and started pacing back and forth within my own little bubble. "The doctor is ready to speak to you. Would you mind following me?"

"I'll wait here, T. Everything will be okay. I promise," Callum said reassuringly.

"Can Callum come, too?" I couldn't remember her name. Beads of sweat rolled down my forehead, yet my hands were as cold as ice.

"If that's what you want? Of course he can come." Rose led us through to a small airy room, decorated with bright colours and filled with comfy chairs.

"I'll go and get the doctor and tell him you're ready. Take a seat and I will be back in a mo." I didn't want to sit. I was too nervous. I'd go crazy. I walked. Even when I found myself on the phone I would pace around the room.

The doctor walked in just minutes later with Rose following, and they shut the door behind them.

It's not good news then.

I couldn't stay positive. There was not a chance. I had to prepare myself.

"Hi, Tamsin, I'm Dr Vasir. I will get straight down to it, if that's okay?" I nodded anxiously. "Your mum is very ill. We've run some tests and it seems the cancer is now at Stage 4, which means it has spread. In your mum's case, it has spread to her lungs. I'm sorry, Tamsin. I know it's difficult to hear, but there is very little we can do for her now, other than to make her comfortable."

"It's not a chest infection?" I had to ask. Just once more. Maybe he'd made a mistake.

"It's not, I'm sorry. We will make sure she feels as little pain as possible, okay?" Rose placed her arm on my shoulder to comfort me. When Mum had got ill, she'd said if she ever had to go to hospital, she wouldn't be coming home. She was right, as always. I hated that, and especially this time, I wanted everyone to be wrong. I wanted to take her home and make her food. I wanted her at my graduation. I needed her, for me.

"Do you have an idea of how long she has?" I hated saying those words. Pain struck my body in the form of lightning bolts with my chest taking the brunt of the strikes.

"Based on her current condition, it's unlikely she will make it through the night," the doctor said, barely maintaining his composure. As the words came out of his mouth, I regretted asking. I didn't need him to put a time on the inevitable. I needed to be back with Mum. Callum got up and shook the doctor's hand before he swiftly left. Rose stayed behind, trying to do the impossible, but not even Callum could comfort me.

"You can stay in this room as long as you'd like."

If anything, I just wanted to get back to Mum as quickly as possible. If she wasn't going to make it through the night, I wanted to be by her side every chance I got. Every minute possible.

I sat on the edge of the hospital bed and clung to her, out of breath after rushing back to her side. She wasn't awake, and her breathing was shallow as if the pain was suffocating her. I wanted to wake her up so we could spend time together. I wanted us to go to the zoo together just one last time. I needed her to tell me how much she loved me, even though I knew. I begged for a miracle as I looked at her almost lifeless body. Less than an hour had passed, and as she deteriorated fast, I knew this time there would be no miracle.

If you love them that much, let them go.

I was selfish to beg for a miracle. Selfish to ask her to stay in pain for me, to stay longer so I could prepare for what was about to come. I couldn't. I really didn't want her to go, but I was selfish to want her to stay.

I watched her chest rise and fall as she took slow deep breaths. I drove myself into a state of insanity, counting the seconds in-between.

Fifteen seconds.
Twenty-four seconds.
Thirty-seven seconds.
Breathe, Mum. Just breathe.

Callum grabbed my hand, but I didn't need him. I needed Mum.

She's not breathing.

Uncontrollable cries left my body, screaming out for her. Her body lay there. Still. Peaceful.

I ached all over, sobbing with my fists clenched, begging for her to come back. I tried to tell myself it wasn't true. I tried to deny what I had just witnessed. I watched my nightmare play out in front of my eyes, but I couldn't snap out of it. This time, nurses didn't come in and cover her with a white sheet. Instead, they rushed in after hearing my cries from down the corridor, only to find me gagging and physically sick with grief.

Pain.

Numbness.

Heartache.

Two separate pieces of Play-Doh, ripped apart from one. The children had won, unaware of the mess they had caused. These two pieces of Play-Doh couldn't be pushed back together. My heart was broken. I was broken. Forever.

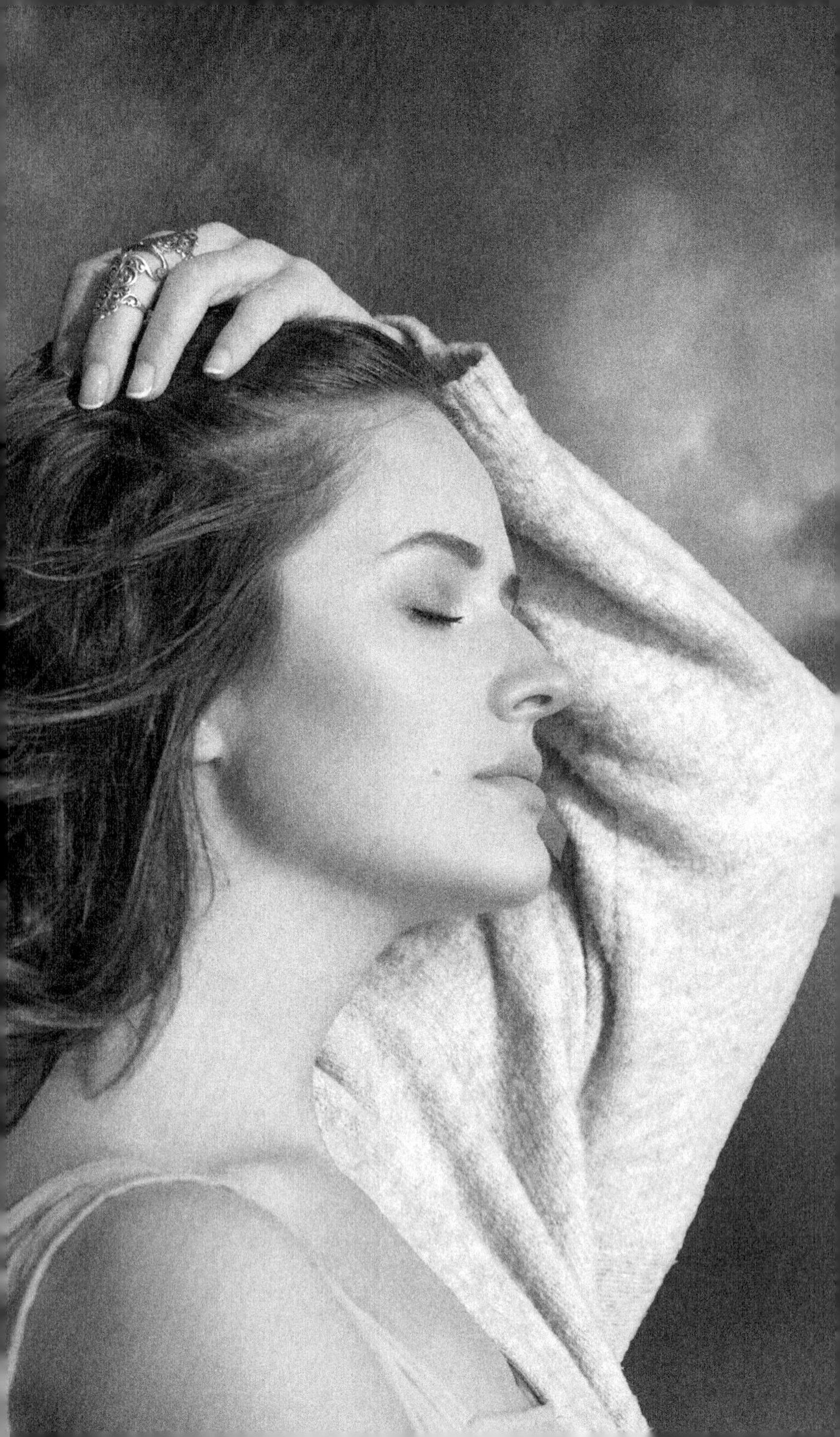

CHAPTER ELEVEN

"Mum wasn't religious, so she wouldn't have wanted any hymns or prayers. Is that okay?" Sarah nodded understandingly. I'd never organised a funeral before. I felt like an idiot asking so many questions, practically chewing Sarah's ear off in the process. The funeral director was the cutest lady I'd ever met. Short grey hair swept across her forehead, and she dressed in all black, as you'd expect. Mum wouldn't have wanted me to endure prayers for her. I did worry about what Callum would think, though, as his parents had raised him to be the good Christian boy he'd become. Most of the time, anyway. I sat in the room with Liam, who held onto my hand the whole time. He'd insisted I didn't go alone, and I was in no position to turn down a friendly face as my world was still crumbling around me. I was as stressed as I'd ever been, talking on the phone every day, appointments and even had to endure friendly cups of tea that were slowly taking over my life. It was a welcome distraction, though, in between the deep sadness that continued to sweep my body when I was just sat there thinking. Thinking about Mum.

"So tell me, what was special about Theresa. What made her unique?" Sarah asked, poised to make notes for Mum's eulogy.

What didn't make her unique?

That would have been a better question. She was a force to be reckoned with. Loving and kind, absolutely. She wouldn't take shit from anyone, though. She was a confident woman, until she got ill. She'd have done anything for me. In a world full of selfish people, I always came first for her. We didn't have much money but that didn't matter to her. In fact, there were times she'd barely had the money to feed herself. Liam told Sarah about a food fight we'd had in the house, trifle plastered up the walls and across the ceiling. Mum didn't care. She brought out the laughter in every situation, and without her, my childhood would have been very different. The funeral had to be perfect. She deserved it. I did worry, though. I worried there wouldn't be many people there to celebrate her life like they should have been.

"How many people will be attending the funeral?" she asked sweetly.

Mum didn't know many people. For a start, she had lost touch with her friend June, and she kept herself to herself mostly. I was the closest person to her, then there was Liam and of course, more recently, Callum. My grandparents had passed, and my dad was nowhere to be seen.

"Three people?" In doubt, I looked at Liam for help.

"Thirty. At least thirty," he said, as if he'd just plucked the number from thin air.

"Perfect. Now, I know we've spoken a lot, but did you know what songs you'd like played? If you don't know, you can email me once you've decided."

I knew. Mum had already picked her funeral songs, though at the time I'd been sickened at the thought. She'd done me a favour, because I wouldn't have known where to start.

Ke$ha - Dancing With Tears In My Eyes.
Avril Lavigne - When You're Gone.
Rihanna - Disturbia.

Once the songs were sorted into their order, Sarah mentioned the small matter of the cost. Mum had left behind priceless possessions that meant the world to me, but nothing that I could or would trade in for money. She wouldn't have wanted a huge ceremony either, nor a lot of money spent on her. Liam and Callum had both offered to chip in before I came to sort the funeral out, but I couldn't accept it. It felt like charity.

It had already been a week or so since Mum had passed. I had to guess, as time seemed to merge into a blurred mess. The only thing that had kept time in check slightly was those dreaded appointments and a bursting calendar of seeing people. University had prepared me for a lot of things, like paying my phone contract, but I'd never had to take care of a whole house before. I had been carefree until losing Mum shoved reality down my throat. Still, she'd raised me to deal with anything life threw my way, so that's what I had to do. Mature up and get it done. I had to take it seriously, but that was going to cause problems, too. Liam was by far the funniest person in my life, but since Mum had passed, every time he made a light-hearted joke I would snap. He'd look at me confused when I would change the conversation immediately and not drop to the floor belly laughing. It wasn't like me. I didn't like myself.

"Callum, I feel like the person I used to be is slowly draining out of me." I lay in bed next to him while he scrolled through his phone.

"What do you mean, babe?" he asked automatically as he continued to scroll.

"I just feel as though I don't find anything funny anymore. I feel like this is making me grow up faster than I want to. I don't want to be an adult and not find things funny because I have to deal with adult crap," I said, burying my face into a pillow, feeling sorry for myself. I always hid my face when I was upset. I hated feeling defeated when people saw me low.

I was strong. I had to be strong.

"Tamsin Cross…"

My full name. I'm in for it.

I buried my head a little deeper into the pillow.

"You may have grown up. You may have even matured. But do you really think that's the reason you aren't laughing as much as you used to? Come on, Tams… You're such an intelligent woman. Yes, you have a little more responsibility, but do you not think you're sad because your mum isn't around? You are trying to use these responsibilities to disguise your emotions and distract you. It's okay to not feel yourself for a while."

He had cracked me. He knew me better than I knew myself. I hated that.

"A little more responsibility?" I said sarcastically.

"And there is the sarcastic comment. Textbook Tamsin." Laughing, he pulled me closer. "I really love you, T."

Tears filled my eyes. I didn't want to admit defeat. He was right. I was devastated, but I had to get on with my life, reach for the stars and grab hold of my goals. For that, I needed to cross the finish line. I didn't know where it was, how long it would take to get there or what would happen along the way, but I had to cross it. Callum kissed my forehead and brushed my hair with his fingertips. As I fell asleep, my tears dried, staining the reality of my emotions across my face for Callum to see.

"Are you getting ready, T?" Callum asked. "Liam will be here soon."

I wanted the bed to swallow me up–anything to escape. Even though I'd said my goodbyes at the hospital, today made it final. Deep down, I hoped I would see her again, that this was all just a crazy dream. Her funeral was closure and I didn't want closure. The past two weeks I had driven myself and everyone around me crazy, as a whirlwind of emotion had swept me and everyone else off their feet. One minute, I would be talking, smiling even. The next, everyone would be drowning in a tsunami of tears. Talking about Mum was hard, but I knew I had to keep her memory alive. In my eyes, it brought her back to life. After I had groaned long enough, I dragged myself up from the bed and dressed myself in the dress that Callum had picked out for me days before. I pulled open my makeup draw, the least organised part of my life, and found Mum's red lipstick lying amongst the clutter. A single lipstick that held more sentimental value than anyone could have imagined. It represented the beginning of my career. Meeting Callum. Mum. It wasn't just a lipstick. It was a time capsule I would treasure forever.

"Are you nearly ready?" Callum mithered, as I placed the lipstick in my handbag.

"Yes, I am. Why is that outside?" I questioned as a

funeral car sat curb-side, right outside my house. "I didn't ask for that. I can't afford it."

"I confess. It was me. I wanted to make sure today went as smoothly as possible. No stress. Besides, Liam bought flowers and they're outside, too," Callum said apologetically. I wanted to be angry, but how could I be?

"Thank you." My arm reached out to Callum, and he came closer. His forehead pressed to mine, as close as we'd been since the spa.

"Today is going to be okay. I promise. Grab your coat. Let's go and get Liam, and make Tessa proud."

The crematorium was barely a drive away. In fact, we spent more time loading the car than we did driving. It wasn't long before we arrived at the crematorium, which looked as if another funeral had taken place before Mum's. Liam subtly pointed to the crowd of people stood close like penguins, trying to keep warm in the autumn cold.

"Your mum would have only cared about you being here today. Scratch that. I was her favourite, not you." Liam laughed to try to lighten the mood in the car that had been silent since we'd got in. "Obviously, I'm joking. I know Tess never wanted a fuss, but all these people are here because they all had the pleasure of meeting her."

"Those people are here for Mum?" I said, confused, as we approached the crowd in the car, faces starting to look familiar.

"Yep. I invited them. Not for your mum, but for you. I wanted you to know that your mum touched more hearts than you think."

I couldn't look at Liam. Instead, I focused on the people outside as I welled up. I wanted to punch him for being so nice. I hadn't even got inside and I'd already cried.

"Liam, you are incredible." Callum said, slapping his hand just above Liam's knee, making a thud and pulling my attention back to them.

"No. You are." He winked. "But don't do that again because you'll turn me on."

I'd usually have rolled my eyes and laughed at them. I wanted to laugh or smile at least, but I couldn't. Inside, I was emotionless. I looked back at my reflection in the window. My expression looked blank. I looked numb; even I could see that. A single tear rolled down my left cheek as I readied myself to get out of the car. It was time to say goodbye for the last time, even though I was in no position to let go.

Everyone stared with sadness in their eyes even before I had taken one step out of the car. The crematorium didn't look much like a church. It was modern with the front covered in large windows to allow the natural light to pour in. I couldn't face talking to anyone, so I put it off as long as I could and shuffled to the front with Liam and Callum to take my seat. *Dancing With Tears In My Eyes* played through the crematorium speakers, filling the hall.

'Here we go. Welcome to my funeral.'

The lyrics couldn't have been more apt. Stocky men in suits carried Mum's coffin down the aisle. We hadn't got to the speeches and people were already in floods of tears. Once Sarah had introduced herself and read out a small poem, I was summoned to the large podium at the front of the hall. It covered most of my body. I wasn't sure if anyone could see me. I knew they could hear me, though; my constant sniffles echoed through the hall. I cleared my throat to speak.

"My mum was..." I mustered between sniffs and then froze, looking at all their faces. I didn't know what to say. It wasn't stage fright. I'd stood in front of bigger crowds at university. It was the fact that no words could ever sum up her life, no eulogy could ever describe to anyone else what she meant to me. I saw Callum shuffle in his seat, trying to coach me into saying more. It wasn't working. Time passed in a blur once more as I stood there looking blankly at the growing concern on people's faces. Liam came towards me and held on to me tightly.

"Theresa was someone you could count on. Someone loving and caring, yet she also had a carefree attitude, which as a teenager I absolutely loved. She let me get away with murder. She had everything. Everything that mattered to her anyway." Liam looked across the room as I followed his gaze with my tearful eyes.

"June, thank you for coming today. I know you two

hadn't seen each other for a long time, but despite that, Tess always spoke about you. She kept that cute clock you gave her as a gift before you moved away. She wasn't carefree when it came down to the clock. She'd always shout '*If you break my clock, I'll break your legs.*' She missed you an awful lot." June's eyes were completely red as she battled to get another tissue from her handbag. She mouthed *'thank you'* to Liam.

"Linda, you haven't seen Tess in forty years. You were childhood friends so many years ago, yet even though all that time has passed, she always told stories of you both frolicking in the playground and getting up to no good." Liam then pointed to our dentist, doctor and the MacMillan Nurse.

"And as for you guys, I'm not sure you realise the impact you had on Theresa's life. You were her escape from the house, the socialising she needed when we weren't around. She didn't look at you as professionals, you were her friends." Liam continued to thank them for everything they had done, and then the hall went silent. I looked to Liam to see if he had finished, pulling at my dress nervously.

"And then there is you, Tamsin. You are the strongest girl I know. She was and would still be so proud of you. You will achieve your goals. You will get to where you want to be, because your mum made sure of that. She's been preparing you for this her whole life. As your mum would say, '*Aim for the sky, Tamsin, but don't stop there*'."

"She was... my everything," I croaked beneath Liam's voice. He looked to me and smiled, still holding on to me tightly.

"I know, I know. I'm sure you will all agree that Tess spread a lot of joy in all of our lives. That is her legacy, as well as Tamsin here. Never let go of those memories she gave us. Let them shine brighter than they ever have. I know for both Tamsin and me, she will always *Shine Bright Like A Diamond*." Liam stepped down and guided me towards my seat. His words played beautifully through my mind, especially the Rihanna reference at the end. Mum would have loved that. I thought no words could ever sum up her life, but Liam had done an amazing job. His words wrapped through my mind for the duration of the ceremony, and it brought me a little peace I desperately needed.

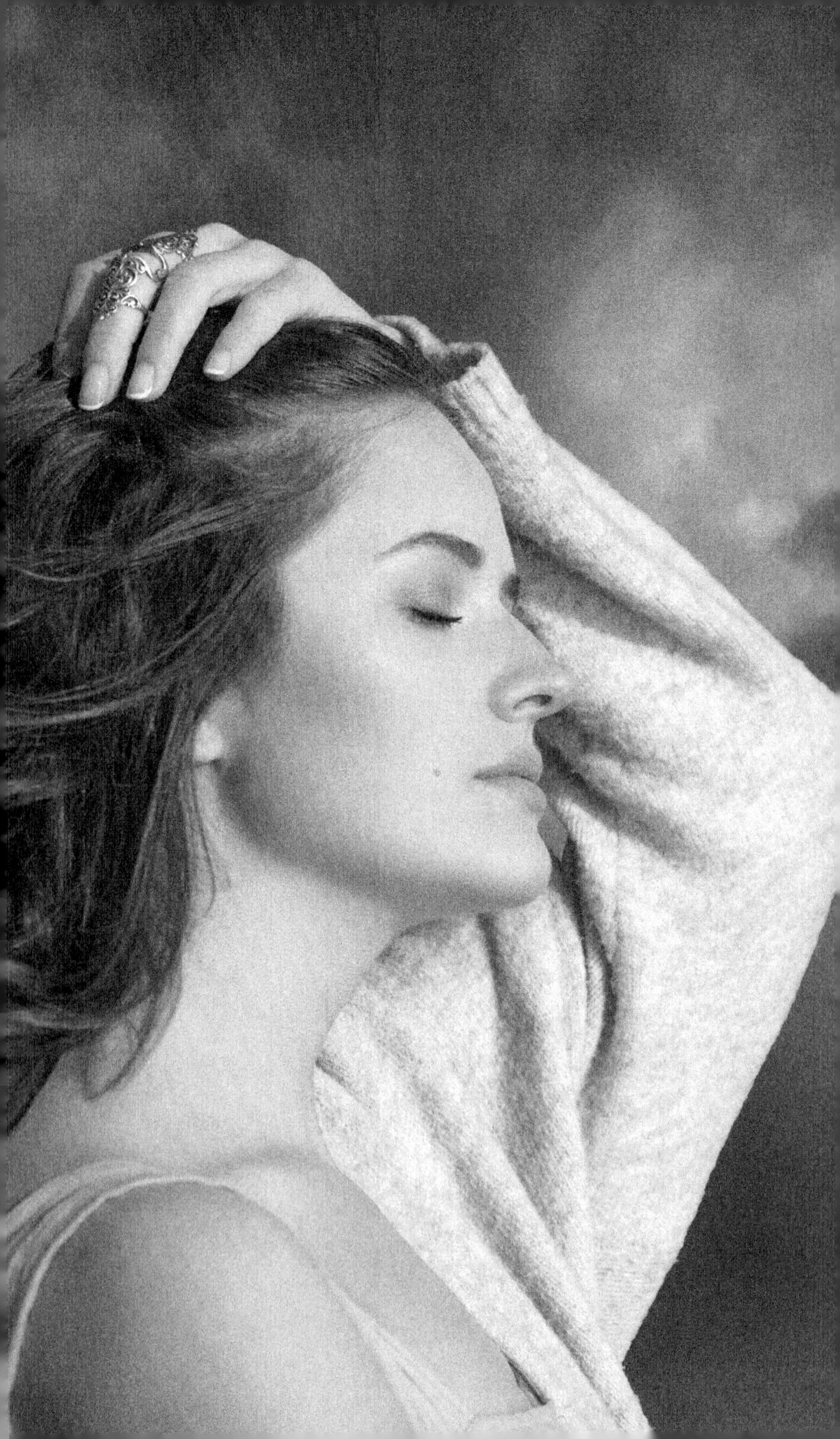

CHAPTER TWELVE

My thoughts, once clear and concise, were far from those of a stable person. I had been cooped up in Callum's room for days, nervous to go home and face the reality of my loss. For how many days? I wasn't quite sure given how often I'd slept. My phone had stopped buzzing, left on the other side of the room uncharged. I was left in peace, with my mind in pieces. Mental exhaustion was taking over, and sleeping was the only real downtime I had from myself, even though I'd locked myself away. Constant thoughts of the past played continuously in a loop of doom that I couldn't switch off as I worried what life would be like without Mum. I didn't know how to pull myself out of this lull, or if I'd ever break free from myself, and the agony I felt inside.

"Liam has called again. Are you still sure you don't

want to see anyone?" Callum said through the door that stood ajar.

"I'm not ready yet."

I wasn't. I hadn't the energy to put on a brave face–a brave face like the polite exchange you have with work colleagues and a checkout assistant.

'Hi, are you okay?'

'Yes, are you?'

'I'm very well thanks.'

These responses were my go to. I'd always tell my friends 'I'm okay', even if I really wasn't. That was normal for me, and talking about my feelings certainly was not. It required a form of energy that I hadn't yet learnt to wield.

"Tamsin…" Liam's voice sounded from the hallway. I groaned as Callum tried to justify why he'd let Liam in.

"You've literally not stepped outside in over a week. Your phone is off. I needed to know you were okay. I had to see you," Liam continued as I shoved my face between two pillows.

"I need space, and I can't deal with anyone right now." I felt more exhausted than ever just speaking.

"I have given you space. We all have. It's time to talk about it. You're bottling everything up like you always do, and it's not good for you."

Liam was right. I hated that. The thing is, I'd probably have said the same to him if the shoe were on the other foot; obviously not literally, as Liam sometimes tried to fit his size nine feet in my size seven heels. I was very good at giving out advice, but never liked listening to it myself. You could say I was a little stubborn. I lifted a pillow off my face and turned to Liam, who was sat on the edge of Callum's bed. My eyes squinted at the bright light that I'd been hiding from all this time.

"What do you want?" I greeted Liam with more sarcasm, but he wasn't bothered at all. He just crept closer.

"I just wanted to see you in person to make sure you're alright. Why did you leave without saying goodbye on the day of Tess' funeral? People were asking after you."

I didn't have the energy to justify my actions, but I knew if I didn't explain he wouldn't stop bothering me.

"The house isn't my home anymore. Mum made it that. I just needed to get out of there, to not have those people asking after me. It just makes me worse."

"I can imagine. I just wish you would have told me," Liam continued. "Look, do you want me to get you anything? Maybe some clean clothes from the house? Anything of your mum's?"

"No, it's fine. I'm fine. I can't hide away forever. I need to go home and sort everything out," I said and looked at them both.

"We're here to help too, T. You don't have to do this alone. We'll manage it together." Callum comforted me. I didn't want to see anyone, but for that short moment while Liam was around, thoughts had stopped swirling around my head.

I stood facing the clutter left over from the wake, along with a deep sadness, a sense of loneliness even. I had been right to leave the last time; the house really didn't feel like home anymore. I didn't know where to start at first, grabbing just the paper plates and cups, and popping them into the recycling boxes. I sat on the floor, surrounded by Mum's things, but my mind was elsewhere. I thought about moving away for good. It seemed logical at the time, and in an instant my mind was made up. What I was unaware of was how much this decision was going to change my life and those around me.

"I'm giving the house back to the council. I'm going to move," I said bluntly as both of the boys looked up from tidying Mum's CD collection.

"What? You can't be serious?" Liam replied, astonished.

"I couldn't be more serious. It's too much being here without Mum. Maybe it's time I got a place of my own. I could rent closer to work."

"So you've spent a week hiding from me and now you're moving a hundred miles south? Really, Tamsin?" Liam's tone changed, as he threw the CD *'Now That's What I Call The 80's'* across the room, which crashed into my handbag.

"You better not have broken my phone." I grabbed my handbag, and started to rummage through it.

"You're making these decisions too quickly. Am I the only one with my head screwed on here?"

My phone was okay, but something else was not.

"Great. I didn't want to see you, and now you're calling me an idiot, and you've broken my mum's fucking lipstick! Just leave, Liam." My tone changed to match his as I slung my bag across the room. I'd never had to speak to him like that before. He shook his head, and as he left, he slammed the front door behind him. All the anger I had housed in my body was released in an instant. Emotions I had been bottling up had spilled over and created a mess–a huge mess in a friendship that had never been fragile. Callum looked at me in despair, like he didn't completely understand what had just happened or the reasons why. After a couple of seconds, I broke down, tears streaming down my face accompanied by whining. Lots of whining.

What had I done?

I had lost another best friend.

It was another few days before Callum and I headed back to the house after the argument with Liam. It was all too much for me to deal with, and even Callum agreed. We sat sorting clutter into organised groups.

"It's going to be so weird moving out. Like when Rachel moves out of Monica's apartment. It's like the end of an era," I said, quoting the *Friends* TV show to the best of my ability. It was all I would watch on TV growing up. I'd convinced myself that they would be my friends in real life or at least that I'd live in a place where I actually spoke to my neighbours.

"Who are Rachel and Monica?" Callum said, straight faced. I rolled up the imaginary sleeves on my t-shirt, ready to punch him with my mouth open wide. "Just kidding! Of course I know who they are." He laughed.

"I was literally about to break up with you."

"I can't have that, can I?" Callum paused for a moment. "Maybe you should move in with me? So instead of you being Rachel, fleeing a wedding and trying to fend for yourself, maybe you could be my Chandler?"

"That's a little gay, you know?" I mocked him, trying to disregard the serious question he'd asked me.

"Is that a no?" Callum asked simply.

Could I move in with Callum? He did live in the next town over, so it would be a change of scenery.

I tried to come to some sort of rationale. We had only been together for just over five months, and it did feel too soon to be considering such a leap into the commitment pool. I loved him, though, and he clearly loved me, otherwise he wouldn't have wanted to commit. I continued to weigh the pros and cons as they wrapped around my mind, hoping I would be able to make a decision without pausing too long.

"Are you sure?" I asked, to stall answering without committing to an answer, like some sort of politician.

"I wouldn't have asked if I wasn't sure. Besides, you've practically lived at mine for weeks anyway. It would be our house, not my house. What do you say?" He had a point. If I moved in, it would be another goal scratched off my list, too. My perfect house. The house I'd dreamed of.

"Yeah, okay then. Let's do this." I said enthusiastically, hiding the small pool of doubt that sat at the bottom of my stomach. He weaved his way towards me through the clutter spread out across the living room floor and pressed his lips softly on mine. It had been so long since I'd felt his touch like that. I craved his touch once more, so as he pulled away I pulled him back in for more. That sick feeling disappeared while I was in his embrace. I had made the right decision; at least, that's what I thought.

———

It took a good few days to move everything out of Mum's house. With the little money she had put aside, I paid for a van to move the items we'd hoarded over the years. Some things were just too sentimental to be thrown away or given to charity, so they were sent to a self-storage unit, which didn't come cheap. Callum encouraged me to make the place feel more my own, so pictures that had once hung in my own room were now placed in Callum's room. *Our* room. There were pictures of Liam and Mum, which at the time filled me with sadness with looking back at how things used to be. I ached knowing I'd never see Mum again, and I was still hurting from my fight with Liam. Callum was in the walk-in-wardrobe, which stretched the length of the bedroom, placing my clothes on hangers, a task I always tried to avoid. I procrastinated by throwing on a mixture of fancy dress costumes I had found while looking through his section of the wardrobe. His laugh was infectious, and spurred me on to try on more of his fancy dress clothes. I hadn't been here for long, but I knew I was going to love it. We were real. A couple. Nobody could take that away from us.

A loud noise echoed through the house.

"T, can you get the door?" Callum shouted from deep into the wardrobe.

"Yeah, sure." I ran down the stairs wearing a lei around my neck, straightening up my Rastafarian hat that sagged from my head.

"Hi! Can I help?" I opened the door and looked at the vaguely familiar man and woman stood in front of me.

"You must be Tamsin. I'm Jaqueline and this is Richard. We're Callum's parents."

I stood there, meeting my boyfriend's parents for the first time, looking like a member of a circus freak show. They didn't seem too fazed by my outfit, nor by the length of time it took me to invite them in.

"Don't you just love what she's wearing?" Richard laughed, directing his question to Callum, who had just peered out at the top of the stairs.

"I wondered what all the commotion was about. What are you guys doing here?" He hugged both of them promptly. I wished I had done the same instead of standing hopelessly, playing with my lei.

"We wanted to come see our son. Is that such a crime? And with Tamsin moving in, we thought now would be the perfect time," Jaqueline said, pulling a small suitcase behind her on a set of wheels.

Not a short stay then.

"I'll show you where the guest bedroom is so you can set down your suitcase. Mind the boxes, though. We're still putting stuff away." Callum looked at me as his parents made their way up the stairs. He mouthed the word *'sorry'* as he followed them up.

"I get what you mean about spontaneous now," I whispered behind him and picked up one of the lighter bags.

"I know, they weren't supposed to be coming until next week," he said in a quiet sort of tone so his parents couldn't hear.

"You knew they were coming next week and you didn't think to tell me?" An angry whisper leapt from my mouth and Callum turned to look at me.

"You've been a little pre occupied locked in my room for weeks. We've hardly spoken. What were you expecting?" he snapped.

Shit. He was right. I couldn't be mad. I had ostracised myself. I didn't know what was happening with my boyfriend, at work or with anyone else for that matter. My emotions were spinning around in an uncontrollable mess; being angry at every little thing that was happening around me and grieving was no excuse. I couldn't take it out on him. I had already done that with Liam.

"Oh, yeah. You're right. I'm sorry. I don't know what came over me. Come on, let's go upstairs or your parents are going to wonder where we are."

We all sat in the lounge together. His parents were as great as he'd said. Callum had nothing to be sorry for. They were kind, hard to keep quiet and generous, too. They handed us a card and a bottle of Moët Champagne as a moving in present.

"Aw, you didn't have to." I opened the card with congratulations written all over, and read their message.

Something to get you started in your home together. Make this Christmas one to remember. Love Jaqueline and Rich xx

Another envelope fell out, which contained a cheque for one thousand pounds. I looked at Callum, astounded. He looked just as shocked as me.

"You've got to be kidding?" I said, holding the

largest cheque I'd ever held in my life. It was a lot of money, to me anyway.

"Mum, Dad, you didn't have to do that. Thank you," Callum said, getting up to go and give them a hug. I was speechless. We sat together as a family–a family I hadn't asked for, because I hadn't needed to. They'd raised Callum to be one hell of a man and I was so lucky to have him and them in my life.

Maybe bad luck doesn't come in threes after all, I thought to myself, mulling over the superstition. First Mum, and then falling out with Liam–I was almost waiting for the next bad thing to happen. I needed to give myself a break. It wasn't happening.

"So, we are thinking of staying until next week, if that's okay son?" Jackie asked, even though it seemed she'd already made her decision. I wouldn't have dared call her Jackie to her face, though. She didn't seem the type to have a nickname.

"That's fine, although I'm going back to work on Monday. I've booked Friday off for Tamsin's graduation, but we'll be out all day. Are you two going to be alright to keep yourselves busy?" Callum asked, reminding me of my graduation. I'd completely forgotten about it with everything that had been going on. I quickly grabbed my phone and loaded the email to check.

"That won't be a problem. We haven't been up this way in a while, have we, Rich?"

"Why don't you both come? I have enough tickets," I interrupted before Richard could respond.

Tamsin Cross
Chester University
Chester Cathedral
Friday 2ND November 2018
Graduation Ceremony at 11:30am
3 guests

One ticket for Mum, another for Callum, and the third ticket for Liam, which I had applied for. He was graduating at the half past one ceremony, straight after mine.

"Are you sure, T?" Callum asked. He looked concerned and I wasn't sure why. He could have looked happy. I'd asked his parents to come so at least he wasn't going to be sat there all alone.

"Absolutely."

Another email loaded as I typed 'graduation' into the search bar of my email account. I glanced down at the email receipt for my graduation gown hire and the picture frames that Mum saved tirelessly to pay for.

Wish you were going to be there, Mum.

I wanted Mum there, but in adult life, I was learning that you didn't always get what you wanted. What I did know? I was going to have the best day, not just for me, but for Mum, too.

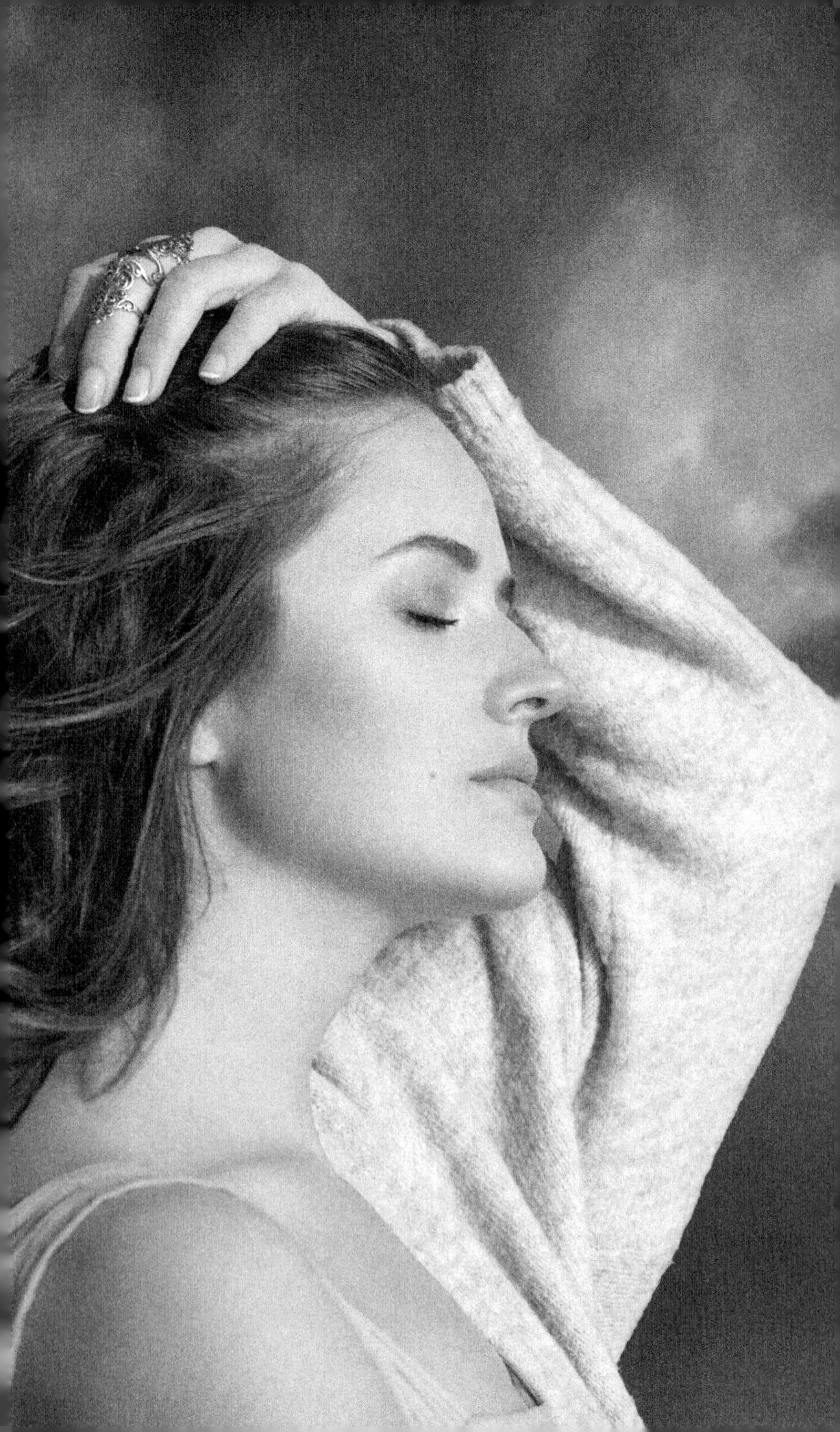

CHAPTER THIRTEEN

I picked up my cap and gown from the leisure centre, and then walked amongst the crowds towards the side of the cathedral along with Callum and his parents.

"See you soon," I said, hugging them all.

"Good luck, brainy boots," Callum said in a dork-ish way, making me snort.

I was ushered in through a side entrance to the cathedral, via a cobbled street lined with large Victorian town houses. I'd always wondered what Chester Cathedral looked like on the inside. I'd walked past it often enough getting to work. Callum and his parents couldn't believe that I'd never been in one before. I followed a long narrow hallway with bare brick walls that looked like something out of *Harry Potter*.

Two large screens were placed either side of stone pillars, and displayed the live footage captured by the camera crew dotted around the main hall. I sat down on the horrible wooden benches that were typical of any type of church. Just minutes in and my bum was already numb. I knew Mum would have complained about the chairs, too. She wasn't there with me, but I knew she'd be proud of what I had achieved. I smiled thinking about her, and a friend from the first year smiled back.

Awkward.

I sat uncomfortably, waiting for eleven-thirty. I wasn't excited, which was not how I'd imagined my graduation day. It was my own fault for watching so much American TV. I half expected everyone to break into song and dance. Although I had worked hard, university hadn't just been about learning for me. It was an escape from my hometown, a binge drinking, all-night working lifestyle, which I'd have gone back to in a flash if I'd been given the chance. Most importantly, it was a big middle finger up to the statistics and a few of my high school teachers. They hadn't been on my side, but I had shown them. My degree was proof that, despite living in a council house, you could beat the odds. Was it hard work? Absolutely, but the people I'd met and surrounded myself with had made it so much easier, and so had the alcohol. Definitely the alcohol.

I looked through graduation caps and gowns to find Callum sat towards the back of the hall looking down at his phone. He looked concerned, annoyed almost. He looked as he had stood at his window, watching me leave. The usual sparkle in his eyes had dulled, and it wasn't something that could be blamed on the lighting in the cathedral. I assumed it must have been his parents, bugging him with questions, as his eyes continued to sink into his phone for most of the ceremony. I practically had no use for my phone; the only people who ever messaged were Mum, Liam and Callum. My eyes kept wandering around the hall, one minute to the stage as the students shook hands with the university's chancellor, the next minute to a young guy in the next column across, picking his nose and trying to subtly wipe it on his gown. My eyes stopped wandering as a woman dressed in a colourful robe interrupted me and asked the whole row to move along and wait at the side of the stage. This was it.

Don't trip over. Don't trip over.

I walked up onto stage, smiled and shook the chancellor's hand.

"Congratulations, Tamsin." His deep voice echoed throughout the hall. The audience clapped as I walked off the stage and around, back to my seat. Honestly, it was underwhelming, but I had done it. All that was left to do was celebrate, in the true university style I had dearly missed.

Once I had fought my way through the crowds of students, I stood close to a small independent wine bar, just away from the hustle and bustle outside the cathedral.

Callum <3
2ⁿᵈ November 2018

[13:04]

Just outside the Cathedral, near the wine bar xxx

I looked up from my phone to see Liam, taking pictures with his family. Even little Jade was with them, holding tight onto her teddy called *Tiger,* even though it was actually a cheetah. Liam looked phenomenal, wearing a sparkling black suit with matching black trousers, all accompanied by his hat and gown. He glanced my way after taking what must have been the hundredth photo, looking at each one to make sure he looked good. I smiled at him and lifted my hand, and he returned a smile before the path between us became crowded once again.

"Congratulations, T," Callum shouted above the noise, raising his arms. "You were so great. Proud boyfriend moment right here."

"Thank youuuuu," I said, shaking my graduation gown towards him, stopping promptly as his parents arrived behind him.

"Well done, Tamsin. Wasn't that just lovely?" Jackie said as Richard agreed. "Let's go and have some food together. Our treat, no arguments." Richard had no choice in the matter; they were paying.

"Aww thanks, Jacki-eline," I said almost calling her Jackie. Not my finest moment.

"When we're done, we will leave you and Callum to continue celebrating as I've booked us into a spa hotel for the evening. We wanted to give you two some space."

"Yes, me and your mother are going to the spa. She booked it last night while I was sleeping," Richard said reluctantly, laughing.

"That's my mum," Callum said under his breath to his dad as Jackie lead the way to a Brazilian restaurant close by that she had quickly looked up on her phone.

"Would you like more?" the Brazilian waiter asked me, with everyone else already taking more meat from the skewer. I wouldn't normally have said no. I was a lover of meat, not in a lewd way, but I craved it. In disappointment, I turned over the green coaster to the red side, which read *'which meat would you like next?'*. The coaster was mocking me. There was no way I could eat anymore. I wanted to, though; it was delicious. Once I turned over my coaster, everyone else around the table followed suit. We had sat in the restaurant for around two hours, so we must have got our money's worth. Well, Jackie's money, anyway. Callum kept taking his phone from his pocket, swiftly checking it every now and again. Normally his phone would have been on the table, but instead it was shoved back into his pocket. I guessed his mum had a rule about mobile phones being on the table while eating, so I also placed my phone in my bag. Jackie told me about her cleaning business and how it had all started. No university degree, because it was different back then. She hadn't even married into the business, as Richard had been a postman. She'd started cleaning houses at the age of fifteen and it grew, and kept growing as it covered the whole of Hertfordshire. She was successful and had worked bloody hard for her money. Her status. Her business was making her money, and if she wanted to she could stop cleaning, but she didn't want to. Working was weaved into her DNA. Jackie summoned the waiter confidently and asked to settle the bill. Jackie and I couldn't have been more different. We shared ambition, but I wished I could bottle up just half of the confidence she had for myself.

"Right. Now that the bill is settled, we're going to head off and leave you young-ones to carry on celebrating," Jackie said, taking her coat from the waiter. We walked out of the restaurant with them and said our goodbyes, as they headed to their car.

"So, where now, clever clogs?" Callum asked, nudging me.

"Anywhere. I'm just so happy right now. Let's make the most of it. A few bars on Watergate Street?" I skipped as I pulled him in that direction, already deciding without Callum's input. I guessed I was more like Jackie than I had originally thought.

"Lead the way, brainy boots." He laughed.

"You are such a nerd... I love it, though." I pulled him close and kissed him, stood in the middle of the street. I didn't care. I channelled my inner Jackie, and took what was mine, because I truly couldn't have been happier.

The bars in Chester were crammed to the brim, looking as though day drinkers would stumble out every time the doors opened. We didn't have to wait for too long for a table, practically jumping into somebody's grave as they left. I sat and snapped pictures of my *Long Island iced tea* cocktail to plaster all over my Instagram later.

"How's work been over the past few days?" I asked Callum nervously. I hadn't been back since losing Mum. I was due back on Monday after Ian kindly extended my compassionate leave. Was I ready? I didn't think I was, but I had to push myself.

"It was nice to go back and see everyone. They were all asking about you. Ian is basically getting everyone ready for the busy Christmas period, you know with the Christmas markets."

"Oh god, really?" I said, even more concerned about my return.

"Yep. Although, I've not had it too bad. I think Roberta has been drowning in interviews for seasonal staff and Darren is constantly being bugged about social media. I don't know whether to feel sorry for them or feel thankful it's not me." We both laughed as it faded into the noise around us. Within that noise, I could hear something distinct. Unmistakable. I could just about make out Liam's voice. He was sat across from us, in another section of the bar, along with some friends I recognised from his course. I wanted to go over, I really did, but the last time we'd spoken properly had been weeks ago. I cleverly justified not going over as Callum would be sat alone if I went. I didn't want it to be awkward. Within a couple of minutes Liam looked over to our table, waved and then kept miming vulgar signs to us, not that I minded. He was practically sat on a guy's lap, and in between flirting he would hold up a hip flask he had very clearly snuck in to show Callum and me. He would persistently wink, pointing to the guy currently feeling his chest. He had pulled.

Good for him.

We were both stubborn. We still needed to clear the air that had stagnated between us, though I knew after seeing him, we were going to be okay. After all, Liam was prone to telling the truth and saying exactly what was on his mind; drunk or sober, it really didn't matter.

———

I sat up in bed with Callum lying peacefully next to me. No matter how hard I tried to get to sleep, I couldn't. There was no off button, nothing to stop the thoughts running around my head like a child on a sugar rush. Sleeping had got that bit easier up until now. It was a sign I wasn't ready for the day of work ahead of me. I had a mixed bag of emotions, eager to see Roberta, Rach and James. I wondered if they'd missed me or even needed me at work. I reminded myself of the copious texts from everyone over the past weeks to ease the anxiety that built high on my chest, starting to weigh me down. I sluggishly got out of bed at four-thirty in the morning, after admitting that sleep was not an option I could take, and made myself a coffee without making too much noise.

"You're up early," I said with my hands wrapped around a coffee mug, hearing Callum walk down the stairs.

"Shitting hell. You scared me." He looked startled, like he hadn't noticed I wasn't next to him when he woke. I was far too awake for the morning, mainly because I'd hardly slept. I couldn't stop laughing.

"Why are you up so early? You don't need to be worried about today, you know?" He said reassuringly.

"I could ask you the same thing. Why are you up so early?" I loved to mess with him.

"I have so much work to do from last week, I'm still catching up on myself." He opened most of the cupboards in the kitchen to find some food to fuel him for the day ahead. I never understood how he could eat as soon as he woke up.

"I'll come into work with you then, instead of waiting until my return to work interview with Ian. I could do with the moral support just getting on the train."

"You sure? You'll be waiting around for a while."

"Yeah. Why not? I'll grab a coffee or something while I wait."

The anxiety of going back to work was eating me up from the inside out. My stomach growled continuously, loud enough to hear over the sound of the tracks that rumbled underneath the train. I lacked energy, despite the coffee at home and the one I'd picked up at the station. I was drained, my resources depleted against my own will, and nothing I tried was bringing them back. I wanted to sleep, even for a few minutes, but no matter how many times I shut my eyes, I'd continue to worry. It was on the train, bile rising quicker than I could control. I admitted defeat. I needed help, but I also knew that I had to get today over and done with. I loved work and Callum had said that going back to work would be a distraction, and he was probably right. The train slowed as it approached our stop. My vision blurred. I was going to throw up. I could hear the train doors beep and open as we arrived, but I couldn't move. I'd be sick if I moved. Callum's voice echoed in my ears.

"Are you okay? You don't look so good at all, T."

I quickly got up from my seat, ran off the train holding my breath and vomited on the busy platform. I looked around and gasped for breath as Callum pulled my hair from out of my face. People stared at me like I was some drunk throwing up after drinking too much cider. Callum rubbed my back as I hunched over. I quickly started to feel better once my body had got rid of everything it didn't want. The worry was no longer in my stomach. It was all over the train station platform and still prominent in my mind.

"Tamsin, welcome back. And my main man, Callum," Ian yelled from across the foyer as I signed in at reception. "It's so good to see you. Are you well?"

I glanced in a nearby mirror. My face looked ghostly with the little makeup I was wearing smeared beyond the point of saving.

"I'm as good as I can be." I smiled weakly. Normally, I would have plastered a huge smile on my face and pretended everything was fine. Nobody would have had a clue, but that time had been very different. I'd come back for a distraction, but so far, being there was more of a reminder that I had been gone. It was too much for my liking.

"That's good. Well, let's just get you settled back in today. We've got your RTW interview today at ten, which is just a formality, but before that, let me catch you up on a few things you've missed as I walk you to your office." Ian placed his arm on my shoulder. A few minutes and friendly faces later, we arrived at my office. A gorgeous bouquet of flowers sat on my desk as Roberta, Sharon, Rach and James surrounded them. 'Welcome back' banners hung from one corner of my room to the other. No wonder Ian had been hovering in the reception area; he'd been waiting for me. I usually loved fuss and attention, but I wasn't sure I could hack it and hold it together. Roberta wrapped her arms around me, not letting go for a while, as the others attempted to surround me with their love. Roberta and I had spent quite a lot of time together; she had become my best friend at work.

"I've missed you so much," she whispered, still hanging on to me.

"Missed you too," I said in a lacklustre voice, lacking the energy to make it sound like I meant it. I needed a coffee or something to at least replace some of the energy I had lost throwing up.

"It's going to be good to have Callum back, too. I only saw him one day last week the little skiver. *Working from home* my arse." Roberta laughed, finally letting me go.

"What do you mean? He's been back since Monday last week. He only had Friday off for my graduation," I said, struggling to think back to last week. My memory hadn't been great. I could barely remember what I had eaten or if I even had.

"Oh, I saw him on Monday, and I'm sure we had an email about staffing. Maybe I'm mistaken. How was graduation? Congratulations!"

"Aw, thank you. Graduation was good, too. Good to get out the house and make myself look nice," I said, trying to not look confused.

He was only off for graduation. I remember he said that to his parents.

"Feeling good will definitely help. You know where I am, yes? Anyway, I will let you get settled back in. Byeeeee." I did love her, especially to gossip with. She knew everything. I stood, playing back what she'd said.

I only saw him one day last week.

He worked from home.

I couldn't stop. If he was working from home, why wasn't he at home?

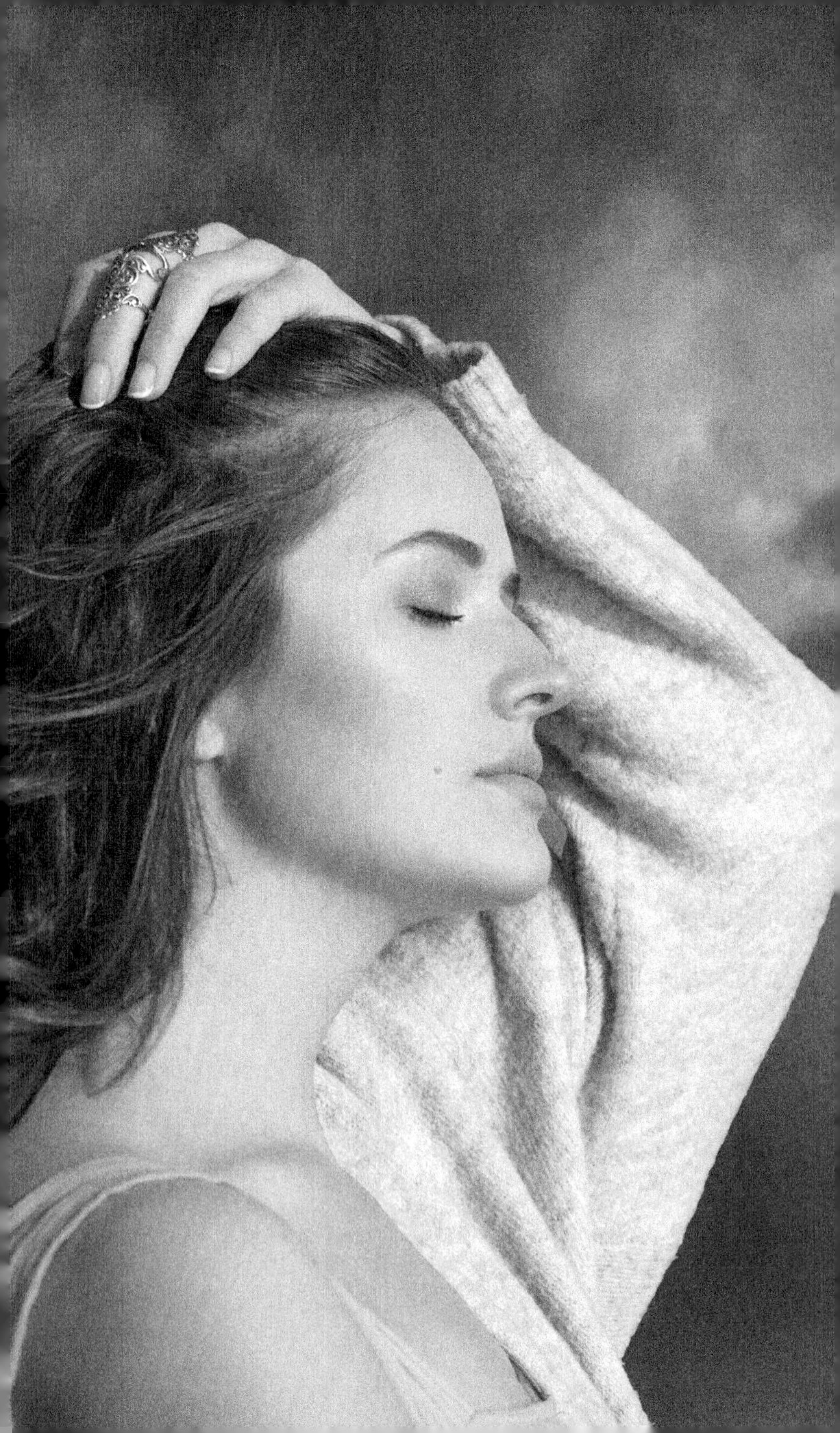

CHAPTER FOURTEEN

The cubicle door slammed behind me, my hands shaking as I tried to lock myself in. My eyes filled with tears while my throat felt like I had swallowed a large pill that wouldn't go down. I didn't want to be here. I wanted to be at home, under a blanket to hide from the world. I wanted to be asleep so I could stop thinking for just one second. I needed to be someplace else, any place, or somewhere I had conjured up in my dreams. I continued to sob, trying to hold back my loud cries every time I heard the toilet door slam. I continued to trace back through the past week, struggling to make a timeline of events in the jumbled mess of thoughts that was my mind. I had been alone with Callum's parents while he was at work, and I remembered him coming in every day, around late afternoon.

Had he been lying, or was Roberta mistaken?

Roberta knew everyone's business. She couldn't be

wrong. Being back at Farden today was hard enough without worrying about something else–about my relationship with Callum. I needed to know the truth, and the only way I'd know for sure was the email Roberta had mentioned.

I rushed to log on to my computer, and tried desperately to remember my password after weeks of not being at work. My memory really was failing me. The time on the desktop mocked me. It had only been minutes since everyone had greeted me in my office, yet it felt like I had been at Farden for hours. Eventually I got into the computer, and sifted through countless emails that had been left unread. I knew only last week's emails mattered to find out the truth. I opened each email, reading them word-by-word, occasionally losing focus.

"Where are you?" I said in frustration as more tears fell down my face.

I had to admit defeat. I couldn't find it. Roberta must have been mistaken. Callum wasn't lying. My memory had clearly served me wrong. I'd gone crazy, turning the smallest inconsistency into a huge deal. I hadn't told Callum what was going on. I wanted to gather the facts before I did, but truthfully, there were no facts to gather. I wanted to leave Farden, but I knew running away from my problems would only make it worse. My irrational thoughts were taking over; I had to distract myself. Coffee. It was imperative I had coffee and calmed down.

I removed the black circles surrounding my eyes and replaced the makeup that I'd wiped away, then stood waiting to be served at the hotel café.

A queue. Great.

The café was never normally this busy. The hotel's profile was rising with all our hard work. Even the foyer was bustling, a real difference from the deserted space it had once been. I wanted to take credit for its success, but how could I? I hadn't been there for over a month.

"Latte, please." The woman in front of me said to the barista. A pathetic excuse for a coffee if you were to ask me, although I was jealous that she was getting her coffee fix before me.

"Thank you," the *weak coffee girl* said, grabbing her drink as she continued.

"Does Callum work here?" she said as I eavesdropped. The barista looked at her blankly as his hands continued to tap the till in front of him, like it was embedded into his memory.

"Callum Dunn?" she pressed.

"I'm sorry, I don't know. Reception may know of him, though," the barista said as he prepared to serve me, looking around the *weak coffee girl*.

That's my Callum.

How does she know him?

"You know Callum?" I couldn't help myself as my mouth took over. I jumped at the chance to speak to her as she started to walk past me. The barista kept on looking at me, but he was sorely mistaken if he thought I was going to speak to him before I found out more about the *pathetic coffee bitch* stood in front of me.

"Oh, yes. He's an old friend. How do you know him?" she asked.

"What's your name?" I questioned, completely ignoring her last remark.

"Louise, what's yours?"

"Tamsin."

We looked at each other, shocked. Gobsmacked. She had heard of me; there was no denying that. I didn't know what to do or say. The barista continued to get more and more impatient, summoning the person waiting behind me to order first. I preferred her as weak coffee girl, not Louise, Callum's ex. Her blonde hair was straightened to perfection, not a strand of hair out of place. She was pretty, which made me hate her more.

"Shall we grab a table and talk?" she suggested reasonably.

"Yeah, just let me grab my coffee."

I sat nervously, opposite a woman who had once been the love of Callum's life. He'd searched for years for her, and yet somehow she was here, right in front of me at our place of work. I didn't know what to think, struggling as questions continued to run through my mind. I tried not to let my mouth run away with itself, but I was confused to say the least. Louise and I looked very different, polar opposites in fact. Her blonde straightened hair looked like something out of a magazine; I could never get my hair that straight. She was tall, about four inches taller than me. I tried not to feel intimated by her.

"So, why are you here?" I asked, genuinely needing to understand what she was doing on this side of the planet.

"I wanted to see if Callum was telling me the truth. He told me he works here," she said confidently.

"You've been speaking?"

"We've been messaging, and I met with him last week at a coffee shop in a place called Crewe."

She's met my boyfriend. In my hometown.

My head dropped as emotion weighed it down. I wanted to punch her, and nothing else. Was she the one in the wrong? Partly, but so was Callum.

He had betrayed me.

It all made sense. That's why he was always on his phone. He was talking to Louise. Roberta wasn't wrong all along. He wasn't at work like he had told me. Little pieces of information started to fit together like jigsaw pieces in my mind. I wasn't crazy.

"So, if you met him last week, why are you here now?" I said, finally gathering my thoughts.

"It's as I said. I wanted to see if he was telling me the truth about working here. He said he needed time to think, and I haven't heard from him since Friday morning. I thought he had lied to me again."

I had no idea what he needed to think about. Why did he need time to think?

Did he still love her?

I hoped not. I tried to answer each doubt in my mind one by one as a way to calm down. He hadn't seen her for years. He told me he loved me all the time. That must mean something. The way we kissed had to mean something, too. We had a physical connection, a spark that I never wanted to go out.

Did he want to be with me?

Surely Louise showing up couldn't change what we had. I thought back to the time I'd read his journal. I couldn't remember the exact wording as my memory failed me for real this time. He'd mentioned something about loving someone else. Had I been blinded by love? It seemed so. The warning signs had been there right in front of me; I'd just refused to see them.

"Lied to you again? I don't understand." I was even more confused than I had been at the beginning.

"He said he would meet me on Saturday evening, but he didn't. Said something about being hungover, and then told me he would meet me next weekend. I can't wait that long for another excuse." Sass rolled off her tongue as she placed her hands on the table. A glistening light caught my eye, reflecting from the diamond ring on her finger. She still had the ring. He'd proposed and she'd never taken it off. I hated her for so many reasons, especially for ruining a part of my life I'd never imagined crumbling to the ground. What I hated more was being lied to. Callum had been talking to Louise under my nose, the day after my graduation. He was heartless.

Callum walked into the foyer, facing me. He saw me and smiled, but his grin soon faded. I had been rubbing my eyes to stop myself from crying, leaving red puffy skin surrounding them. I didn't want to seem weak in front of Louise, but controlling my emotions wasn't going well. He continued to walk towards me, about to open his mouth until he noticed the blonde hair of the girl sat across from me. He knew that I knew. He stopped dead in his tracks. I would have thrown hot coffee over Louise to know what was going on in Callum's head. I'd have thrown it on her for free. I smiled weakly as I thought about the coffee ruining her pristine hair and makeup. Louise turned to Callum and flashed a smile.

"Why are you here?" he asked her, looking as if someone had just robbed him of his livelihood. I couldn't tell if he was unhappy to see her, or unhappy he'd been caught out.

"I came to surprise you, sweet," she addressed him in a way that disgusted me to my very core.

How dare she talk to him like that?

I was sat right across from her.

"T, it's not how it looks. I promise you."

How could I believe him? He had lied through his teeth. I was distraught. I tried very hard to hide my feelings, but I couldn't. I knew they were written all over my face. Callum had hurt me, and he knew it.

Did he really think he was going to get away with it?

My blood boiled as I desperately held onto my emotions.

"How is it not how it looks?" I asked rhetorically. "It's perfectly clear to me. If you had nothing to hide you would have told me. I don't know you anymore." My voice rose, depleting the very little energy I had left.

Ian walked out of the office behind reception after hearing me shout.

"What's going on?" He questioned, looking between the three of us.

"Callum has been cheating on me. That's what's going on." Tears streamed down my face in anger, as my voice continued to rise.

"I was going to tell you I had met with Louise. I just needed time to process things. Please, let's go somewhere and talk?" Louise sat looking smug, sipping her latte and watching with her eagle eyes.

"That's a good idea. Let's all calm down and go talk in my office," Ian said calmly, oozing a sense of authority. It was the first time I had heard him sound stern. People were looking at us. They were looking at me. But I didn't care.

"You wanted time to process things? Let me give you all the fucking time you need. We're through," I screamed, enunciating the swear word to make it clear I was livid. I continued in a rage, and knocked the coffee to the floor as I grabbed my bag in frustration. I stormed out of Farden onto the streets of Birmingham, looking like death. I couldn't look back. The streets were blurred from the tears puddling under my eyes and condensation that built up on my glasses. I must have walked for a mile or so before I found a bench to rest on, with no one daring to ask if I was okay. The things Callum and Louise had said played over and over in my mind, tormenting me and twisting the past as though it hadn't just happened.

I needed time away from you.
We've been messaging behind your back.
I love her, T.
You're nothing compared to her.

All I could do was listen. There was no hope for me. That positive person I had always tried to be was no more, sucked from existence. I had lost everyone. There was nothing more life could throw at me to knock me down. I had nothing left. I missed Mum. I needed her now more than ever. I missed Liam. He'd know what to do. Callum had kicked me while I was down, so low that I was in the pits of hell.

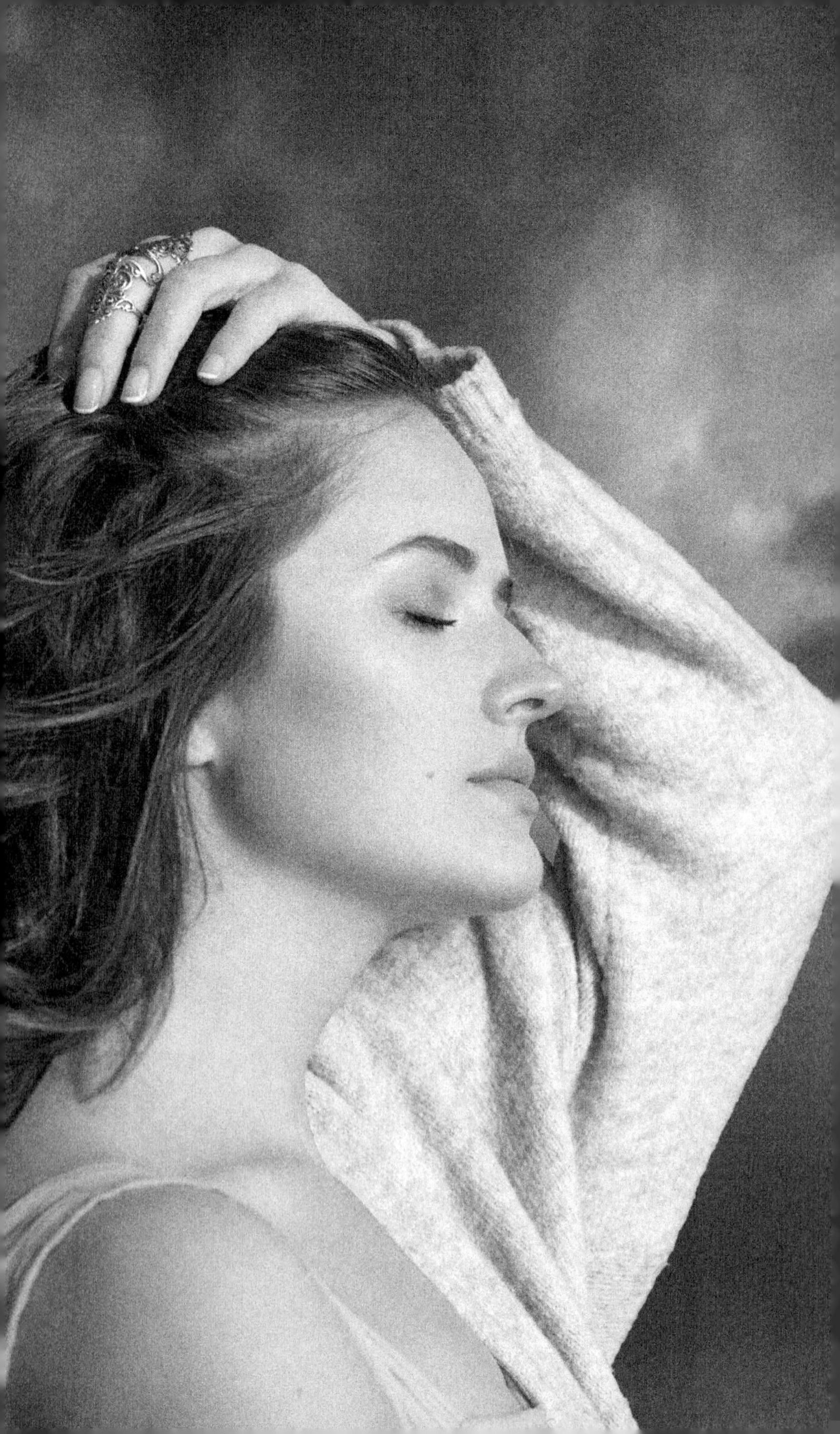

CHAPTER FIFTEEN

I knocked desperately at Liam's door, frozen and soaking wet after the walk from the train station. The rain was heavy, lashing on my bare arms and drenching my hair. I didn't care that it was raining, not like I normally would have. I didn't even care that I looked like a wet rat that had been dragged from one end of a sewer to another, barely holding on to its life and fighting for its next breath. I couldn't warn Liam I was coming. I knew I had to see him in person. I knew I had to grovel. In the midst of everything that had happened, along with the exhaustion that had taken over my body, I could barely remember what our fight had been about. The door opened, followed by a downpour of tears and thunderous cries. Liam stood at his door, shortly met by his little sister Jade being her usual nosy self.

"We're over. Done. Me and Callum," I said, blubbering as the rain continued to pour down on me.

"Go inside to Mum," he told Jade, shooing her back into the house. "Come here." He stretched out his arms to hold me, as if our fight didn't matter anymore. No dead air, just complete love for each other.

"I'm so sorry, Liam. I'm sorry this had to happen for me to apologise. I'm sorry I've been a shit friend."

"Shhhh, it's okay. I'm sorry, too."

There was a long, comfortable silence and I felt the warmest touch I'd felt in a while. The most comfort I had felt in a long time.

"Can I stay with you? Until I can get back on my feet?"

"Of course you can. Now, let's go inside and get you clean and dry. I can't be seen with you looking like this," he said with his hand resting on my face, trying to make me laugh. I tried to laugh. I did.

"Does this mean you aren't moving a hundred miles away anymore?"

"I'll only be moving if you're coming with me." I smiled and held him close again. Liam was the only stable relationship in my life. He was all I had. I wasn't going to be a fool and let that go for a second time.

I slumped onto his bed with a sigh. Liam's room was spacious and had a high ceiling. There were still marks up there from when we'd flicked slime onto the ceiling as children. Three mannequins stood tall in one corner of the room, all with unfinished garments hanging on them.

"So, what's happened?" he asked. I knew it wouldn't take long until the questions started. I had to tell him, even though I didn't want to talk about it. I knew getting it off my chest would be good for me. I gave good advice. Most of the time my brain was right, but half of the time my heart didn't want to listen.

"I'm so exhausted. Can we talk about it another time? I will tell you, I promise," I said, almost pleading.

"Don't worry, it's fine. Why don't you get some sleep? After all, this is now half your bed," Liam said, wrapping his arms around me once more.

"Just half my bed? You know I hog the bed and duvet," I joked with him, trying to forget all that life had thrown my way in such a short space of time.

"Oh yeah. Is it too late to change my mind?" We both laughed. I realised while I lay in bed, cocooned by the duvet, that I was no optimist. I'd been through a mess, and as much as I'd been trying to look on the bright side, somehow I'd always ended up looking at the negative. Not when I was with Liam, though. He was the optimist. His infectious personality would take over me uncontrollably, and made everything right again. I was lucky to have him. Liam shut his bedroom door and I drifted off to sleep, quicker than I had in a long time.

I woke to the door opening and the smell of food

rushing into the room. The scent of bacon clung to my nose and my stomach grumbled.

"Someone's hungry," Liam's mum said, smiling.

"I think I may be." I smiled back. With everything that had been going on, I had forgotten about food. I'd completely lost track of time. Diane woke me up just in time for tea and instructed me to go downstairs to fill my plate. My senses had been correct—bacon with new potatoes and peas. The potatoes were covered in butter, of course. My mouth watered in anticipation and my taste buds leapt in joy.

"This all looks so amazing. Can I contribute?" I asked Diane while everyone else was sat at the table, already digging in. Jade sat playing with her peas, eyeing up Liam's bacon. He always saved the best until last.

"Nonsense. You aren't giving me a penny and that's final," Diane said sternly. I wasn't going to argue. She was a proper mother figure, about five years older than my mum. She was a hugger, too. Every time I saw her I would find myself nestled between her huge breasts. She tried to hide them, but they weren't the easiest to conceal.

"Only if you're sure. Thanks, Di." She'd always let me call her Di, for as long as I could remember.

"Of course I'm sure. The amount of times your mum took care of Liam while I was at my lowest. I couldn't be more grateful. This is pay back." Diane's motherly instincts kicked in as she took me under her wing. The reason my mum and Liam had been so close was because of how much time we'd spent together when we were young. He was like a brother to me. Stuart put his arm around Diane and smiled. He was quite a stocky guy, taller than Diane, although she was quite small anyway. Liam had got his height from his birth father. Diane had struggled for a long time with her mental health, and it was all down to Liam's Dad. Aggressive. Possessive. A drunk. It started when Liam had told them he was gay. At first it had been fine, but his dad started drinking more and more. When he was drunk, he was a knob. Liam blamed himself for the breakdown of their marriage, even though I'd told him countless times it wasn't his fault. Things happened for a reason, and that's what I had to start telling myself, too.

"We're all good now, though, right, kids?" Stuart addressed Liam and Jade as he reassured Di. You could have bottled up the love around that table and sold it. I knew I would have bought some. My phone rang just as I pressed my fork into the crispy bacon that sat on top of the boiled potatoes. It was Farden.

"Do you mind if I get that? It's work. I don't think I'll be able to eat if I don't." Diane nodded. Bile churned in my stomach with worry.

"Tamsin, it's Ian." I knew from the tone of his voice he was annoyed.

"Hey, Ian." Before I could say anymore, he cut me off.

"I am absolutely disgusted at your behaviour in the

hotel lobby today. In front of guests. I won't tolerate it. I know you've had a lot to deal with, and for that I am sorry but what you did was inexcusable..."

I was fired.

I hadn't worked my six month probation period. I was screwed.

I couldn't stand there and grovel on the phone. I had to defend myself.

"You mean what Callum did *was* inexcusable?" I said, brushing off the blame, even though I had sworn. A lot.

"Callum has told me everything. I know what's been going on. That still does not give you the right to treat the hotel, your colleagues and friends with such disrespect." Ian had taken sides. Callum could never do any harm to him.

"Ian, when are you going to take your head out of Callum's arse and realise he was meeting up with his ex-girlfriend while he should have been working? I'm done with this crap. I quit!"

I quickly hung up, not wanting to hear another word from Ian. Liam's family all looked at me, their mouths agape, aside from Jade who was still playing with her food, completely oblivious to the world around her.

I couldn't be fired. I had to quit my job. It was damage control. I had to leave with a shred of my dignity intact. I'd tried to extinguish the fire that was my life, and it was working. The fire had been doused, leaving a pile of rubble surrounding me.

Fuck.

"I guess you want to know what Callum did, right?"

I sat in their lounge with my unconventional family. Jade was sat on Diane's lap, a true mummy's girl, dozing in and out of sleep while clinging onto her teddy. Stuart, Liam and I played a card game called *Bullshit*. We had to change the name, though, otherwise Jade would be shouting it at school. She was so easily influenced. So instead we shouted *pineapple* each time we suspected a cheater. Stuart won most of the games. He was hard to read, not like Liam who would act overly confident every time he lied about the cards he placed down. I thought about playing poker with him and the amount of money I'd win because of his awful bluff.

Then I wouldn't need a stinking job.

It was nice to feel normal after I'd told them about what had happened between Callum and me. After a while, everyone went upstairs to sleep, Jade carried up the stairs by Stuart, limply resting on his shoulder.

"I'm gonna need to go shopping tomorrow. I don't really want to be turning my thong inside out to wear." I lay in bed wide awake next to Liam. I didn't need to sleep. I was still rested from the nap I'd had earlier.

"I was thinking about that. We can go shopping, but you aren't buying clothes you already have. I'm going to message Callum now. I will pick up as much stuff as I can and throw it in my car," Liam said, grabbing his phone from the bedside table.

I lay there silently. I didn't want to know what he was saying or to be any part of it. Honestly, I didn't want him to go. Liam was protective of me, a real brother figure. I half expected him to call Callum and yell, or go and egg his house. He didn't, though. He knew that would stress me out. A few minutes later, Liam's phone vibrated on the table.

"It's sorted. I'm going tomorrow morning. Callum isn't working. Once I'm back, we can go for a wander around town." He grazed my arm to reassure me.

"Okay. Only if you treat me to a Starbucks."

———

The next morning, I woke up to a vacated bed. Liam had already left to grab some of my things. I tried to ignore the anxiety that was creeping up slowly, and kept chanting things I had read.

It's out of my control.

I can only change the way I think about things.

They were correct. I had no control of the situation aside from my reactions, both physical and emotional. I threw on a pair of Liam's jogging bottoms and a t-shirt that was left on his dresser. He'd either left them out for me or couldn't be bothered putting them away, either way, they were mine. I made my way downstairs to find Diane cooking breakfast on the stove—full English. She was a feeder, entirely my kind of woman.

"We can't have you going hungry now, can we? The

boys ate their's already." Before I could ask where everyone else was, she continued. "Stuart took Jade to school and Liam went out to... well, you know." I sat down at the dining table and watched Diane cook. A freshly poured coffee appeared next to me and I argued with her to let me wash up in return. Liam's car pulled up in the drive. You could hear the gravel crunching under his tyres from inside the house. He came bursting through the door with bags filled with my stuff and placed them in the lounge.

"Hey, you. I grabbed as much as I could," Liam said as he continued to lug more in through the hallway.

"Thank you." I leapt up and started to root through the bags to find fresh underwear.

"That's the most energy I've seen you have for a while. Good sleep?" Once he'd asked, his eyes scanned me. "I see you're already stealing my clothes. You have good taste. You could have worn mum's, though. Actually, her bras are way too big for your perky pair." He quickly grabbed my boobs, wobbled them playfully and ran upstairs, grabbing a bag on his way.

"That's my boy," Diane said, laughing and shaking her head as she put the dishes away.

Yep. That's my boy.

Coffee ran through my body like it had been injected intravenously. I had the energy of a five-year-old once we got back from town. It was either the Americano or the sugar syrup that I'd requested for extra flavour. I'd even handed a few CV's out in town after updating it on my phone and printing it before we left. I had to get my life back on track. Being at Liam's house wasn't a burden to anyone and I loved it there, but I couldn't stay forever. I needed a fresh start—a new chapter in my life to forget about Callum, even though I knew it would be hard. He had become such a huge part of my life, and Mum had adored him. All for nothing. One thing I could guarantee: Liam would be right by my side and the only constant I needed.

There was a small knock at the door.

"Get that for me, sweetie?" Diane asked Liam, even though it was an order.

"Ugh fine. Why am I always the one who has to answer the door." Liam moaned while getting up from the couch. I looked at Diane and she rolled her eyes in a funny way.

"Drama queen," she said, and I had to agree.

"Tamsin, door!"

Someone was at the door for me? I didn't need three guesses. I knew who it was. Callum stood on the doorstep, soaked from the rain that had caught Liam and I off guard walking around town that morning. Liam walked past me and made it clear he was going to be in the next room if I needed him.

"Why are you here? I thought I'd made it clear. We are done." I had calmed down a lot since then, but not enough to greet him properly. I stood by everything I'd said.

"Tamsin, please listen to me. I didn't tell you that she'd made contact and I'm fucking stupid for that, but believe me when I tell you there is nothing going on between Louise and me." I could hear the pain in his voice. He was begging for mercy; he didn't have to be on his knees.

"Really? She was wearing the ring you proposed with."

"What was I supposed to do, Tamsin? Snatch it off her? Rip her ring finger right off? It was her choice to keep wearing it, not mine," he said, losing his cool.

"Fair enough, but you're still an idiot for not telling me she'd travelled all the way from bloody America to come and see you. It's insane."

"She didn't come from America to see me. She lives in the Cotswolds somewhere. She lived in America for a while, though. She lived in New York for years with her dad while he was out there for work. She went to school there, too. That's why she has such a strong American accent. I knew she was from the UK, but I thought she'd moved to America permanently. That's why I couldn't find her all that time. I was looking in the wrong place."

"That fills me with so much love and joy. I'm made up for you," I said sarcastically.

"Please, T, I'm not done."

"Well, I am. I told you before and I'm telling you again. I'm done. You lied. Worst of all, you needed time to think. If I really meant so much to you, you would have told me straight away and not needed to think at all." I slammed the door in his face. A sigh escaped me as I rested against the door. The worst was over.

"She was pregnant," I heard from the other side of the door.

She was pregnant?

The thought echoed, repeating on a loop.

They have a child.

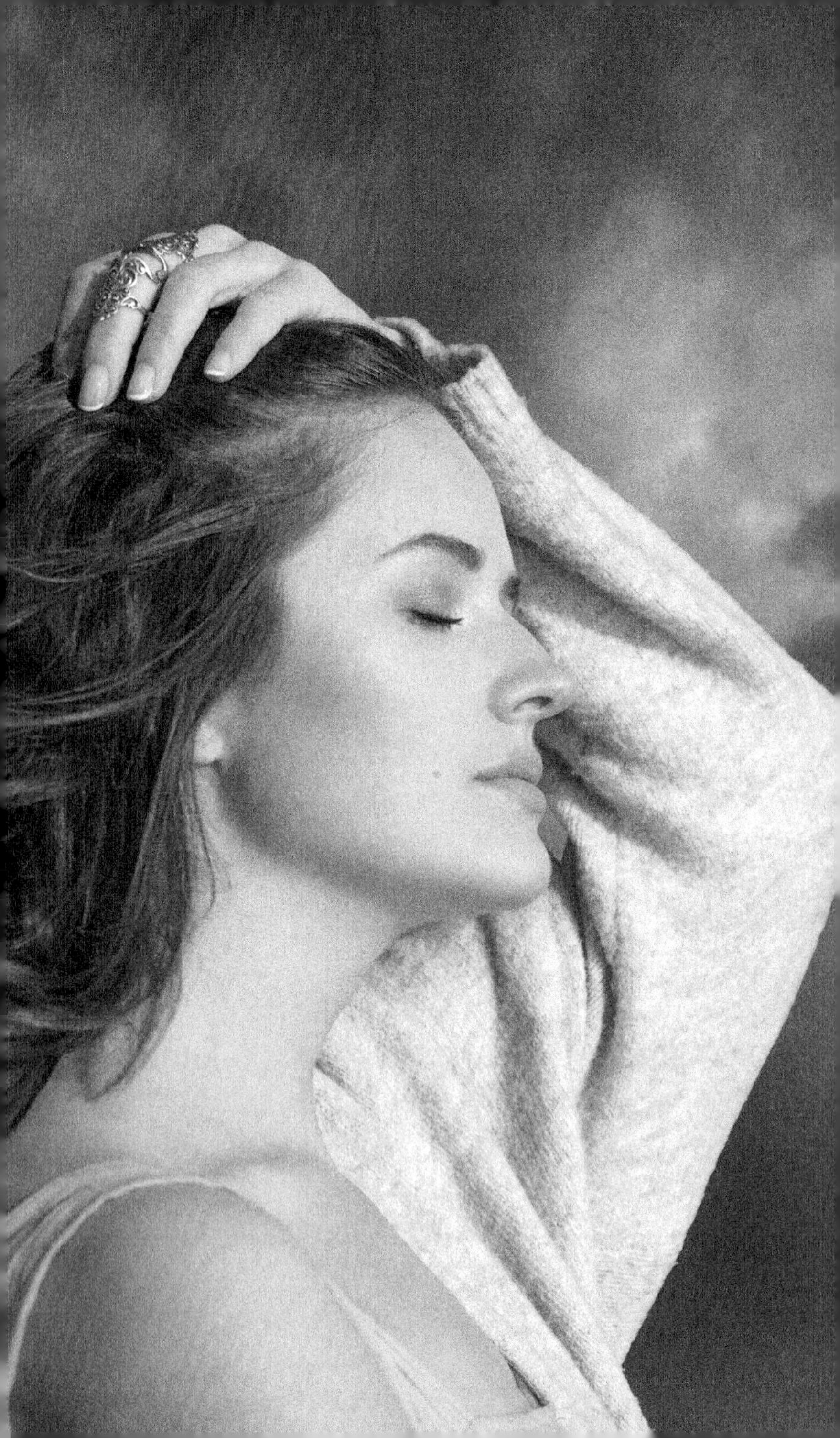

CHAPTER SIXTEEN

With my back against the cold wooden door, my body limply slid to the floor.

Callum has a child.

A growing pain spread like wildfire throughout my body. I had been upset about him lying. He was an idiot, but somehow I'd still had hope that we would work things out. Hope that he would explain, apologise, and we would work through the mess that had become our relationship. Hope that I would be able to move back to his fancy house. Hope that I'd be able to get a new job, kiss him goodbye in the morning and hello in the evening. Hope that we would live our lives together, but separate. Separate in our careers—working together was doomed from the start—but together in love. That hope had vanished into thin air. I couldn't be the third person in a relationship, living each day as number two with his love child coming first. That was without even the mention of Louise. She could use that poor child as a puppet in whatever master plan she had for Callum, just to get her claws in. I needed closure. I needed to hear him out, give him what he wanted and close the door on what we'd had. I got up and pulled the door open.

"Does this mean we can talk?" Callum asked softly.

"I'm not going to make you choose, Callum. You have a child. I'm not going to be the person who gets in the way of a family," I said, getting straight to the point. It was like ripping off a plaster. Quick and painful.

"I don't have a child. I did. It's so hard to say it without saying it."

"Say what, Callum? I don't understand."

"She had a miscarriage. Louise. That's what I needed to think about. That's what I needed to process." He paused for a while. "I was going to be a dad, T."

It was the first time I'd seen Callum cry. He still looked pretty, even though he was soaking, shaking to the bone.

I'd been wrong.

Wrong about Callum.

Wrong about Louise.

I was the idiot, too quick to snap. Too fast to judge.

"I'm so sorry." I apologised for a multitude of reasons—for his loss and Louise's. I couldn't imagine the pain they must have gone through. I was sorry for jumping to conclusions and not hearing him out. Sorry for tossing away a relationship that mattered more than I wanted to admit to myself.

"It's hard. I didn't want to bring you into this. I know I should have told you, but with everything else going on, I didn't want to make your load heavier than it already was."

Each time Callum spoke, I imagined holding him. I wanted to take his pain away, just like he had done for me.

I love you.

I wanted to say it, but I couldn't, not yet. I held back.

"Louise is doing alright, too. She had her family around her once it happened. She was trying to protect me. That's why she left. I can't cut ties with her." He was shaking. This was his only demand. He still wanted to speak to Louise, but was worried to hear my response.

"I understand. Of course I do." How could I not? She'd done nothing wrong, aside from stalking Callum but I guessed if I'd been in her shoes I would have probably done the same, or worse.

"I'm not here for an apology. I understand the way you reacted. I'm here for you. I want you to take me back. Take back all those things you said about us being done. I need you, T. I need your shoulder to cry on, just like you've cried on mine. I need you next to me in bed so I can stop thinking about what could have been and think about my life with you. You have been through so much crap that would be unimaginable to most people.

Some of it with me, some without. Let's promise to go through the rest together?"

He was such a smooth talker and knew exactly what to say. His heartfelt words made goosebumps rise on my skin. His expression said it all, too. If words could sweep me off my feet, then those were the ones.

"Can we have each other without the crap please?" I lightly mocked his question, but a beaming smile appeared on his face.

"Fine by me." Callum moved closer, his arms widening to hold me as beads of rain fell from them. It had been around twenty-four hours since I'd last seen him, but for some reason, I craved his touch more than ever. I'd missed his smell and the warmth that surrounded us. I'd missed grazing my fingers across his chest, down to his abs, and I'd missed his fingers lightly stroking the bottom of my back. His lips pressed against the crook of my neck, and as he let me go, I could still feel his touch lingering on my skin.

"I know you aren't here for a sorry, but I am. I take back what I said about you and Louise. I jumped to conclusions. I was exhausted. I couldn't process anything else aside from what I was already thinking. I want you to know that I'm going to get an appointment at the doctors. I need some help. I've been drowning and part of me still is. Liam is my life jacket and you are my whistle; I just need a boat." Admitting to myself that I'd been drowning was one thing, but talking about it was another. It was hard to get the words out, but I felt accountable to Callum, to myself. There was no going back. I had to get help for sure.

"I'm sorry for not seeing you were drowning. You put on such a hard front that sometimes you are impermeable. Cancer was eating you up emotionally, and it's been forcing you to make irrational decisions. It isn't like you, T." Callum stroked my hair as he continued. "I'm here for you and I'll support you in whatever adventures you want to go on. Whatever journeys you need to take, I'll be by your side. I'm not losing you again. You have me… and Liam." Callum looked up and smiled as Liam stepped around the corner. Callum mouthed *'thank you'* to him, like him being there was some sort of set up. It was. Of course it was. They had been conniving together like two best friends.

"Coming in for a brew?" Liam asked, and Callum looked at me to ascertain whether it was okay.

"Coffee okay?"

We must have sat together for a couple of hours. The mess of the past disappeared over time, and it was like normal. We introduced Callum to the game *Pineapple*—game after game he became easier to read. Callum couldn't stop talking; in fact, Liam and I were acting as his medicine, numbing his pain as our infectious laughter echoed through Liam's room. Jade nipped in every few minutes once Diane had picked her up from school. She would talk our ears off until she got bored, and then she'd come back a few minutes later with something new and interesting only a five-year-old would find fascinating, like a paper clip or a piece of bubble wrap.

"What's with the fancy costume over there?" Callum asked, pointing to a sequin dress in a sky blue colour that sparkled underneath the ceiling light.

"Ahh, the blue one is a custom order I'm doing for a drag queen from Chester. She's held a gay night for nearly twenty years, and she wanted a bespoke dress for her anniversary night," he said naturally, like it was no big deal.

"That's awesome…"

"I'll say. Oh my god, this is amazing," I jumped in, cutting Callum off. "Is it for Miss Mirage?" I asked, already one hundred percent sure it was her. She was the best-known drag queen in Chester while we were at university and long before.

"Yeah, who else?" Liam exclaimed.

"So what does this mean? I can't believe I didn't know." I knew why I didn't know. I was too busy wrapped up in my own mess and I'd neglected Liam.

Not anymore.

I was incredibly proud; this was huge.

"Well, I've also reduced my hours at The Tap. It's about time I did something that relates to my degree. You know how much I love fashion. I guess this is just a twist on the couture fashion I used to design in university." Liam did love fashion. He would always read my mum's trashy magazines and in high school, he'd save up his money to buy the latest edition of *Vogue*. He would spend hours drawing stunning silhouettes.

"I'm so proud of you. How did this come about?" I asked, more and more intrigued, catching up on a part of his life that I'd zoned out of.

"Oh, I slept with him," he said casually.

"LIAM!"

"What? It got me the job, right?" He laughed. "Instead of an awkward morning after sex, we got talking and it turned into a job opportunity. A well paid one for that matter. The dress making, not the sex. I pride myself on not charging for that." He winked at Callum, hoping for a reaction. Callum flirted back. I'd have been worried if I hadn't known he was comfortable with his sexuality.

"Well, I can't say anything. I don't even have a job and I can't exactly have sex with someone to get one," I said, looking at Callum, teasing him. "But no, I'm glad I quit before Ian fired me. New beginnings and all that."

"Ian wasn't going to fire you. You know that, right? He may have been the angriest I've ever seen, but he told me he was just going to suspend you for a while. He didn't want to lose you for good. You're one of the best at Farden."

Damn.

Had I really just quit a very well paid job, out of this awful town, for no reason? No. Callum was the other reason. I couldn't face going back there with him. Having everyone look at me like a crazy person. Being judged for a reaction based on the situation unfolding there and then. There was no way I was going back to that. I had a chance, an opportunity for a new era of Tamsin. Tamsin 2.0. A chance to recreate myself without the mess everyone knew about. Without the sympathy of people knowing I'd lost Mum and been left alone. Scratch that. Not completely on my own. I had Liam and Callum.

"Well, things happen for a reason. I don't know what that reason is yet but I will soon. Call me crazy, but I think I'm happier without Farden. Onwards and upwards," I hummed positively.

A lifetime of desire for material things suddenly didn't matter—a coffee machine, a big house with a gorgeous chandelier or even a car that glistened. I had always wanted to be the CEO of some big company. After all, I had worked hard. In the midst of aiming for the stars and achieving the goals I had spent my childhood planning out, I had forgotten about what was truly important and neglected my friendship with Liam. That once bustling road of friendship had become a one-way street, and that had to change. Liam was making something of himself, designing clothes and putting his fashion degree to use, and I'd been too busy in my own little world to ask about him. My life was eating me up and spitting me out, each time taking something away from me that I couldn't live without. Enough was enough. I dragged my moping, imaginary body off the ground and grabbed life by its invisible balls.

Mess with me all you want, life. Ruin my plan, put a stop to the goals I've worked so hard for, but you can't take away my relationships. I'm responsible for those.

And with that, my body regained its posture and the fog in my mind started to clear.

Ready for my next journey.

Set for what was in store.

Go. I was going to go like I never had before.

I took my phone from my jeans pocket and dialled the doctor's number, memorised from when Mum had been ill, instead of searching for it within my contacts. It rang then played an automatic message, but I held for reception.

"Hello, Weaver Surgery. How can I help?"

"Hi. My name's Tamsin Cross," I said nervously, stumbling at almost every word. "Can I have an appointment with a doctor? I've been struggling and need some help." I didn't want to say any more. Thankfully, I didn't need to. They knew.

"Can you come in this Thursday evening? We have an appointment at five-forty with Doctor Falkon."

"That's great. Thank you. I'll see you then." In relief, I hung up the phone and received a text confirming my appointment. I had taken the first step in gaining control of my life, and it had been easier than I'd thought. Next, the appointment.

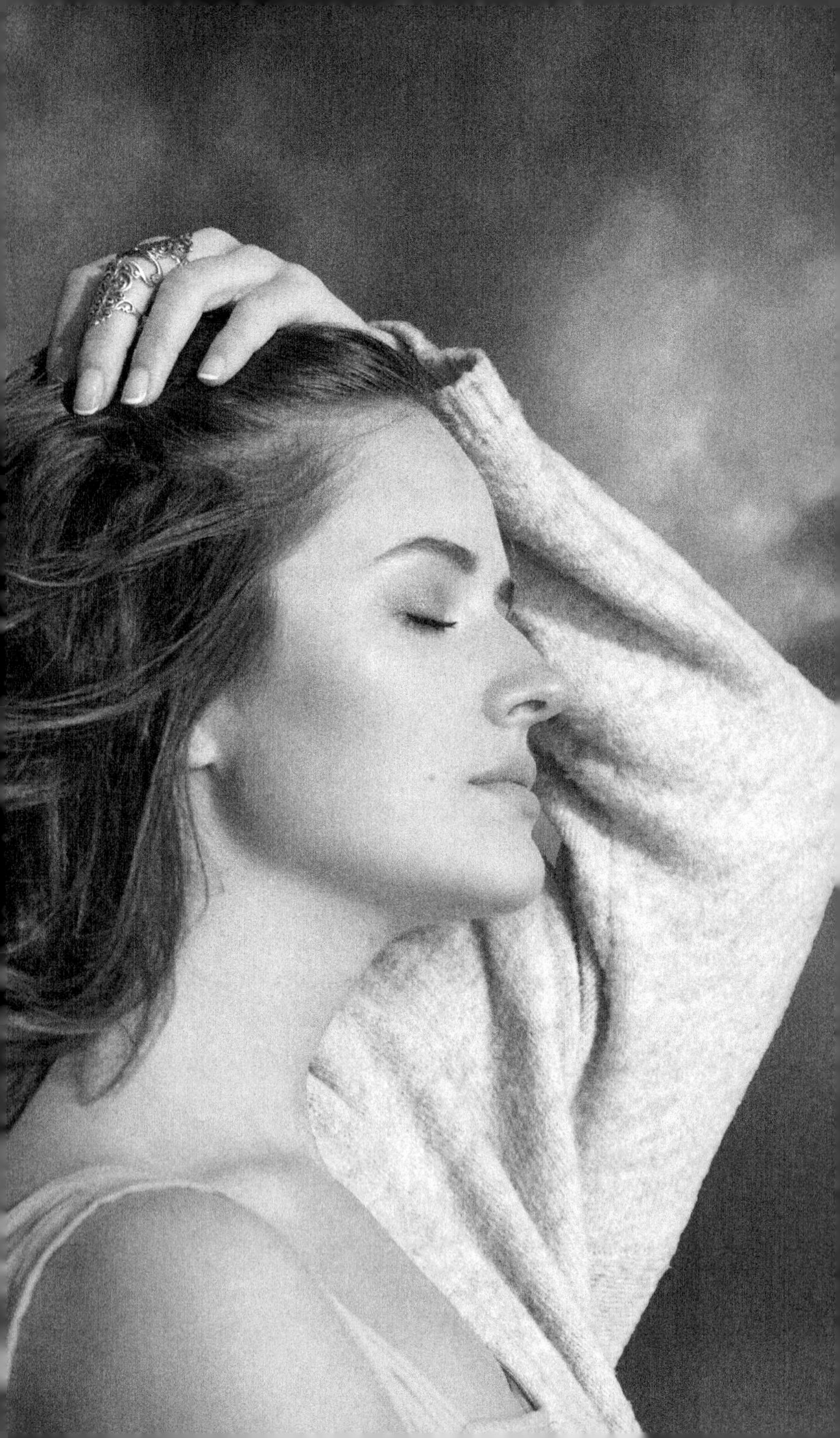

CHAPTER SEVENTEEN

I arrived at the doctor's surgery promptly at five-twenty, nervous for an appointment that left dread pooling at the bottom of my stomach. Once I'd waved Callum off after he'd dropped me off in the car park, I made my way to the front desk. The waiting area was eerily quiet, so much so I could hear the receptionists talking about what they were having for tea as I walked through the door.

"Hi, Tamsin. Here to see Dr Falkon?" the elderly receptionist asked. She always seemed to remember my name despite me never remembering hers. It was a small surgery, a family practice that had grown considerably over the years. You couldn't have stopped my mum from going to the doctors; she loved to chat. I mean, she'd been registered at the surgery since she was a child herself, and never missed one of her asthma reviews. Me on the other hand–I usually had to be dragged to the place. I hated talking about myself and answering all the questions. This time was different, though. I knew I had to talk to start to feel myself again, the way I had at university.

"Hey, you. I am, yes," I said, getting straight to the point.

"I've let him know you're here, my lovely," she said softly, but before I could say thank you, she continued, "Tamsin, I just wanted to say how sorry I was to hear about Theresa. I couldn't get the time off work to come to the funeral. There was no one to cover me, but I did ask the doctor to pass on my love. If you ever need anything, I'll be here at this desk, as always." She walked around the desk to give me a hug.

"Thank you," I croaked, struggling to conjure up any more words as an unexpected lump grew in my throat, trying to stop myself from getting emotional. She rubbed my arms and led me over to the seating area to wait for the doctor. I sat on my phone, mindlessly scrolling through social media, and opened the occasional GIF sent by Liam in attempt to calm me. He'd wanted to come, and Callum had, too, but I needed to be alone. As my name appeared on the screen, I had to drag myself down the corridor. I knocked.

"Come in," I heard from behind the door. "Ah, Tamsin. Take a seat." The door shut behind me. "How can I help?"

I sighed. The lump in my throat was growing larger

by the second, to the point I could taste the anxiety and upset in my mouth.

"I don't feel like myself anymore. I'm really struggling. I feel like my life is out to get me. I feel like I'm fighting a losing battle. I can't escape." I huffed between words, trying to hold back the dam of tears, even though a few had already escaped.

"That's understandable. Did this start when your mum passed away?" Doctor Falkon's voice calmed me. It was a simple question. I could answer that.

"Yes. Well, maybe a bit before."

"Okay. So what exactly has happened since?" he probed further.

"The funeral was hard. I locked myself away at my boyfriend's house for about two weeks after, pushing everyone away. My best friend and I fell out and I had graduation without Mum. I keep on jumping to conclusions, making irrational decisions about everything, and to top it all off, I have no energy." I couldn't cry. Not here.

"Jumping to conclusions? Irrational decisions?"

"I thought my boyfriend was cheating on me with his ex-fiancé. I kicked off at him in front of everyone at work and then quit my job." Word vomit poured from my mouth as I quickly tried to tell him everything so I could stop talking. I gave a little smile to disguise the emotion I was feeling inside.

"It's okay to cry, you know? There's no one in this room you have to protect."

That was it. The walls I had once built to protect myself crumbled. I couldn't keep them up. Floods of tears poured down my face as if the walls had never been there in the first place. I couldn't stop them. I didn't want to. I needed someone I didn't know to understand the pain I was going through and avoid the sympathy from my two favourites.

"I think some counselling would be beneficial. You have been through a lot and talking to someone impartial will help. Have you taken anti-depressants before?" he asked as he scrolled on his computer. I guessed he was looking through my records, or lack of them. I shook my head. "Okay, well I am going to prescribe you twenty milligrams of Fluoxetine. They should help with how you are feeling. They aren't magic pills and they won't work straight away. You may have some side effects, but once they start working in a few weeks, I think you may find yourself feeling more energetic and more like yourself."

"Thank you. It means a lot, and thank you again for being there at the funeral." I sighed again, but this time with relief, letting out the anxiety that I'd pent up inside for so long.

"Don't mention it. You'll get a call in a few days with an appointment. Look after yourself, Tamsin."

"I will. Thanks again," I said walking out, holding on tight to the prescription and self-help sheets that Dr Falkon had printed for me like it was a matter of life or death. They were my lifeline–tickets to becoming me again.

After being in the pharmacy longer than in the doctor's surgery, I arrived back at Liam's house, concealing the tablets in my pockets like some sort of drug mule. I wasn't ashamed of having to take anti-depressants; at least I didn't think I was. I just didn't want the whole Wright household to know. I bypassed the living area and went straight upstairs to Liam, who was busy working on the blue sequin dress. It was taking shape, and looked like a gorgeous, flowing gown.

"So, how was it?" Liam said, not for one second taking his eyes off the dress and sewing machine in front of him.

"Good, I think. He said I need counselling, and I think I have to agree with him. He also gave me these." I took the tablets from my pocket and flung them onto the bed next to where he was working. "He thinks they'll help with my energy and my thoughts. He said there may be a few side effects but I'm not too worried as long as they help in the long run." I slumped onto the bed and lay there with my phone in the air, scrolling casually. It was so easy with Liam, no effort to be around him at all. A text from Callum buzzed onto my phone.

Callum <3
8th November 2018

[19:42]

Will you be coming home tonight, T? I'm worried xxx

I hadn't told him. I hadn't told Callum I was staying at Liam's for a few more days before heading back to his house. Becoming absorbed in my own thoughts and problems had become the norm. I wanted to take things slow, spend more time with Liam, and make up for the lost time between us. I needed that, for me.

[19:48]

Not tonight. I'm gonna stay at Liam's for a few days to get myself back on track and spend some time with him. I feel like I've forgotten about him recently. I hope you understand. We're okay, I promise. I can't wait to be snuggled up in bed next to you. I'll give you a call tomorrow. I love you xxx

With the reply sent, I placed my phone on the side table next to me and turned my attention to Liam. After all, he was the reason I'd stayed. Liam was still adding sequins to the bodice of the dress, placing them with precision.

"The dress looks great. You should try it on when you're done," I said, eager to see the finished dress on someone other than a poorly shaped mannequin or draped over the side of the sewing machine.

"I'd love to, but it would hang off me. Although you've just reminded me, it's nearly finished and I need to organise a fitting with David before Friday."

David was Miss Mirage. We had been on first name basis with him since before the end of first term at university. Every week without fail we would go to the club, get drunk and dance dramatically in front of the DJ booth, constantly requesting songs. Any other DJ or drag queen would have hated it, but not David. Whether it was because he fancied Liam or whether he took joy in our carefree dance moves, I didn't know, but he'd always made time for us.

"Oh yeah, it's his celebration night soon, right? Oh god, Liam, I miss it so much. It's not even been a year since our last Tuesgay night out. What I would do to just rewind and go back to when life was simpler."

"Well, you're in luck," Liam said as he got up and opened his bed side table draw. He handed me two tickets. *Miss Mirage Presents Tuesgay's Big Birthday Bash*. "You didn't think I would go to all this effort and not see my dress being worn in person, did you? Besides, it's an excuse for us to get drunk and do filthy dancing against each other." Liam winked and slut dropped to the floor, raising his hips in the air as he slowly got up.

"So rude. You just want another excuse to sleep with David." I stated the obvious.

"Nah. Fitting is another excuse to sleep with David. Tuesgay, on the other hand, means freshers."

I was wrong. I should have known.

After a few hours of back-and-to chitchat, and a delicious meal cooked by Diane, I took my tablet and headed to bed. I lay awake for what seemed like hours, listening to Liam snore while he slept as soon as he pulled the cover over him, until I drifted off.

A freezing wind filled the room from the open window Liam had left open. I could feel chills all over my body, even with the duvet covering all but my face. My phone lit up, showing a text from Callum.

Callum <3
15ᵀᴴ November 2018

[02:13]

Don't bother coming home. Louise would have come home to me.

I tried to wake up Liam who was still soundly asleep next to me. Another text appeared on my phone.

Gayboy x
15ᵀᴴ November 2018

[02:14]

I sleep to escape you. Leave me alone, Tamsin. You pushed me away so I can do the same to you.

Once I'd read it, he sat awake, not speaking, holding his phone. The bedroom door opened and my surroundings suddenly changed. I was in my childhood bedroom, sat in my old bed and the room was filled with all of my things.

"You need to tidy up in here. It's a pig sty." The voice filled me with warmth.

"Mum?" I said, wanting to reach out and take hold of the shadow in the doorway.

"Who else would it be?"

"You're really here. I knew you would come. I love you, Mum." I could feel tears rolling down my face. My emotions raged, not knowing whether to feel happy or sad.

"I'm here, but I've got to go now. You quit. You gave up. So I gave up, too."

"Mum, don't say that. I'm sorry. I've failed you. Please don't go. Mum! Mu..."

———

"Tamsin. Wake up. Are you okay?" Liam shook me lightly, until I came around. "You were shouting in your sleep again and breathing really heavily." Just as I had started to sleep better, my luck had turned with an influx of nightmares. It was the second night of nightmares; both times I'd been woken by Liam. A week of nightmares in a row wasn't a coincidence. Liam put it down to the side effect of the tablets I had been taking, just like they were making me throw up. I could just about keep down one meal a day, which was not like me at all. I made a call to Weaver Surgery, and told them about my vivid dreams and sickness. The dreams haunted me, my thoughts drifting to them uncontrollably all day. Later that evening, I received an email from Dr Falkon.

Dear Tamsin,

I'm sorry for the delay in getting back to you. The symptoms you have described are listed as possible side effects. If these are mild and you can cope with them, the symptoms should ease over the next week or so. If they get worse, stop taking the tablets and come in to see me so we can discuss a different medication.

I hope this helps and take care.

Dr Falkon (MRCGP)
Weaver Surgery

I couldn't *not* take the tablets. Getting myself back on track wasn't going to be a quick fix, as the doctor had said. Throwing up meals and having weird dreams was a price I was willing to pay.

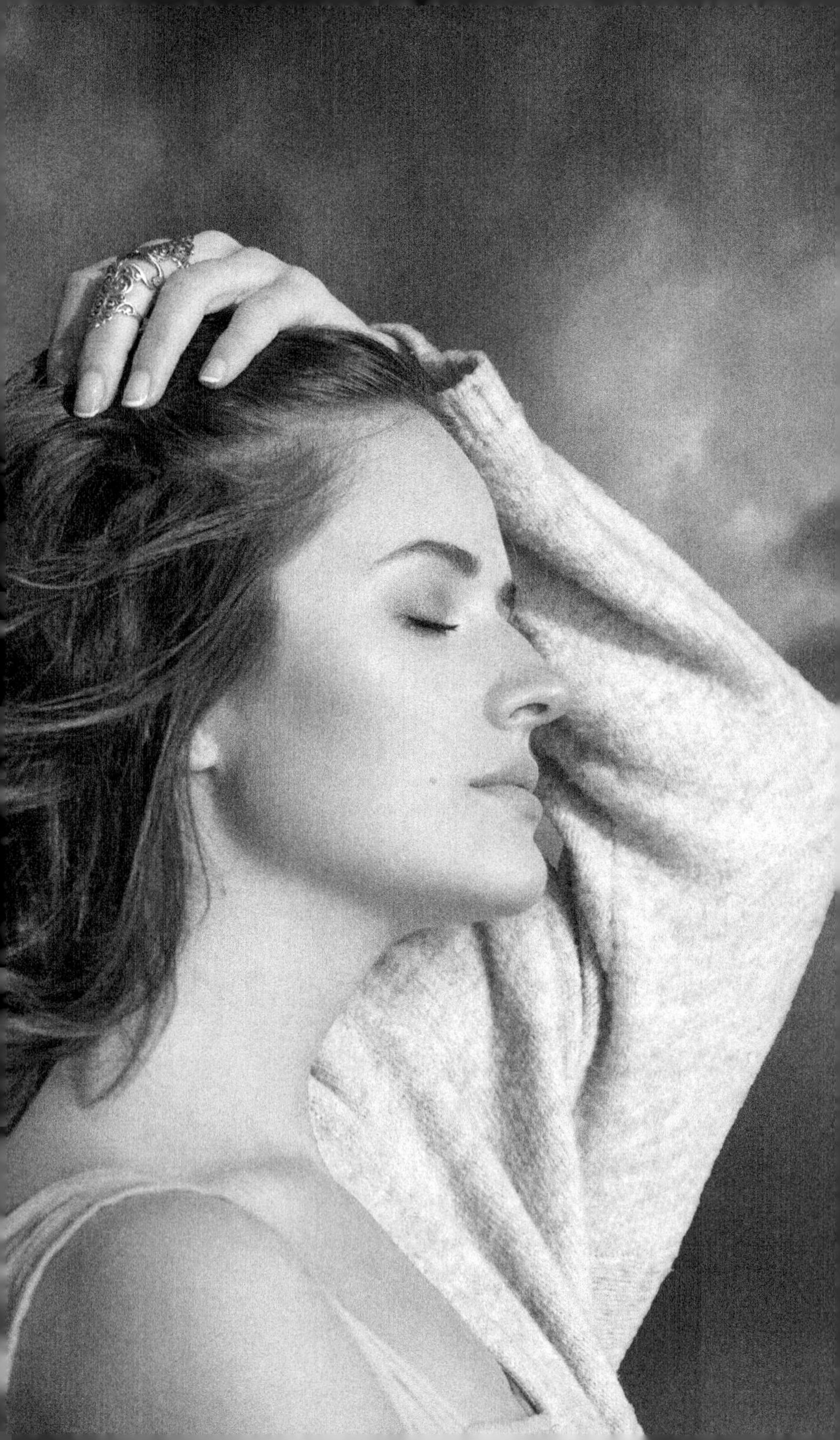

CHAPTER EIGHTEEN

The Gal, The Guy & The Gay
19TH November 2018

[10:11]

Thought I would set up this group chat with my two favourites. You guys okay?

[10:12]

Liam: You that bored, hun?

[10:12]

Callum: Yeah, some of us have work you know ;)

[10:13]

Yes okay, I'm bored sat watching the same programmes every day. Diane has got me watching Jeremy Kyle re-runs now. I'm sure I just saw my old neighbour on it!

Also, working my arse! Look how quick you both responded!

[10:15]

Liam: The bar is quiet and Grindr is boring.

[10:16]

Callum: I was just eager to speak to you, T ;)

Miss you x

[10:16]

Liam: Ew. Gross.

[10:17]

Callum: Just because you don't have a special someone lol

[10:17]

Liam: Special someone? I'm gonna be sick.

[10:18]

Now now, boys!

Jezza has just brought out a human male version of Toothless from How To Train Your Dragon. You are distracting me.

[10:19]

Liam: This was your group. Speak or leave.

P.S. How you feeling? Stopped being sick?

[10:19]

CALLUM: YOU'RE BEING SICK? WHAT'S UP?

[10:24]

LIAM!

UGH I'M FINE. THE TABLETS ARE MAKING ME A BIT SICK. NOTHING TO WORRY ABOUT.

LIAM LEFT THE CHAT.

[10:25]

CALLUM: WHY DIDN'T YOU TELL ME?

[10:27]

I WAS GOING TO COME ROUND TO YOURS TONIGHT AND TELL YOU, BUT LIAM JUMPED THE GUN...

DON'T WORRY I'M OKAY.

[10:29]

CALLUM: YOU ARE STILL GOING TO COME TONIGHT, AREN'T YOU? MOVE BACK IN. LET ME LOOK AFTER YOU. YOU'LL HAVE THE WHOLE HOUSE TO YOURSELF WHILE I'M AT WORK. YOU CAN DECIDE WHAT YOU WANT ON TV INSTEAD OF WATCHING JEREMY KYLE WITH DIANE LOL

[10:37]

I WILL BE MOVING BACK IN SOON, JUST NOT YET.
ALSO, JOKING ASIDE, JEZZA WAS INTENSE TODAY!

[10:39]

CALLUM: I MISS YOU, T X

[10:39]

I MISS YOU TOO X

Callum <3
20ᵀᴴ November 2018

[13:45]

IT WAS GREAT TO SEE YOU LAST NIGHT. I WISH YOU COULD HAVE STAYED. I WASN'T READY TO LET GO OF YOU AT ALL. STAY LONGER NEXT TIME? X

[13:48]

I WILL, I PROMISE X

[13:49]

GOOD! WHAT HAVE YOU DONE TODAY? X

[13:52]

JUST BEEN WITH LIAM. HE'S NOT WORKING AT THE BAR TODAY. WE'RE GOING OUT TONIGHT TO TUESGAY, WHICH SHOULD BE FUN. HE'S A BAG OF STRESS ATM THOUGH X

[13:55]

WHY? CAN'T DECIDE WHAT TO WEAR? LOL X

[13:57]

YOU LAUGH BUT THAT IS PART OF THE PROBLEM HAHA

He has also been contacted by two other drag queens for a custom design before Christmas. Miss Mirage has clearly already been showing off her dress before her big evening!

Oh, and he said yes to both of the queens and now he is ranting to himself, covered in bits of material, panicking he won't get them done in time x

[14:02]
Rather you than me! Pass on my congrats to Liam though. That's fantastic. Shame I'm not seeing you again tonight. I hope you have fun with Liam though. Where are you staying? Stay safe please x

[14:05]
I'm sorry. I think Liam mentioned something about a hotel, I know we're staying in Chester.

I will. You know me x

[22:49]
So, it turns out we are staying at Miss Mirage's. Typical Liam I guess. We're heading to the club soon. We've got VIP tickets which is exciting. I've never been a VIP before x

[22:54]
Are you sure you are okay with that? Do you want me to come pick you up later? Enjoy living your best life tonight x

[22.59]
No, it's okay. I'll be fine. Besides, you have work tomorrow x

[23:01]

I don't mind. You not drunk yet?

[23:10]

Not yet, hopefully soon though! Just walking to the club now. I love you x

[23:11]

I love you too xx

21ST NOVEMBER 2018

[00:16]

I've just got into bed. Late one for me. Hope you are having a nice time dancing to cheesy music. Text me before you head to sleep xx

[03:56]

I m gonna gey ya

[04:10]

Ioutside xxxxxxxxx

GAYBOY X
21ST NOVEMBER 2018

[11:29]

Where are you? Are you okay?

[11:35]

Mum says you aren't at home. Where are you?

[11:37]

Tamsin??

[11:40]

Hey, I'm at Callum's house. According to an email I received, I got an Uber to his. I was so drunk last night, I fell up a step into Callum's front door and hit my neck on the door knob so now I have a huge bruise that looks like a hickey. I was sick all down my dress and on his doorstep, so I apparently stripped off in the hallway and tried to have sex with him. I'm such a mess.

[11:45]

I'm weeing myself. That's brilliant. Tried to have sex? You mean you didn't?

[11:49]

Nope. No sex. Apparently a slobbering, slurring drunk women isn't sexy, even to a man who loves her. We haven't had sex since my graduation night. And before that, probably before mum passed away. I'm gagging here.

[12:22]

Ouch. David and I feel for you.
P.S. Sorry for the delay. Just had sex.

[12:23]

I hate you.

The Gal, The Guy & The Gay
21ˢᵗ November 2018

[16:36]

Guys, it's nearly Christmas so I thought we could set up Secret Santa?

[16:40]

Callum: You do realise Liam left the group? I'm on my way home btw x

[16:41]

Oh shit. One sec, I will add him now x

Liam was added to the group.

[16:43]

Liam. I want to do Secret Santa. You in? This has nothing to do with my lack of funds.

[16:46]

Liam: Sure! What's the budget?

[16:47]

Callum: £40? Something like that?

[16:48]

THE WHOLE POINT OF THIS IDEA WAS SO I COULD SAVE MONEY. IS IT TOO LATE TO WITHDRAW? HAHA

[16:50]
LIAM: YEP. I HOPE I GET YOU CALLUM.
[16:51]
CALLUM: ;)

[16:52]
EW. GROSS.

I DIDN'T TELL YOU GUYS. I GOT A LETTER TODAY. MY COUNSELLING APPOINTMENT IS NEXT WEEK. HOW QUICK WAS THAT?

[16:55]
CALLUM: THAT'S GREAT NEWS. I HOPE IT HELPS. I'M STILL WORRIED THAT YOU KEEP ON BEING SICK :(

[16:55]
IF IT WILL MAKE YOU FEEL BETTER, I WILL SPEAK TO THE COUNSELLOR ABOUT IT, BUT MY GP SAID THE SICKNESS SHOULD PASS SOON ANYWAY.

[17:10]
LIAM: HURRAY! I'M GLAD YOU ARE BEING SEEN QUICKLY. MUM WANTS TO KNOW IF YOU ARE HOME FOR FOOD TONIGHT? WE'RE HAVING GAMMON AND EGG WITH CHIPS.

[17:14]

I'm going to stay at Callum's if that's okay? But I will come tomorrow in the day to see you both if you aren't working?

[17:15]

Liam: No worries xoxo

Gayboy x
21ST November 2018

[17:17]

Need sex that bad?

[17:18]

You can talk! Haha
Don't judge me. She deserves it.

[17:20]

Did you just refer to your vagina as a she?
P.S. Judging you. Not for needing sex. That's allowed.
Judging you for having a vagina.

[17:24]

Yes I did! She says hello. Now can we stop talking about my vagina, Callum has just walked through the door.

Liam's Mum
22ND November 2018

[12:10]

I just wanted to tell you how much you mean to me, all of you. I know I told you in person, but it just didn't seem enough. Thank you for taking me in when I had no one else to turn to. You made a very cold and lonely girl realise she has family closer than she realised. I look up to you. You raised such a gentleman in Liam. I'm so incredibly lucky, and that's without mentioning gorgeous Jade. She is turning into a clone of Liam. I'm not sure if you should be worried or thrilled. I think Callum will be over tomorrow to collect the rest of my things. Keep an eye out for the postman over the next few days, I hope it says thank you better than these words. Lots of love, Tamsin xx

[12:47]
That brought a tear to my eye, Tamsin. We're lucky to have you. Our door is open anytime. You know that. You didn't have to say thank you. That's what family is for. Love always, Diane xxx

Gayboy x
22ND November 2018

[13:04]

I was going to message you thanking you for everything as well, but since you called me a soppy cow, you don't deserve the sop.

[13:07]
You're welcome x

The Gal, The Guy & The Gay
23RD November 2018

[15:20]

LIAM: YOU TWO WANT TO COME OUT TONIGHT?

PUTTING DRESSES TOGETHER FOR PEOPLE IS TAKING THE FUN OUT OF ACTUALLY DESIGNING THE FASHION AND I'M IN THE MOOD TO SHAKE MY GROOVE.

[15:25]

CALLUM: NOT FOR ME, SORRY. TAMSIN HAS JUST GOT IN THE BATH SO SHE MAY BE A WHILE RESPONDING :)

[15:27]

I WON'T, SORRY. MY STOMACH ISN'T GREAT TODAY.
HOW ARE THE DRESSES COMING ON? IF I CAN HELP IN ANY WAY, YOU KNOW WHERE I AM.

[15:28]

CALLUM: I THOUGHT YOU WERE IN THE BATH?

[15:29]

I AM. I ALWAYS TEXT AND PLAY ON MY PHONE IN THE BATH. I'M NOT WEIRD.

[15:31]

LIAM: BOOOOORRRRINNNNGGGG.

I'LL MESSAGE THE GIRLS.

THE DRESSES ARE FINE, BUT JUGGLING EVERYTHING ELSE IS STRESSFUL. I'VE HAD ANOTHER TWO PEOPLE ASK FOR A PORTFOLIO WHEN I DON'T HAVE ONE. I'VE ALSO GOT TO ARRANGE FITTINGS, AND SOMEHOW WORK ALL OF THIS AROUND WORKING AT THE PUB AND AROUND EVERYONE'S SCHEDULES. RANT OVER.

[15:36]

As I said, you know where I am. Struggling to find ways to keep myself busy at the moment.

Callum <3
23ʳᵈ November 2018

[15:36]

Send nudes ;)

[15:37]

You're such a perv.

No nudes. Come get the real thing.

The Gal, The Guy & The Gay
25ᵗʰ November 2018

[14:25]

Liam, will you hurry up and click the bloody link. I want to know who my Secret Santa is!

[14:30]

Liam: Done.

[14:35]

Callum: Everyone happy with who they have? I know I am.

[14:37]

Yep. I hope you both know I am going to find out who you both have. I'm going to make it my mission.

[14:38]

Callum: Doesn't that defeat the object of 'SECRET' Santa?

[14:40]

Yes, but I don't like secrets. I'm going to create the Anti-Secret Santa Society, or ASSS for short.

[14:42]

Liam: She's always like this. Every year in uni it was constant. In final year, the girls and I decided we would lie to her about who we all had so it would be a surprise. She was not happy! I'm surprised you aren't used to this side of Tamsin yet.

[14:44]

Callum: That's brilliant. Every day is a learning day with Tamsin...

[14:45]

I am here you know!

Mum - ICE 1
27th November 2018

[11:08]

Hi Mum. I'm sat waiting for my Counselling appointment (early as usual). I know you aren't going to receive this text, but I just needed to tell you how much I love you. I don't know what's going to happen when I go in there and talk about my feelings. I've never spoken about my feelings to anyone other than you. I don't like to. You were my person. My best friend. I guess that's why I'm in this mess right now. It's not even been two months and I'm already screwed in the head. Everyone around me is holding their hand out and offering me help. I want to reach out and grab them, I do. I just wish you were holding out your hands to catch me like usual. I've just realised you're still registered as my emergency contact. I guess I best change that. You can have two people, right? I'm so bad at this. But anyway. I miss you more than I could ever put down on paper. I think about you every day and that will never change. I promise to keep remembering you every day, to share our memories with the world. I promise every Mother's Day I will still buy you a gift that you would hoard away for years because it was special to you. I will hoard it for you. Callum won't be happy though. I also promise to keep working on myself. I couldn't have asked for a better person to prepare me for my future. I've got to go now. I love you lots and lots, like Jelly Tots xxx

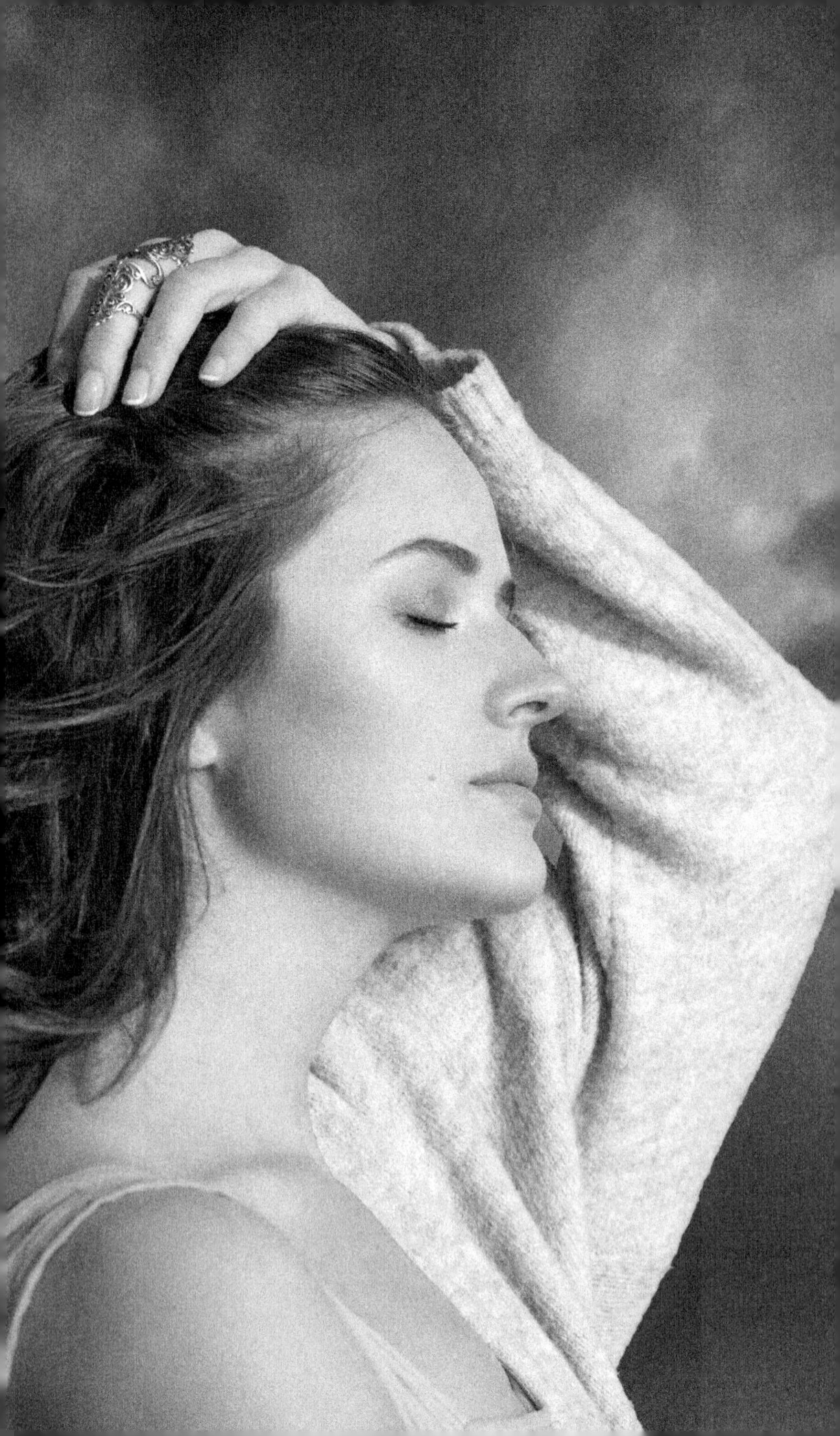

CHAPTER NINETEEN

"Good morning, Tamsin. Please take a seat." The counsellor sat down firmly in her chair. "Let me introduce myself before we get started. My name's Elizabeth Hackett and I'm a counsellor and psychotherapist. I've been providing sessions for just under eight years now, both with private sessions and for the NHS." Her voice was soft, but despite her soothing voice and the dimmed lights along with the water feature sat trickling and humming in the corner of the room, I couldn't relax.

"Hi, Elizabeth," I said, pulling the collar of my dress away from my neck nervously.

"So, what's prompted you to be sat with me today?" The questions had started. I was being calmly interrogated.

"I don't really know where to start. I guess I've not

been myself since Mum passed away," I murmured, sat opposite Elizabeth.

"I'm sorry to hear that." She looked directly at me. Surprisingly, it wasn't uncomfortable and I didn't mind telling her more. Elizabeth left me no choice anyway. She remained silent until I spoke again.

"That's okay. I've felt really low, lonely and unloved. I was pushing away people I care about. I thought Callum, my boyfriend, was cheating on me. I quit my job. I've been having nightmares and I keep throwing up my meals but I think that's the medication the doctor put me on around two weeks ago. I'm going to book an appointment after this to see my doctor," I ranted, quickly firing the information across to her. I had to tell her about the doctor's appointment. I needed her to know I was feeling at least a bit better, almost like damage control so she knew I was capable of looking after myself.

"That seems an awful lot to go through in such a short space of time. No wonder you aren't yourself." I sighed in relief. She understood.

"I guess I have, yeah."

"So would you mind if we start at the beginning? Let's talk about your mum."

"Mum had Cancer. She was diagnosed while I was in my last year of university and passed away in October. I graduated this month, but I just wished she could have been there to see me. I spent a long time caring for her, and before that, we were practically inseparable anyway. Then in an instant it had vanished. I was left with a massive void in my life." I found myself rambling. I couldn't stop. I was comfortable. "I felt as though the void was eating me alive. I felt numb and I guess that's why I locked myself away. I was trying to hide away from myself and how I was feeling." I paused for just a second to catch my breath that was escaping faster than I wanted it to.

"So were you alone? Who have you had to confide in? You mentioned Callum?" She was listening to my every word.

"I wasn't alone, but I felt alone. Callum is my boyfriend, and I moved in with him soon after Mum died. I also have my best friend, Liam. I think I realised I wasn't myself when I started to push Liam away. We argued because I wanted to move away and he broke Mum's lipstick. I'd never argued with him before. We're okay now, but while I've been trapped with my own thoughts, he's been getting on with his life. He's started his own little business, and I had no idea, all because I was stuck in my head constantly dealing with my life. My mess. He offered to help. He always does, but I don't want to accept it. I want to deal with this myself. That's what Mum and I did. We fought together and dealt with everything on our own." My hand was clenched around a cushion on the sofa, as I painfully spoke about the past.

"I understand, Tamsin, and talking here will help get rid of these thoughts and demons you speak of. It does seem your heavy reliance on your mum has caused an emotional trauma. I want you to know, you are grieving and it's completely normal to feel how you are feeling. It does justify your behaviour. You mentioned quitting your job and pushing away your loved ones? They are prime examples of changes in behaviour that results from a trauma," Elizabeth said in a soothing manner, showing off her eight years of experience within the field. "I also don't believe you are vomiting because of the medication. Usually mild side effects like nausea and vomiting only last a few days. I feel your vomiting may be fuelled by your anxiety. I think it's your body's way of grieving."

Overwhelmed, I nodded along, trying to process everything she was saying.

"So what you are saying is how I am feeling is how people may feel with a physical trauma?" I stared blankly at her.

"Absolutely, the grief shown in both emotional and physical trauma are quite similar, so I would say your behaviour has been normal, under the circumstances, but we both know that without the trauma, you may not have reacted in those irrational ways, so we need to put a plan together and get you back to the old Tamsin. Each time you come, we will delve deeper into how you have been feeling, but before that I want to give you some techniques to manage your anxiety." Elizabeth started with a simple breathing technique, focusing on one object in the room and slowly taking one breath, in and out. She then told me that setting small goals would help. I'd spent my whole life setting goals, so that was going to be a piece of cake. The hour-long session was closing in on us fast, and before it was over, Elizabeth left me with another thought.

"It seems that you came here today worried about pushing away your loved ones. I want you to know that they will understand. Don't feel like putting yourself first is ever a bad thing. Self-care is a priority. Think about what they say when you get on a plane. If the cabin loses pressure, oxygen masks will fall from above, and they always tell you to give yourself oxygen before helping the others around you. It's okay to do that. If you don't have oxygen yourself, you won't be able to help the others. Look after yourself and I will see you next week."

After saying thank you, I left the room, the thought still wrapped around my mind. It was a comparison I wasn't going to forget. I mattered, and that was okay. I wasn't going to neglect my relationships; I'd already learnt that lesson. I'd also learnt that spending all my resources and focusing them on how I was feeling was fine, too. A smile graced my face as the door shut and I looked over to the receptionist who was already walking over to me.

"How was that, Tamsin? Are you okay?" she whispered quietly so nobody could hear. Before I could answer, she jumped in again, "She can be a bit scary, can't she?"

"It was good and really useful. She asked a lot of questions, but I needed that. It's made me think a whole lot more, and do you know what? I can honestly tell I am going to be okay." I smiled at her sincerely. The journey to feeling myself again was going to be long haul; I knew that, but determination filled my stomach where all the angst had once set up camp.

I'm going to be okay.

The town centre was bustling with people carrying shopping bags full of toys in preparation for Christmas Day. Christmas had to be the best time of year. The smell of cinnamon poured out of the cafes, the friendly smiles from people passing in the shops and you couldn't beat the deals. I loved going into Boot's to buy presents, but often I'd end up buying two gifts and keeping the free ones for myself. They were free, after all. I swanned around the aisles, finding joy in the smallest of things. I loved to shop, even if I wasn't buying anything. I loved the interaction and browsing. A lot of the time I'd be day dreaming. I picked up Liam's favourite concealer and foundation for his Secret Santa present before heading to the '3 for 2' aisle to fill my basket. My face lit up as I grabbed a Disney Princess Ariel makeup brush set for Liam, and some Marvel merchandise for Callum. I only had to buy for Liam this year, but I couldn't not give Callum a present. The Marvel slippers featured all the Avengers on the front and were perfect for wearing in his house. *Our house*. It was only fair that the pair of Smelly Cat socks I placed in my basket were for me. I continued to walk around, touching almost every item I passed, and found myself looking at the lipsticks.

Mum's favourite lipstick. She loves this colour.

I dropped the lipstick in my basket without thinking, out of habit, and then it dawned on me. I had forgotten Mum had died. I'd forgotten she wasn't going to be around for Christmas. No annual trip to the Christmas markets together, where instead of browsing, we'd end up getting drunk on mulled wine, Baileys hot chocolate and any other alcohol abundant Christmas drink we could find. No watching Christmas movies, drowning in duvets, and no Mum's Christmas dinner. Her gravy could have been used as a currency in our house. It was so delicious I'd always made deals with her to give me more. I stopped in my tracks and tried to hold back the tears that were building up inside my lids. I stared at the shelves, not making eye contact with anyone, because I'd feel weak.

"Do you need any help?" a store assistant asked. I looked up, tears blurring my vision, barely making out the bold black colour of his glasses.

"I'm okay." I said swiftly.

"Are you sure?" he asked, concerned at seeing tears falling down my face.

"Positive." I sniffed, and continued to walk around the store, not ready to face another person and pay. I could have run out of the store, but I didn't, so that was a win for me. Inside, I wasn't holding it together, my emotions fighting to see the light of day.

The self-checkouts.

I avoided speaking to the checkout lady and placed my basket on the self-checkout counter. I scanned the items one by one, including the red lipstick, which I held onto longer than any of the other items.

Card Declined - Please Try Again

I pulled my card from the reader looking around, rubbed the chip and placed it back in.

Card Declined - Please Try Again

"We've been having trouble with that self-checkout all day. It may take a couple of tries," the assistant said, swinging the checkout fob around her neck.

"I'll just try a different card." I awkwardly reached into my purse and held onto my credit card. It wasn't the machine. I'd run out of money. I had dreaded looking at my bank account online, so I hadn't bothered. I was embarrassed to say the least. I hated being in debt. This was the first transaction the credit card had seen since my first year of university.

"Ah there you go, that's all gone through," the lady said, reading off the screen.

"Thank you." I grabbed my bag and quickly tried to dart out of the store. A Macmillan volunteer stood collecting donations near the exit. I flustered and reached again for my purse, this time tipping out any change I had into the bucket before leaving.

They need the money more than I do.

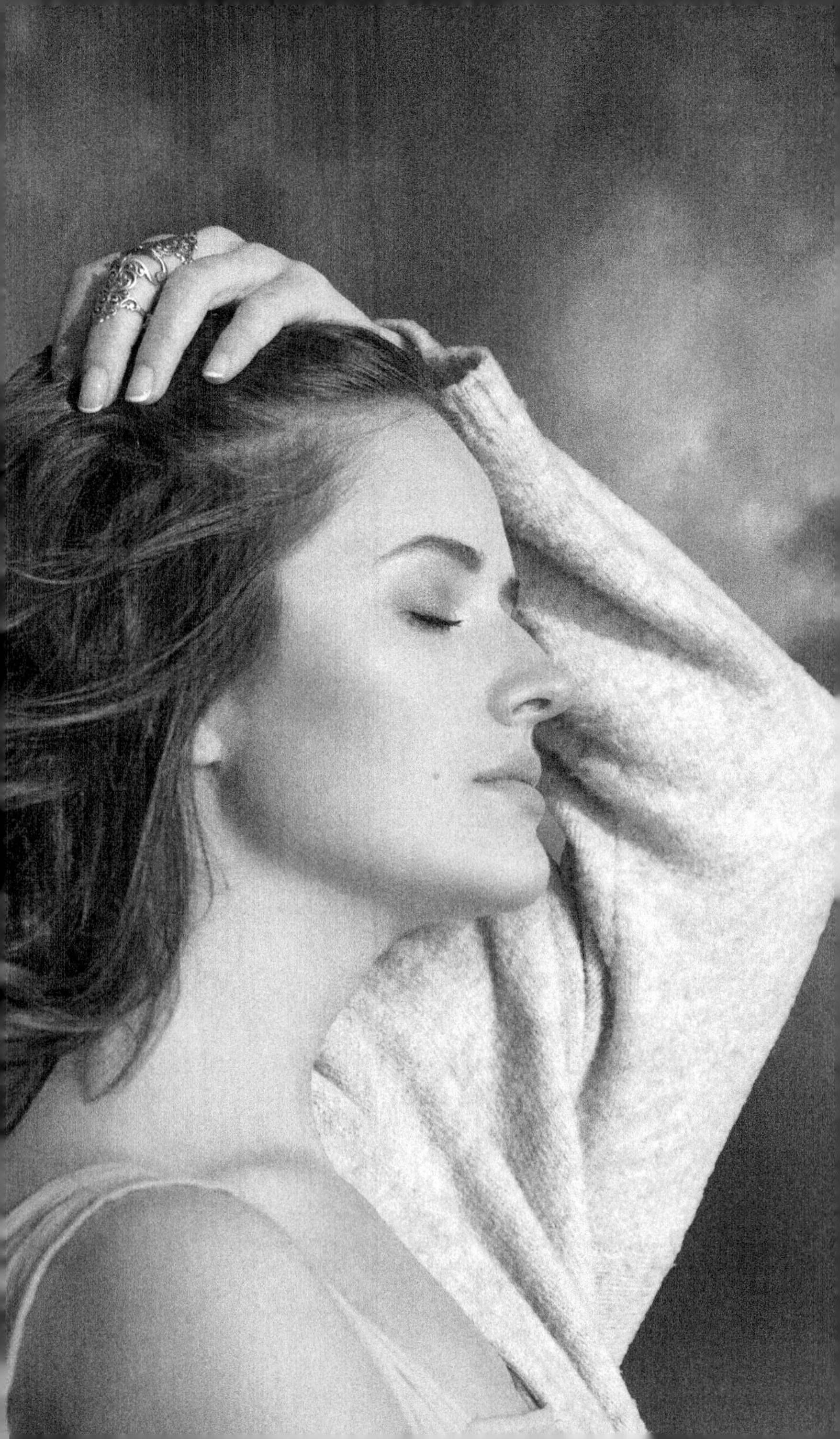

CHAPTER TWENTY

I shuffled through the front door with the shopping bags that clashed against my thighs, and placed them on the kitchen floor. Travelling back from the town centre didn't go as planned. A taxi wasn't an option—they didn't accept card and my small town didn't have the luxuries of Uber just yet. Instead, I got on a bus, using what little money I had on my debit card. Passengers filled the seats and stood in the aisle of the bus like sardines, jerking forward in time as it stopped at *every* goddamn bus stop. I was the epitome of a Brit. I hated queues, public transport, and when you held a door open for someone and they didn't say thank you. That was the worst.

I sat on one of the breakfast bar stools with all of my body weight slumped against the table, and contemplated my latest predicament. I had no money. No job to earn money. I was all but ready to give up, let the vultures come and scavenge on what was left of me. It was atrocious timing, too. Christmas was just around the corner and I had less than ten pounds to my name. Luckily, I'd bought presents for my favourites, so they weren't going to go without. I had to show my love to them, and try to make up for how I'd been acting for the best part of a month.

I spent the rest of the day cleaning the house, waiting for Callum to return from work. It took me back to the routine I'd had when mum was ill. I'd cleaned from top to bottom, not because the house was dirty, but because it was a distraction. It was hard to clean around the clutter anyway.

Callum didn't know the extent of my financial problems. He knew I wanted to do Secret Santa for that reason, but I had to tell him I was struggling, talk about how I had no money and form a plan together to sort me out. That's what couples did. What families did. Until then, I cleaned.

My counsellor would be proud.

"Honey, I'm home," Callum said theatrically, his voice carrying throughout the house.

"You're such a cheese ball," I yelled back at him.

"I could definitely eat some cheese balls right now," he said, greeting me with a soft kiss to my forehead. I caressed his cheek, which was covered in light stubble, darker than usual. The smirk on his face began to change, as he looked deep in my eyes. They were brighter than I'd ever seen them before, or maybe I'd only just started to pay attention to them. I locked my hands at the back of his neck and pulled his mouth closer to mine, placing another kiss on his soft lips.

"What was that for?" He spoke softly, his forehead resting on mine.

"I've just missed you. That's all." I wasn't lying. I had missed him. His affection. His everything.

"You seem in a good mood. So it went okay today?" He planted another kiss on my lips while waiting for me to respond. His fingers played with a piece of my curled hair that had fallen out of place as he leant over me intimately.

"It did. But enough talk, for now anyway." I pulled him in closer once more, craving his touch I'd not felt for so long. I'd been deprived of him, but that was my own fault. His knees forced my legs to close as he climbed onto the chair, astride me. His lips wrapped around mine and our tongues twisted together in unison. As our lips were still locked together, his hands fell from my hair and left a tingling sensation from my shoulder blade to my breasts. His mouth, buried in the crease of my neck, left a trail of wet kisses that drove me crazy. I let out a slight moan, which spurred him on further. We had been physically starved of love, and it was time to rightfully reclaim what was deserved.

I lay on the sofa, panting, catching my breath as the material below stuck to me. Every inch of Callum's body lay bare against mine, only parted slightly by the sweat beads between us. His intimate touch left me quivering for more, as he stroked from my breasts down to my waist. We gazed at each other, longing for the love we had. The glisten in his eyes was captivating; I couldn't look away. Every so often, he planted a kiss randomly on my face, his eyes still inviting me in for more. He playfully nudged my chin with his nose, wanting me to move a certain way so he could kiss me some more. He loved me. Cared for me. I could tell. His eyes said it all. It had been so long since our last time, and nothing else mattered as we lay there.

"Was that the door?" He practically jumped out of his skin and dove to floor as he realised he was stood with nothing but his socks on, in front of the living room window. Our clothes had been launched across the room as we'd passionately ripped them off each other. As Callum attempted to redress himself, another knock thudded against his front door. I just lay there, too tranquil to care after the sex.

"Coming!" Callum shouted.

"Didn't you say that around ten minutes ago?" I teased him, still lying quite happily on the sofa.

"Shhhhh." He blushed slightly as he got up after fighting with his clothes. I looked at the ceiling, practically in a trance, in my own little world as Callum answered the door. I was then slowly pulled out of my daydream by the distinctive sound of Liam's voice.

"Don't go in there," I heard Callum shout from the

hallway. I grabbed the sofa's throw with haste and wrapped it around me, concealing all my curves. Liam walked into the living room with a huge grin on his face, and I tried to play it cool, but my beetroot face had already snitched.

"Have I interrupted something?" he asked rhetorically, smug as anything. "Oh well. Hope you were finished. I want Chinese and I know you guys will get it with me. Mum's got them all eating healthy crap today and I want to treat myself after working so hard." Liam had a habit of making himself at home no matter where he was. We could be sitting in a bar and he would take off his shoes to get comfy.

"You're the boss." I laughed, still trying to hide my bare skin. I wasn't going to argue about getting Chinese. I'd been craving it myself. I just had no idea how I'd pay for it.

"I'll let you put some clothes on..." Liam shuddered at me in an over-dramatic way and nudged Callum as he went through to the kitchen. "Hey, stud," he said in a seductive voice and winked at Callum, being the usual flirt he had no trouble being.

"Oh god. He saw me, didn't he?" Callum asked, all of a sudden very self-conscious.

"No. Don't be silly. He's always like that around you. I thought you were used to it." I laughed, fixing my hair as Callum gathered my clothes for me.

"I am used to it. But I've just been naked. Any other

time I would encourage flirting. I love to mess with him, but... like we've just had sex."

"I have no idea what you are getting at. It's fine. Look. Let me ask," I said, preparing my voice to shout. "LIAM, COME HERE!"

"No. T, don't." Callum looked awkward as Liam walked through from the kitchen.

"Callum is worried you saw him naked. Did you?" I asked bluntly, trying to make a point.

"No, why? Should I have?" Liam asked, joking in his usual way.

"See? Now, will you both go and get the Chinese menu and decide what you want while I get dressed." They both turned for the kitchen, and left me to get dressed. My curls had become a matted mess, from my scalp right down to the split ends I so desperately needed sorting. I was about to uncover myself and get dressed as Liam peeked half his body around the living room door frame.

"Lucky bitch," he said, flashing another wink in my direction, and used his hands spread apart to portray a rough size of what he clearly had seen.

"I know, right!"

I looked down the menu trying to find something tasty, but cheap. Unfortunately, my eyes were always bigger than my belly when it came to food. I always ordered *way* more than I needed.

Not anymore, not until I get a job.

I tried to make a meal by combining side dishes in hopes it would work out cheaper.

"So, I will have a portion of chips, a fried rice and a small gravy," I said, my mouth filling as I thought about the salt and pepper chicken dish.

"Is that it? Are you okay?" Callum looked confused, and well, Liam looked speechless.

"Yeah, I'm fine, just not too hungry. I had a big lunch," I lied in embarrassment. Callum had never worried about money. His parents saw to that, and Liam had worked since the end of high school. He was always coming up with new ways to save money, including sneaking alcohol into clubs, where pretty much all of his disposable income would be rinsed if he didn't.

"You can order what you want. Both of you. I have booked in six bespoke dresses over the next two months, and today I handed in my notice at the pub. Tonight is on me." Liam insisted I ordered more food, and well, he didn't have to tell me twice. Callum popped the cork on a bottle of champagne that he'd been saving for a special occasion.

It was embarrassing to admit that I was in this position, having no money to my name, especially as my emotional resources were finally restoring. With the help of medication, counselling and my two favourites, I was healing. I had to tell them both I was struggling. It was the right thing to do so I could heal some more. I reached into my bag and pulled out the red lipstick and placed it on the table in front of me. I plucked courage from deep inside and opened my mouth. I was so full of nerves, they poured out of my mouth quicker than the words. No more bottling things up.

"I went shopping today, for Secret Santa presents. I saw this lipstick, the same as the one she gave me, and thought it would suit Mum. I put it in my basket without even thinking," I said as both of their faces saddened. "It's okay. You don't have to say anything. I'm okay, but when I got to the till, my card declined. I had to buy all the presents on my credit card. I've run out of money and I don't know what to do." I looked down, unnerved after confiding in them.

"Okay, that's tough, but you know we're here for you, T. We're a team, and we'll get you through it. Right, Liam?" Callum said, reassuring me, wanting Liam to affirm him.

"Absolutely. I'm here for you, but I need you to be here for me, too," Liam said cryptically. He knew I was there for him so I struggled to understand what he meant.

"What do you mean? We're best friends. I'm not going anywhere."

"That's right. We are best friends, and we help each other out when we're in need. I'm in need, just like you. There is no way I can fulfil all of these drag orders and manage my new business, too. I need to focus on the designing of fashion statements, but I need you to be my business manager." I was gobsmacked. He must have been joking.

"Are you being serious right now?" I jumped out of my seat, overcome with a feeling of hope.

"I'm not saying it's going to be mega bucks. I'm still getting on my feet, but we can work out a commission structure and wage on all the bookings you get for me. All you would need to do is manage my diary, put a couple of posts on social media, the sort of stuff you could do in your sleep. Oh, and you can do all of it from home. And, we would get to spend more time together. There is literally no downside. I need you, especially if I'm going to continue doing this as long term as I'd like. Let's combine our expertise, Tamsin. We will be a force to be reckoned with. What do you say?"

"Absolutely fucking yes," I screamed and practically jumped on him with excitement. "Oh my god. I can't believe it. When can I start?"

"Tomorrow. Tonight, we are best friends. Tomorrow, business partners."

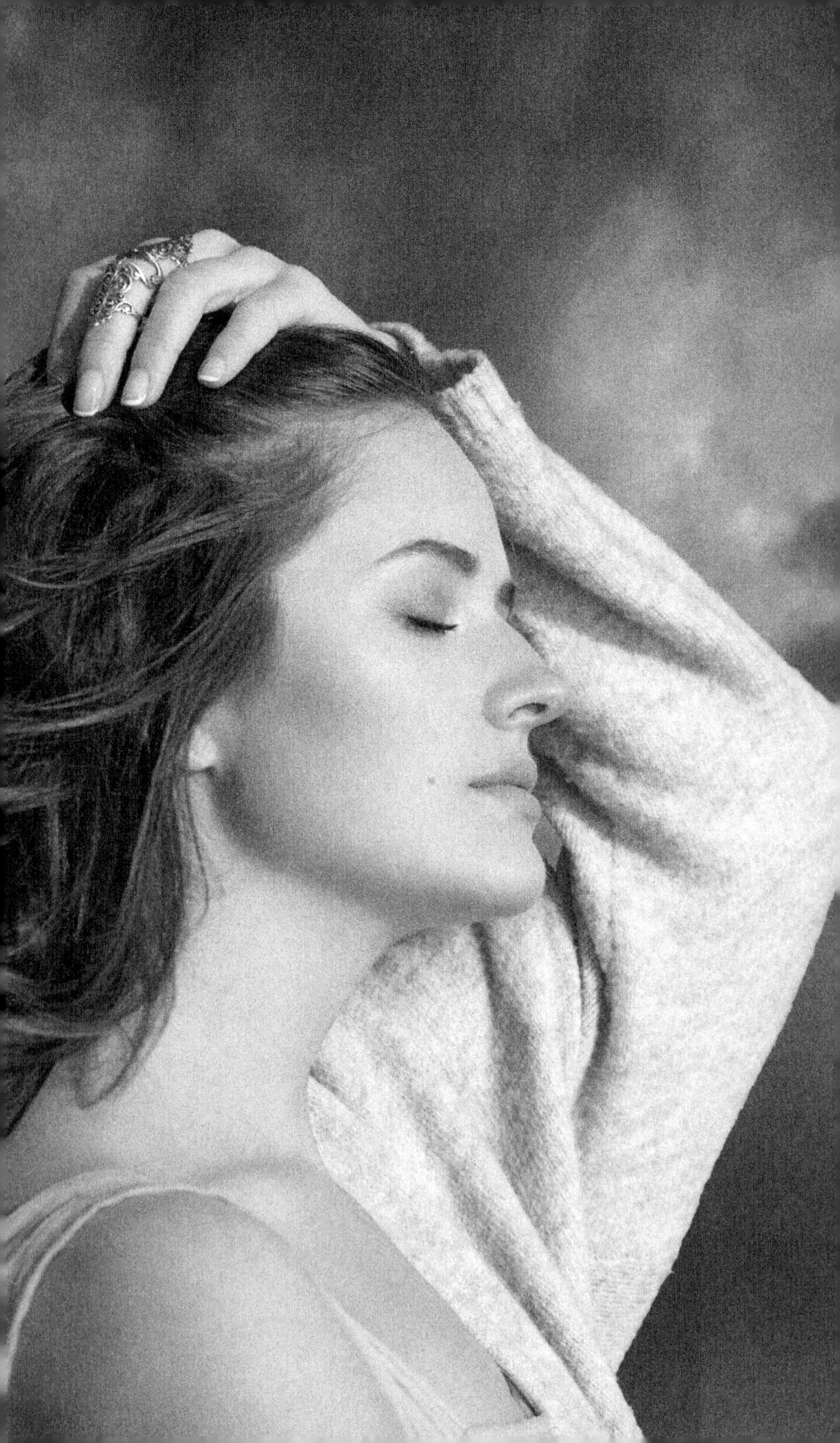

CHAPTER TWENTY-ONE

A couple of weeks later, I woke on Christmas Eve morning with such a huge grin on my face. I hadn't been sleeping well over the past few weeks and I normally slept for Britain. Despite not having much energy, I was feeling good. Great in fact. Christmas was my absolute favourite time of the year. The counselling sessions had been helping tremendously, too, and even though I wouldn't be going through the usual traditions with Mum, I'd accepted it. There was no way to bring her back, and that was okay. Callum had even taken me to the Christmas markets. It was hard, not walking around with Mum, laughing at the smallest of things and tasting all the free samples we could get our hands on. We still got drunk, though, which was nice. It was nice to feel normal again. Happy, even. Especially with Callum.

That morning paved the way for a new tradition.

Callum's parents were coming to our house for Christmas, and we were expecting them any moment. Callum had already left the crisp cold bed, no doubt trying to make the place look like a showroom before they arrived. I admired that about him. I grabbed my phone and made my way downstairs, catching up on my notifications from the night before.

Gayboy x
24ᵀᴴ December 2018

[9:45ₐₘ]

See you at 2pm for Secret Santa. Can't wait! xoxo

Liam was clearly in a good mood, too. He was never one to put kisses in a text, unless he was drunk or flirting. I had to admit to myself that the thought of Liam meeting Jaqueline and Richard did make me shudder with nerves. Liam had spent most of his life trying to fit inside a box that society called acceptable. Our time at university had taught him it was okay to be different, and so he'd embraced it. I'd embraced it, too. Liam had a way with words, and a filter he often chose not to use, but that was what made him, well, Liam. I couldn't ask him to tone himself down, to tweak his personality like some sort of robot. If they didn't love him, tough.

"Liam is coming at two." I shouted behind Callum, sneaking up on him while he tidied the coat closet.

"Jesus, how do you do that? You're like a ninja." He

jumped out of his skin. I wished he'd have jumped out of his clothes. That plain white t-shirt was a staple of his wardrobe. It made him look good, and he knew it. His biceps bulged from the seams, not wanting to be contained. I wrapped my arms around his torso, holding onto his abs like they were a rock-climbing wall.

"I'm sorry." I kissed his neck, tiptoeing and still holding onto him. "I'm gonna go get some breakfast. I'm absolutely starving. Join me when you can. Or I can come help you in a bit if you want?"

"You don't need to help, T. I'm all good," he said softly once I released him from my caring embrace. "It's not like you to be hungry in the morning, You've been eating breakfast loads recently," he pointed out.

"I hope you aren't calling me fat," I shouted, as I started pouring the shredded wheat into a bowl.

"Will you help prep some of the buffet food soon? My parents will be here in about an hour and I don't want to leave it all to Mum," Callum shouted through from the hallway. It was a good job he lived in a detached house. His neighbours would not have been happy with how much we yelled.

"That's fine," I howled back with my mouth full, still shovelling more cereal into it. More recently, the side effects of the medication were easing. I wasn't being sick nearly as much as I had been. Two weeks earlier, even the thought of preparing food would have made me ill. Once I'd finished my cereal, hoping I hadn't got milk stains on my dress, I started to prepare the buffet.

Buffets were the best. All the food you could ever want or imagine in one meal. And you could help yourself and pile your plate sky high without anyone judging.

With a swing of the front door, and the noise of the handle crashing against the wall, Jaqueline emerged, shortly followed by Richard.

"We're here. Happy Christmas Eve!" she gracefully bellowed from the hallway, kissing Callum on his forehead before shuffling towards me, carrying gift bags filled with presents. "Be a dear and get my suitcase from the car," Jaqueline said to Richard and Callum, before squeezing me tight.

"Hi, Jaqueline," I said, smiling, still nuzzled close to her. She released me and stepped back, looking me up and down.

"Don't you look beautiful? That dress is stunning. Are you feeling better now?" she asked lightening the interrogation with a compliment. To be fair, my red sparkling Christmas Eve dress was gorgeous. Jaqueline knew about everything, and although it hadn't been my decision to tell her, I knew it was for the best. My counsellor agreed that being honest and not bottling up emotion in front of the people closest to me would help me in being true to myself. Callum had come clean about Louise, too, and of course Jaqueline had been distraught. Callum was her only chance of becoming a grandmother, so naturally it hit her hard. They'd even cancelled their Christmas holiday and decided to spend it with us.

"I'm doing really well. Starting to feel much better," I said confidently. It had been a while since I'd started to be able to talk about my feelings with confidence. I'd spent months not knowing whether I was coming or going. It had been an emotional rollercoaster that derailed itself every day or so before it was finally able to re-join the tracks.

"I can tell. You look as if you're glowing. You have colour in your face. It's about time. I can't wait to spend Christmas with you, Tamsin. Now, you go and relax, watch some Christmas TV and enjoy yourself. I'll do the food." I wasn't going to argue. Peace and quiet in front of the television was a no brainer, but I knew why she wanted that. She was very particular about food, so this way she was in control.

Gayboy x
24ᵀᴴ December 2018

[13:57]

On my way. Hoe Hoe Hoe.

I showed Callum the text Liam had sent. He was a genius.

"Oh god. Should we warn them?" Callum laughed, referring to his parents.

"I'm sure he will be on his best behaviour." I hoped so.

Christmas songs filled the whole house while

Callum's parents pottered around each of the rooms making our home look even more festive. They hung extra baubles from their house on our tree to give it that *Jaqueline approved* look. I could just about see her rearranging the tinsel that had been wrapped around the hallway bannister.

"I'm here, bitches." Liam walked in without a knock, shouting at the top of his voice. I looked at Callum in horror and he returned the same look of panic.

"You must be Liam. I'm Jaqueline. Nice to meet you," she said in a posher than usual voice.

"Hi, Jackie. Sorry about saying bitches."

"Don't worry about that. It's Christmas."

Callum and I both sighed in relief. Although, not only had he sworn but he'd also called her Jackie. I rolled my eyes.

He gets away with everything.

"Who's ready for Secret Santa?" Liam walked into the lounge carrying a gift bag and placed it under the tree amongst the others, before sitting on the floor like a child fidgeting on a sugar rush. He was wearing a grey jumper with bits of glitter subtly woven through it, paired with black skinny jeans. He hadn't bothered to take his shoes off. That was typical of him.

"I think we're ready. I'll go get Dad from the kitchen if you guys want to set up?" Callum jumped up from the sofa to hustle him into the lounge, and Liam helped me pull the presents from under the tree. I kept Callum's presents nestled under so he had something to open on Christmas Day. Liam was as giddy as ever, smiling and laughing at everything. He had worked incredibly hard over the past few weeks, finishing the orders he had taken for completion before Christmas. His fashion made my job easy. Every time a drag queen was seen wearing his work, I'd get dozens of enquires through the social media pages I had set up for him. They were turning out to be an unintended online portfolio and he had gained just over five hundred page likes in just three weeks.

We all gathered together in the lounge, sat in a circle surrounding the presents on the floor, and each took it in turns to open them. I gave Liam his makeup as well as a bottle of Prosecco I'd purchased at last minute to get to our present budget, and he was thrilled. Liam gave Callum a very revealing Christmas themed jock strap, which made everyone laugh. Even his mum continued to surprise me and chuckled. Callum also opened a stylish shoulder bag, which Liam had very clearly taken the time to personalise. CD had been sown into it in bright cotton. His gifts put my lousy makeup and Prosecco to shame.

"Oh wow. That's amazing. Thanks, Liam." Callum got up to give Liam a hug and then sat back down, grabbing a gift bag on his way. "And this is for you, T. Happy Secret Santa. Sorry it's not much. You can open your real present tomorrow." He passed me an alcohol shaped bag with a card perched on the top. I instantly went for the present first, out of habit, revealing a bottle of champagne. He couldn't have known me better. I then opened the card and started to read.

> *Tamsin. Thank you for being you. The past six months have gone so fast. Loving you has been like a whirlwind, and that's not a bad thing. Every moment with you is exciting. It's a laugh. 90% of the time, it's sarcasm, and I love it. I love you and every little thing about you. Never change and always be yourself. Here's to our future, starting with our very first holiday together. Mark your calendar and grab your passport because on the 12th February we're going to Lanzarote. Love you forever. Let's make memories xxx*

My mouth sat agape with everyone around me smiling in anticipation. I'd never been abroad before. Liam and I had been planning on going to celebrate finishing university, but once Mum had got ill, those plans went straight out of the window.

"He's taking me to Lanzarote!" I squealed in excitement, stumbling across the floor to grab hold of Callum. I couldn't believe it.

"I love you, T."

Liam tried to persuade Callum to take him instead,

claiming it wasn't too late to get out of his relationship with me. He was such a comedian. Callum's parents loved Liam, too. Every time he opened his mouth, their laughter was deafening.

"You can open your gift from us tomorrow, Tamsin. I'm going to go start the hot food now. Everything should be ready in about forty-five minutes," Jaqueline said as she popped off to the kitchen.

"You're staying for food, right?" I asked Liam.

"Do you even have to ask?"

A distinct smell poured from the kitchen and filled my nose. I started to gag as bile started to turn in my stomach.

Not again.

I rushed to the downstairs bathroom, knowing that in a few seconds I would be violently sick. The last time I'd been sick was around two days before, so it was getting better. I just about made it into the downstairs loo before my vomit filled the bowl. I could hear murmurs from behind the closed door, as Jaqueline and Richard became concerned.

"I'm okay," I said, in between catching my breath and throwing up. I sat on the floor with my elbows resting on the toilet rim and my hands holding back my hair. I had become used to throwing up. I knew once it was over I'd feel better.

"Are you sure you're okay?" Richard's deep voice bounced off the bathroom door.

"What made you feel sick?" Jaqueline interrupted.

"I'm fine. I'm used to it. It's the medication. It's made me more sensitive to smells," I quickly said, making sure not to look away from the toilet to avoid mess.

"Sweetie, can I come in?" Jaqueline knocked at the door and I hummed in response. She shut the door behind her and placed her hand on my back, rubbing it gently.

"Tamsin, it's not the medication that's making you sick. I think you might be pregnant."

My elbows fell off the toilet and my body went limp. I sat there listening to the bustling of voices echoing in the hallway. How had I not realised sooner? I was pregnant.

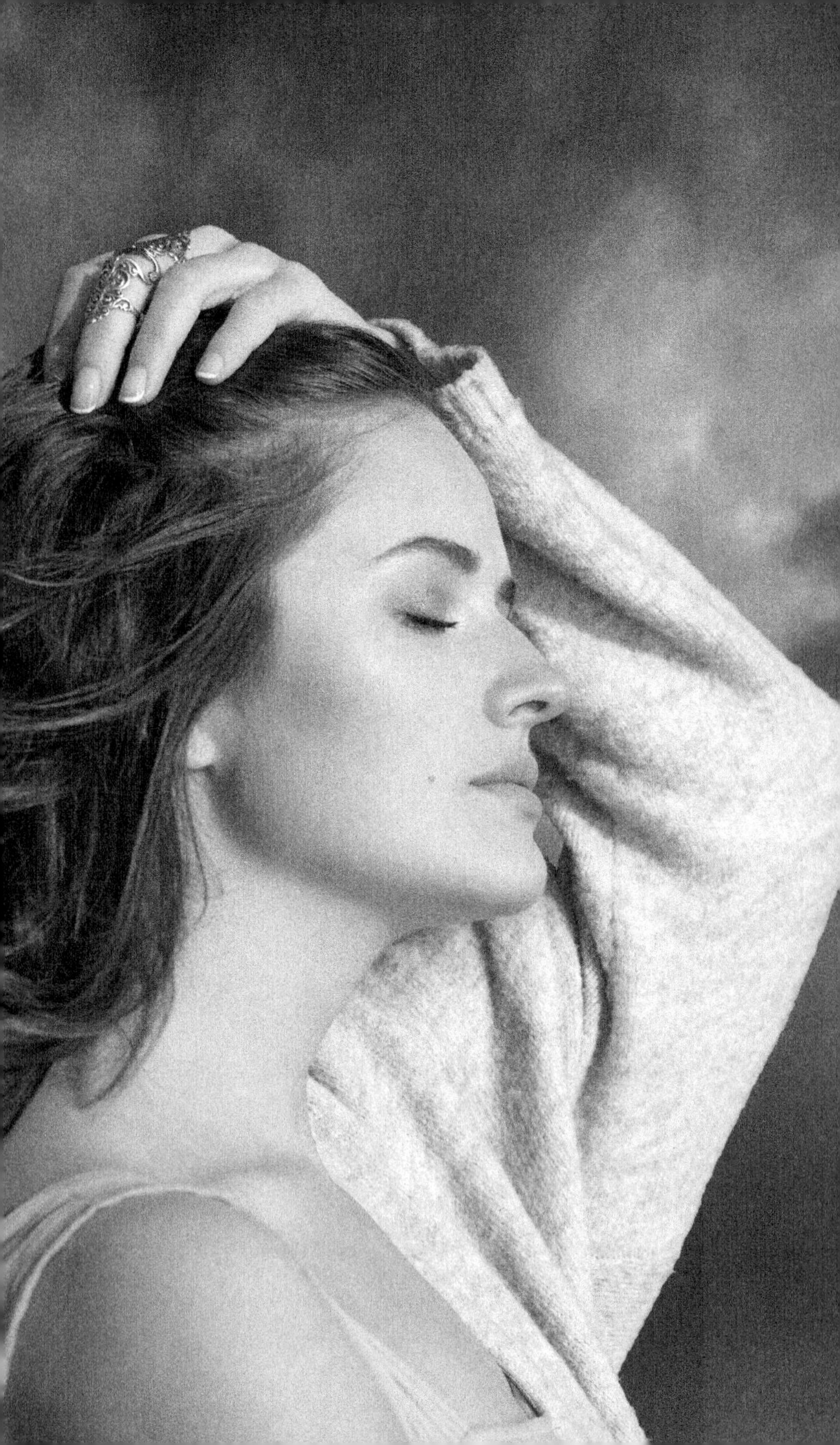

CHAPTER TWENTY-TWO

Christmas Eve turned into an explosion of emotions. Callum rushed to the local pharmacy to get me a pregnancy test and came back with five of them, just to be sure. My whole family, including Liam, stood outside nervously while I tried yoga moves, attempting to figure out which one was most effective to wee on a stick. I took each test, drinking pints of water in between, not quite sure how I'd feel if it was positive. Each one read positive. There was no denying I was pregnant. I should have realised. Even the doctor should have. Liam and Callum had an excuse, as they didn't have a clue what to look out for. I waited until I'd finished all the tests then opened the bathroom door to tell them. They surrounded me, eager for the news, all of them with smiles plastered on their faces.

"It's positive. I'm going to have a baby." Before I

could finish, cheers roared through the hallway. I tried to hide my mixed emotions, thinking back to how I'd thought my life would turn out. I'd had a plan, which had now been screwed up like a piece of paper and tossed in the bin. I felt I had no control once again, and that shook me. On the other hand, I knew I wanted to have a child. I'd just always thought it would come in my thirties, along with the job security and marriage I had hoped for before then.

"I'm so happy for you. I'm going to be a grandma," Jaqueline said, tearing up. Richard shook Callum's hand, which ended in a blubbering man hug.

"As if you're up the duff," Liam said jesting, but I knew it came with love.

"I know. I don't know if I'm ready to be a mum. What about the money? Babies are expensive, and loud."

"That's what Uncle Liam is for. To look after it when you need a break. To make them laugh instead of cry. To teach them that it's okay to sleep with more than one person in a day," He said laughing, and for once Jaqueline looked horrified.

"LIAM!" I tried not to laugh myself.

"No, but seriously. You mentioned money. Callum has a good job, and you work for me. I know it's not a proper income yet, but it's more of a reason for us to be great. We will succeed." Liam held onto my hand and grabbed onto Callum.

"I told you this before. We're a team," Callum assured me.

He was right. We were a team. Every single one of us was lucky to have the other. I knew we would make it work. My support system was something of a comic book, surrounded by my own personal superheroes. I didn't have to worry at all.

Once everyone had calmed and Callum's parents had offered us money, emotional support, and babysitting for life, we sat together in the lounge. The Christmas lights twinkled creating patterns across the living room walls.

Jaqueline and Richard had gone to another room, making calls to announce the news. I knew my mum would have been doing the same if she'd been there. Knowing her, she would have organised a party. I sat against Callum, with his arm propping a pillow up for me to rest against. I'd thought he couldn't get more caring, but I was wrong. I sat staring into space, barely listening to Callum and Liam talking constantly about the child on the way, until their conversation caught my attention.

"So I will make you a deal. You go near her vagina while she's giving birth and I'll hold her hand while she's pushing," Liam said in a serious tone.

"Why can't I hold her hand? I don't want to see that," Callum said terrified.

"NO ONE IS GOING NEAR MY VAGINA!" I

commanded, both of them sitting awkwardly. Liam giggled; he couldn't keep a straight face for too long.

"I'm hungry," Liam pointed out.

We hadn't had food yet, but finding out someone was pregnant took priority. I blamed Jaqueline. She clearly didn't care much for cooking those mini sausage rolls now that she was going to be a grandparent. Pure selfishness.

"I think we could all eat. I will go get everything ready." Callum to the rescue, again. I had struck lucky with that one. Liam continued talking about the baby, questioning me, asking things that hadn't even had chance to cross my mind. It was good; it made me think. It made me realise how unprepared I was even though Jaqueline had already promised to pay for all of the nursery furniture.

"Do you want a boy or a girl? What about names? What will you call it?" he quizzed as if I was on some sort of TV show, not telling me if my answers were correct or not.

"Woah, Liam. One question at a time." I tried to calm him. "I don't mind either to be honest. Don't get me started on names. You know I have my plan, baby names written down so I wouldn't forget."

Madison if it was a girl and Mason if it was a boy. That's what I'd planned anyway. But as I'd realised, plans changed.

"Can you go to our room a sec, T?" Callum asked, interrupting me.

"Yeah, sure." He sounded serious. I walked upstairs into our room to find his journal sat open on the bed. I remembered how reading his diary last time hadn't ended well, so I was dubious to see it. I approached it slowly to find that the top clearly read my name.

Tamsin. I've left this out for you so that you can read it. It's okay. I want you to. Christmas Day hasn't arrived yet and I can already tell it's going to be the best one yet. I know this time of year is going to be difficult for you, and that's okay. I know your mum would be over the moon right now. She would probably be organising some sort of gathering to show you off. Having a baby isn't part of your plan right now. I know we've spoken about that. It wasn't part of our plan, but now it is. I couldn't be happier.

Anyway, you'll notice that there are no more pages in this journal. I've ripped them out. The past few years have been crazy for me, too, and I found peace by writing everything down, but now I have you. I don't need to write in here anymore. I know that whatever my concerns or however I'm feeling, I can talk to you. I hope that you can do the same with me.

Sometimes I wish I was better at saying these

words to your face, and I promise I will try to get better. I'll need to, now that I can't leave you any more notes in here.

I love you, T.

I'd spent my life fighting against the tide, trying to plan out every little detail of my future. I'd grown up thinking that plans, goals and aspirations were as one, but they were entirely different. My life had been planned before my eyes, way before my eighteenth birthday, and I really should have let fate decide. I couldn't lose anyone else. I'd had my fair share of pain so maybe this baby was the ray of sunshine I needed, along with Liam and Callum.

Was I going to be with Callum forever? I hoped so.

Was I going to work for Liam for the rest of my life? Probably not. I knew he'd always be around to bug me, though.

Was the rest of my life going to be filled with more drama and things I couldn't control? Absolutely.

All I had to do was live for the moment and enjoy the calm in the storm that was my life while it lasted. This baby could be what defined me. Not a job. A home. A car. Instead, someone that I could love eternally and they could love me back.

Just like me and Mum.

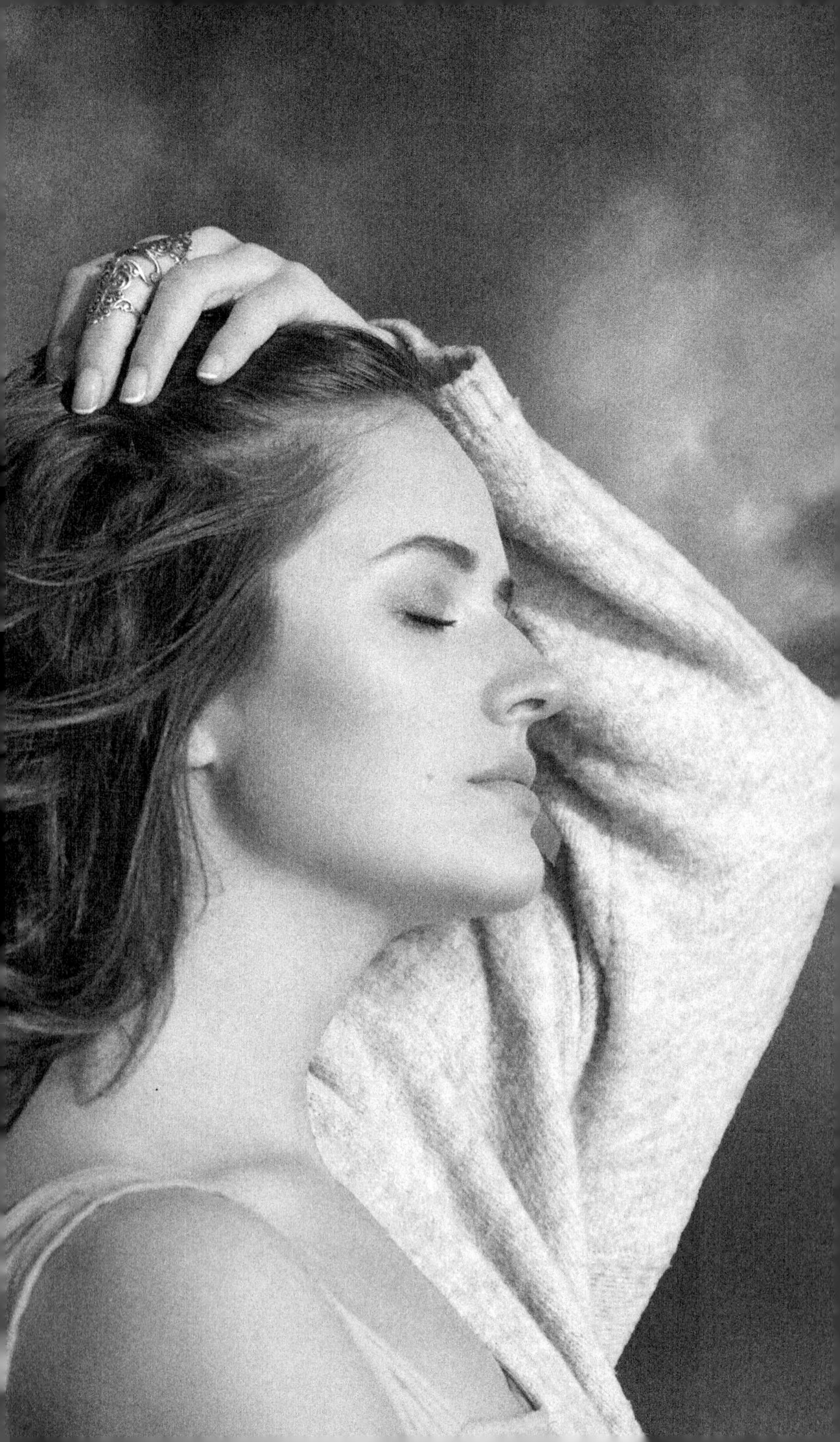

EPILOGUE

"You didn't both have to come, you know?" I said to Callum and Liam as I sat on the hospital bed, waiting to be examined. They looked like a pair of nervous gay dads, waiting to find out if the baby was okay.

"This is fancy shit, isn't it?" Liam said, looking around the room. He wasn't wrong. I was half expecting the walls to be covered in posters of cartoon wombs. Instead they were a clean white. Not one mark. Instead, there were two flat screen TVs and even a plant. I did not fit in, but what was I expecting? Jaqueline wanted only the best for us, so we had to go private.

We sat waiting for the nurse to come back. She'd trotted off after introducing herself as Joy, and had been gone for a while. It felt a long time, anyway.

"So, today is your first scan. Are you nervous?" she said in a strong African accent as she burst back into the room. I nodded. "You don't have to be nervous. I'll scan your tummy–the gel will be cold–and then we'll see your baby on the monitor," she said reassuringly as she put on some disposable gloves.

"So, will I find out how far gone I am today?" I asked nervously, trying to get comfy and not slide off the hospital bed.

"Yes, and the gender if you'd like."

As Joy continued to do her thing, my eyes wandered around the room anxiously. Nerves I had never felt before filled my stomach, unlike anything I had felt in the past. Even more than waiting for the grade of my degree to be posted online. The other two sat still on their chairs, practically on each other's laps, waiting for the nurse to open her mouth. Their eyes followed her movements.

She wasn't joking about the cold gel.

I wasn't looking around the room anymore, but fixated on my stomach and the screen in front of me.

"If you look here, this is your baby." She pointed to one of the TVs, with the image appearing in wide screen. You look around fourteen weeks, so the baby must have been conceived around the first week of October," she said, seeming certain.

At the spa. Just before Mum died.

With that thought, she turned up the volume on the TV. The heartbeat. I was overwhelmed and struck with emotion. There was no point in holding back the tears, not any more. Not in front of Liam and Callum.

"Would you like to know the gender?" Joy asked.

I looked at Callum to see if he wanted to know.

"Yes," he said eagerly, before I could gauge whether he did or not by his facial expression.

"Congratulations. You're having a baby girl." Joy was as excited as the rest of us. You could tell she loved her job.

I was having a girl. Growing my very own person. I could barely get my head around the fact that I was having her in the first place.

"We're having a girl." Callum came over to me, held my hand and kissed my forehead that was sweating after hearing the news. I looked into his eyes lovingly as if nothing and no one else mattered. Liam wrapped his arm around Callum's shoulder, joining us. Our moment.

"Tamsin, do you have any name ideas?"

"Well..." Before I could answer, Callum looked at Liam as if they'd already decided. "We think she should be named after your mum."

"Tessa," Liam jumped in. "Or Tess for short."

Perfect.

ABOUT THE AUTHOR

D J Cook, or Danny, lives in Cheshire with his annoying yet lovable partner, and even more annoying siblings. He has a Special Guardianship Order for his sister since his Mum lost her fight with cancer in 2013. Danny uses books as an escape from reality, because who wouldn't want to be in House Tyrell, sipping wine and watching The Hunger Games unfold before their very eyes? When he isn't consumed by a world full of books, he binge watches TV series and plays Xbox. If he disappears, you'll either find him at IKEA or in the bath.

Printed in Great Britain
by Amazon